AF335386

A Blind Man and His Monkey

R.D. Roldan

ISBN 9780578462578 (Paperback)
ISBN 9780578462790 (Epub)

A Blind Man and His Monkey / R. D. Roldan

This book is biographical fiction. It reflects the author's present recollections of experiences over time. Names and characteristics have been changed, events have been compressed, and dialogue has been recreated.

For information or to order books:
R.D. Roldan
PO Box 3093
St. Francisville, LA 70775

www.rdroldan.com
author.rdroldan@gmail.com

To my mother,
Everything good in my life began with you.

To the people at "The Oaks" and the real Fr. Garcia,
You will live forever in my heart.

To my wife,
You are the very center of my life.

"Wherever they might be they always remember that the past was a lie, that memory has no return, that every spring gone by could never be recovered, and that the wildest and most tenacious love was an ephemeral truth in the end."

Gabriel Garcia Marquez
One Hundred Years of Solitude

Chapter 1

It has been one year, two months, and seventeen days since your funeral and I still have dreams about you almost every night. The dreams always start the same way: A rainy Saturday morning in early December of the year 1981. Five boys spread out throughout a small sacristy, two sitting on a couch, two leaning against a kitchen countertop, and me, sitting on the floor by a rusty filing cabinet in a corner of the room, my knees resting on my forehead. All five of us weeping loudly.

You were exactly five weeks shy of your fifteenth birthday when you killed yourself, I was almost sixteen, and you were my closest friend and roommate.

I have tried hard to repress the events that led to your death, but my memories have a life of their own and make themselves seen and heard at some of the most inopportune moments. I still see you in all our favorite places and I talk to you in my mind all the time. When I forget you are dead, I become very sad and angry that you don't answer my questions or join me in my rants. Our conversations have become one-sided, internalized, and void of any real meaning. I miss hearing your voice, laughing at your silly humor, and listening to your colorful commentary about politics, religion, and the painful events unfolding in our fair city and country these last few years.

I have refused to accept any roommates since your death and the staff have made allowances for me because they know how much I still miss you. I look at your bed every morning and remember how you used to talk in your sleep, often disclosing secrets you never meant to tell anyone. I miss seeing how confused you got when I asked questions related to those confessions.

"Hey, Alex, how is your dad's broken arm healing?" I would ask.

Confused, you would say, "How in the hell did you know about my dad's horse-riding accident?"

By the time you killed yourself you had unknowingly disclosed that your cook had a child confined to a mental institution, two of your teachers were having an affair, your parents were having countless arguments about his workaholism or her friends, and your family's driver may have been connected to the Medellin Cartel. Of course, to be fair, you never spoke in full sentences and I had to guess the rest of the story, but my guesses were always right to your annoyance.

I have been meeting regularly with Fr. Garcia and he believes I need to keep a journal of my feelings and grief. He fears I am becoming more depressed with time and he may be right. I have become a stranger to my family who can't barely get a word out of me anymore. When I am home, I am usually hiding under a book on the terrace, sleeping, studying, or quietly eating my meals. Even my brother, Juan, who used to make me laugh as much as you did, has been unable to comfort me, and this is driving him crazy. I feel guilty about this and I fake a quick laugh at his jokes from time to time, but I haven't had a good laugh since our last weekend at "The Oaks." My mother believes you took my spirit with you when you died and I silently agree with her, but I don't ever say it.

I have become so introspected and somber that I feel like a silent spectator in my own life. I still feel guilty that, somehow, I missed the opportunity to help you and I am so angry at you and the whole world that I feel completely void of any love and compassion for anyone. My role in the events that took place after your funeral brings me some comfort, but it is always an ephemeral feeling that doesn't last, like the sudden smoke of a snuffed candle.

The other day, I was riding a bus from Bello to Medellin's center, when a phrase, long forgotten, came to my mind,

"In this family we deny, repress, and move on."

I broke into a sad quick laugh, followed by quiet tears I tried hard to hide from other passengers. Some memories have the power to change our moods and transport us to places and times we would rather forget. I suppose the opposite is also true, some memories lift us back to places and times when we have experienced indescribable joy and peace. The memories of our brief friendship, when we were young and naïve, bring me joy and deep pain at the same time. Some may argue that I am still very young at seventeen, but I feel very old and jaded. I have some of the despicable characters I met after your funeral to thank for the loss of innocence I have gone through.

"In this family, we eat our young with pride and chase them with a cup of black coffee."

Several weeks ago, I agreed to write your story, not just because it is "good therapy," as Fr. Garcia calls it, but also because I don't want to ever forget you. This process has opened wounds that remain raw, and my mind has had to face for a second time some of the worse people I have ever met. I do hope that when I am done telling this dark and painful tale, I will feel some peace of mind. I am searching for light at the end of a very dark tunnel and I am tired of feeling empty, useless, and angry.

My recurrent dream was a good place to start the story. Five boys spread out in a small sacristy, adjacent to a large and modern church in Envigado, Colombia. As I started writing, I focused on each of those boys faces as a photographer maneuvering his camera to bring his subject into clear focus. But, no amount of zooming in helped me recognize any of their faces. I had only met them briefly the night before at your wake, and I could barely recall their names.

Do you remember watching *Sesame Street* when we were growing up? I used to like those episodes where the commentator compared four items, three of which belonged to a set or pattern and one which obviously did not. I still remember the catchy songs, "One of these things is not like the others. Which one is different? Do you know? Can you tell which thing is not like the others? I tell you if it is so." I felt just like the thing that didn't belong. The scene in the dream was foreign to me. These people were not my friends and I had little in common with them. Yet, I was there.

I met these four boys the night before at your wake at an upscale funeral home in your hometown. I had lived in Medellin for six years by then, but I had never been to Envigado. In fact, I got lost several times trying to get there. I still managed to arrive almost an hour early. It had taken me almost two hours to get there, but, nothing short of death or dismemberment would have prevented me from attending your wake.

I had met your mother briefly about six months before. When I arrived, the family and a small army of volunteers were setting up the hall, arranging chairs and couches for the visitation, making coffee in the parlor's modern kitchen, and setting up trays of sandwiches. Your mother recognized me as soon as I walked through the door. She looked frail and exhausted. It was obvious that she was upset. How could she not be upset? You were only fourteen years old and you were her only son. I cannot imagine the pain of losing a child at so young an age, especially the way you died. She must have been consumed with grief, guilt, and regrets.

Your mother ran to me and gave me an uncomfortable hug. I tried hard not to smile, when the hug reminded me of our first meeting almost a year before. It seemed like time had gone by so fast. One moment we are two young teens trying to discover our place in the world, and the next day, I am at your wake, trying to deal with the debris of the dangerous hurricane you left behind. I recognized in your mother that which I had seen in myself as I entered the hall and passed a set of ornate mirrors hanging at the entrance hall. The combination of hours of crying, little food, and no sleep made her look ancient and sickly. The same combination of factors made me look emaciated and pathetically small.

Still hugging me, your mother whispered in my ear, "If I forget to say it later, please know that I am grateful for your friendship to Alex. It meant a lot to him. He talked about you often."

She started crying softly once again. Her tears falling on my back, while mine were falling freely on the front of my shirt. I remained still, not knowing what to say. Back then, I tended to be very uncomfortable in most social situations, especially in conversations with adults. Ironically, I was a well-known public speaker in our circles, but, when it came to one-to-one encounters, I always felt anxious and insecure. It was as though my brain refused to work properly when the person in front of me was older than fifteen. Adding to the discomfort was the fact that I came from a family who never hugged or kissed, and who felt uncomfortable showing emotions in public.

After the interminable hug, your mother accepted my offer to help in the setting up of the parlor. My job was to go through a box of framed photographs and to choose six or seven pictures that could be displayed on a table near the front entrance of the funeral home, right underneath the wall of mirrors. The funeral director was a wiry, anxious, eager-to-please, little man, wearing John Lennon glasses. He still had the long hair popular in the 1970's but considered out of fashion in 1980. His ill-fitted suit seemed too tight around the collar, and I thought he looked like a boy getting ready for his First Communion.

"Choose pictures that fully capture Alex's essence." He said, looking at me, under pressure to return to the kitchen where someone had dropped a tray of sandwiches, creating a commotion only he could fix.

Obviously, the man had never met you. I remember thinking how curious that expression was, "To capture the essence." Can anything at all ever capture a man's essence? Is this even possible? Even the clearest picture represents nothing more than a millisecond of a person's life. It can never capture the soul or tell us about the internal struggles, the dreams and aspirations, the fears that keep us up at night, and the small victories and humiliating failures that define our lives.

I didn't argue with the man because I soon realized that he and I had something in common. I too was so eager to please that I would have done almost anything he asked me to do. And, like him, I showed a deference for the wealthy and powerful that I seldom showed people whom I considered my equals. This was not a conscious effort on my part, but rather, an unspoken rule I had internalized as I grew up. In our society, the wealthy were often honored with titles like "Don" or "Doctor" even if they had no formal education. They were treated with the respect and fear often shown only to the clergy. As a result, most wealthy people expected preferential treatment, blind obedience, and unquestioned respect.

I chose several pictures that showed you in a favorable light. I had no other choice. None of the pictures showed your obsessive preoccupation with death, your irreverent sense of humor, the depth of your faith, your love for the outcast and the underdog, your beautiful baritone voice, your annoying tendency to pick your teeth in public after every meal, the grandiose gestures you used to show someone your love, your almost pathological passion for all things dangerous, or your tendency to chew with your mouth open and to talk with a mouth full of food. No picture showed your mood swings, the incredible heights and terrifying lows. And no picture could ever show the impact you had on everyone who ever met you.

"In this family we look our best or die trying."

Your mother introduced me to a group of your friends. Carlos, one of the boys, was your cousin. He had traveled with his family from Miami for the funeral. I was told later that the two of you had been very close until his family immigrated to the United States when Carlos was three years old. The family had kept a beautiful house in the city and a large plantation in Rio Negro, a prominent area of the state. Carlos had not seen you since he was five years old. The family used to vacation in Europe and had not returned to Medellin in many years.

This was understandable. In the late 1970's the wealthy in Colombia had reasons to be cautious. Kidnappings had become a popular way for street delinquents and organized groups to fund their criminal enterprises; small businesses were often shaken down for protection money; and the police and military demanded their own pound of flesh in the form of bribes. In fact, the only difference between the military and the cartels was the fact that the military wore uniforms and committed their crimes in the daytime. In any case, your cousin barely remembered you and seemed out of place, although it was obvious that his family was well respected and admired by those in attendance.

Two of the boys were your friends from the Anglo-American school you attended in the city. The American School, as it was popularly known, was an exclusive complex of impressive buildings, sports facilities, and the latest in modern technology. On par with most American boarding schools, the school provided bilingual residential and day school programs for the children of diplomats and the Colombian elite. Since you lived in the neighborhood, you had attended the day school since kindergarten. In fact, John, one of the boys I met that day, had become your friend from your first day of school. He was almost as short as I was at five feet six inches, a whole inch taller than I. He had a nervous energy about him that was quite unsettling. Unable to pay attention for more than a few minutes at a time, John drifted in and out of conversations, often leaving the speaker in mid-sentence. At first, I thought he had a mental disorder, but later I learned that John was high for twelve to fifteen hours a day. The rest of the time he was religiously dedicated to sleep.

Michael, the other school friend, was sixteen years old and the son of an American diplomat on assignment in Medellin. I never asked what type of diplomat he was because we had more blond and blue-eyed teachers, vendors, and low-level diplomats in Medellin in the 1980's than at any other time in history. Some of us at school would often laugh and suggest that the American Central Intelligence Agency needed to hire a more diverse work force. After all, if you are going to infiltrate a Latin American nation, the least you could do was to send us people who looked like us.

The fourth boy was your neighbor and best friend, Cesar, and his name is the only one I didn't have to force myself to remember when I started writing this story. His role in the events that unfolded after your death has haunted me since your funeral and, I suspect, it will continue to affect me for many years to come.

Chapter 2

Gathering the five of us, your mother had introduced me, saying, "This is Joe." Then, as if responding to their inquisitive looks, she added, "He was Alex's best friend at camp."

She paused for a second, fighting a new wave of tears. "He was the last person to speak to Alex before he..." Unable to finish the sentence, she broke down in uncontrollable sobs.

Your father ran to her side and enveloped her in a bear hug, quickly taking her to an adjoining private room. Before leaving us, your father turned and looked straight at me, with a mixture of anger and pain. He held his gaze for a few chilling seconds. I had never met him before, but his imposing figure, his impeccable and expensive suit, and the few strands of gray hair on his temples gave him an air of sophistication. He looked like a man used to being in charge. The fierceness of his look was threatening and unsettling. He seemed to be trying to pierce into my soul to see what laid there.

"He knows," I remember thinking. "My dad doesn't know shit." You had told me on that fateful last call. But, facing him this way, I wasn't so sure.

Your friends introduced themselves and I quickly forgot their names, but I still remember the contrast between themselves and me. They were upper class Envigado boys with prominent last names, a private education, and the delicate mannerisms of the wealthy. They had French tutors, maids, chauffeurs and wore the latest and most fashionable clothes. They vacationed in San Andres Islands, Bahamas, and Miami. I, on the other hand, was as ordinary and low middle class, as it was possible to be back then.

Contrary to most Latin American countries, where there are just two social classes, the poor and the rich, Colombia had always had a middle class. My family owned a working farm in Alta Vista, a small mountain town approximately one-hundred and twenty miles north of Medellin. They also had a home in Bello, a working-class suburb outside of the city, known for being the home of Marco Fidel Suarez (1855-1921), a once illustrious president of the republic. I attended an affordable parochial school, worked most afternoons selling popcorn at a local park, and never vacationed outside of the farm.

Cesar, your neighbor, approached me as the rest of the boys dispersed. He wanted to know about our last conversation.

"How did he sound?" He asked.

"What a stupid question." I remember thinking, but I said nothing.

It was obvious that, although we were all upset, Cesar's anguish and grief bordered on despair. He looked like he had not slept in days, surviving on strong, black coffee and cigarettes. We all smoked back then. Marlboro lights were the preferred brand, but I smoked Salems. Remember those? They smelled like Vapor Rub and tasted like shit, but I had heard somewhere that smoking menthols was recommended by American doctors for people with Asthma. The way I looked at it, "If menthols help prevent asthma, they must be good for you." Years later, I learned that no cigarette was good for you and tobacco leads to cancer and death.

"What do you mean?" I asked Cesar, a bit defensively.

There was an intensity in his voice that made me very uncomfortable. I also didn't know him well enough to trust him. Not surprisingly, you had never mentioned him in any of our conversations, in the same way that you never mentioned my name to any of your other friends. I could have been upset by this had I not known you as well as I did. You had a remarkable ability to compartmentalize and inhabit different worlds without letting your life in one world affect or interfere with your life in another. I belonged to a world light years away from your school and your town. There was something about Cesar that I couldn't put my finger on. All sorts of red flags were warning me to exercise caution around him.

"*In this family, we eat our young...*" I had a suspicion that by the time your funeral was over, I would know exactly what you're saying meant.

"Was he upset? Did he say anything about me? He insisted. There was something odd about the way Cesar asked the second question, "Did he say anything about me?"

I could see there was guilt in his eyes, as though he felt personally responsible for your death. Before I had an opportunity to answer, he lowered his head and started crying. He had an almost refined way of crying - quiet, soft, dignified. I observed him quietly for a few seconds and noticed for the first time how handsome he was. He was approximately six feet tall and had clear blue eyes. His facial features, blond hair, and bone structure made him look like a well-bred Castilian prince. Thinking about him now, I could compare him to a blond Dorian Gray, the iconic character of Oscar Wilde's famous novel. If it weren't because of his very distinctive local accent, one could almost think that Cesar was a Northern European ex-pat living in Medellin.

The next day, I learned that Cesar had an American father and a very prominent Colombian mother. An only son and heir apparent of a vast fortune, the boy had been educated in London until the age of nine, when his father relocated his fashion business to his wife's native city in search of cheaper labor and better weather. During the five years the business had operated in Medellin, the business had grown to include several high-end clothing stores, a factory which manufactured high fashion garments for various renown American designers, and several commercial and residential real estate buildings.

"He was happy, or at least he sounded happy," I answered evasively.

Cesar looked at me intently, trying hard to decide if he could trust me. Unsatisfied with my answer, he pressed on, "What did he say about me?" He asked a second time, enunciating each word slowly, with a pronounced emphasis on the word "me".

I ignored his attempt at intimidation and answered him, "He was the same Alex we know. We talked about camp, his plans for the rest of vacation... You know, stuff like that. He didn't mention you at all."

Cesar seemed satisfied with that answer, but, suddenly, he remembered those episodes from *Sesame Street* about things not belonging to sets. He asked, "Who are you again? And, how did you meet Alex?"

The subtext of the questions was obvious. In a sea of mourners at the wake, I was the only one who didn't seem to belong. Nobody knew who I was, and nobody believed that I was just a "camp friend." There was no universe they could imagine where you would have befriended a short, bespectacled, emaciated, working-class boy from the wrong side of the city. All your friends had a common background. They belonged to a social class filled with unspoken rules and controlled by norms no one had to write in a secret manual because they all knew them instinctively and adhered to them at all costs.

Life was lived within circles. A person was born within the small circle of a particular family and town; lived his life around the same people, streets, schools, and institutions; dated locally and within his class; and married, had children, and settled in the same general area where he grew up, continuing the pattern began by his ancestors generations before. And, even when movement was possible from one town or city to another, most people settled in the same areas where members of the extended family lived.

Education or wealth made it possible for some to advance to wider circles. It was often possible for a well-educated person to marry above his social class. It was also possible for what Americans call "New Money" to be welcomed into circles formerly reserved for the aristocracy. In families like yours and Cesar's, however, the boundaries were reinforced strictly. Those within the circle had the freedom of movement reserved for the upper classes. Those outside of the circle had little to no chance to get in. This is just the way life was, and no one made too much of it because there was nothing we could do about it.

It was difficult for me to imagine your friendship with

Cesar or with any of the other friends I met that night. You were so carefree, so willing to buck social conventions, so comfortable around peasants and pissants like me. Perhaps the real problem was understanding how you could have chosen someone like me to be your friend and confidant. What was it that you used to say? I think the expression involved a blind man and a monkey. "I love you like a blind man loves his monkey." That's it. I never understood the phrase, but I never tried to understand much of what you said anyway. Sometimes you spoke in riddles, and that was okay. It was your way.

I have a theory about how you and I became friends, but please bear in mind that it is pure conjecture. I believe the Church was the great equalizer for us. More specifically, a vocation to the priesthood. Criticize the Catholic Church if you must but give them credit for the powers they have bestowed on the clergy. In a country like ours, priests were a class of their own. Regardless of last name, background, or ministerial aptitude, priests were always regarded as superior to all. They were special in the eyes of the masses, men of great faith and wisdom who needed to be respected, feared, and obeyed.

Priests were the only group of people I knew who had the ability to move freely from circle to circle, forwards and backwards, aided by the respectability of their profession and the power of the Church. Priests were confessors to prostitutes, advisors to popes, patrons of the poor, friends of the rich, chaplains to crooks, and dinner companions of fools. To count a priest in your list of friends was to see yourself on the side of all that was sacred, good, and pious, - a benefit to the salvation of your soul.

For many generations, good Christian families of all socio-economic classes thought it was their duty to give a son to the Church. Just the idea that a young man was interested in a vocation to the priesthood was enough to garner him a fair amount of sympathy and good will among members of his and other social circles. I believe this is where you and I come in. We both were attracted to the idea of service in the priesthood, and we felt a deep call to serve those at the margins of our crumbling world.

By the time I met you, you had decided that the antidote to the shallow and self-centered ways of those with whom you grew up, was to become a humble and simple priest. Of course, as you said many times, some adjustments needed to be made. "The Church ordains, but the heart mandates." Plainly said, you did not agree with and did not intend to obey the celibacy rule.

Chapter 3

As you remember well, what your mother called "Camp" was in truth a retreat and conference center called "The Oaks." Founded by Fr. Wilbert Garcia in the 1960's, the large Center could house over one hundred people for weekend retreats and conferences. Fr. Garcia's family had been the founders of "Antioquia Beverage Company," better known as "ABC Cola." They were the country's equivalent to Coca-Cola and just as successful by Colombian standards. Fr. Garcia had invested millions of pesos of his personal fortune to create a truly beautiful oasis outside the city limits.

We learned the history of the Center early on, and you told me once how Fr. Garcia became the Director of Vocations for the Archdiocese of Medellin in the early 1970's. This meant that he was responsible for helping young men, like you and I, discern whether they were called to the Roman Catholic priesthood before we were accepted to seminary. Fr. Garcia moved the vocations office from the Diocesan headquarters to "The Oaks" in the early 1970's and started inviting those interested in the priesthood to monthly retreats during their senior year of high school.

In 1975, Fr. Garcia had an epiphany. Most of the first-year seminarians who dropped out of seminary left because they had a difficulty making friends, felt lonely, and became homesick. If he moved the year of discernment from the last year of high school to the first, by the time these young men went to seminary they would have a large group of friends they had made over four years. Going through seminary with friends would reduce dropout rates. In short, life in general, and a ministerial life in particular are always easier when they are lived out in community.

To test his theory, Fr. Garcia asked all priests in the Archdiocese to identify young people in their youth groups who were in the ninth grade, showed some leadership abilities, and had an interest in the priesthood. He then started to invite these youth to monthly retreats and conferences, with a heavy emphasis on relationship building and faith formation. These retreats became very popular, and soon Fr. Garcia had hundreds of young people attending retreats every month.

The success of his idea posed another problem. Fr. Garcia did not have enough staff to manage these large retreats. He asked rectors to identify one or two of their brightest students and to nominate them for a leadership school at "The Oaks" where they could be trained as peer mentors. This is how the "Leadership School" began. As you know, I was chosen by my rector in 1980, when I was just fourteen years old. By then the school had been in existence for three years and some of its graduates were serving on staff, training the next leaders and teaching the "Exploration Retreats" for the hundreds of kids interested in the priesthood. Some of these graduates were my mentors when I began the program.

The leadership school met every weekend from Friday to Sunday for an entire year. And, both you and I loved the idea of a weekend boarding school. We had assigned rooms, shared all our meals with the clergy, were required to participate in daily morning and evening prayer, and attended Sunday mass together every week. Late Fridays and Saturdays were spent learning Holy Scripture, practicing public speaking and teaching, and talking about our faith, our dreams and aspirations, and our daily struggles with home, school, and peers. It was a loving, supportive, and incredibly fun atmosphere for any boy my age.

You may remember how Fr. Garcia believed the only way to build a positive youth culture was for the youth to spend as much time together as possible. He demanded that all the youth enrolled in the leadership school spend all our vacations at "The Oaks," including the entire month of July and six weeks in November and December. During those lengthy stays we had assigned chores in addition to a rigorous program of daily learning, liturgy, and sports, under the watchful eye of Fr. Garcia and his team.

A selected group of those who successfully completed the first year of leadership school were invited to stay for a second year as mentors of new students. And this, my dear friend, is how I first met you in January of the year 1981. You were fourteen years old and I was about to turn fifteen.

Being your mentor meant that you and I shared rooms and spent most of our evenings talking until late at night, drinking beer and rum, and smoking cigarettes. As conservative as people in Colombia were, there was a certain freedom at "The Oaks," which was a complete mystery to our parents and churches who sent us there. There was an implicit understanding that none of us had chosen celibacy yet, we were still kids, and there were more important matters to worry about than smoking or drinking in moderation.

I remember our first meeting well. I was already in our room when your parents dropped you off at "The Oaks."

As soon as you entered the room, you exclaimed, "Hello, sweetheart." Remember that? Then you added, "It is an honor for you to meet me."

Startled, I got up from my desk to greet you. I extended my right arm, ready to shake your hand, but you bridged the gap between us in one giant step and gave me a bear hug.

"Handshakes are for pussies." You raised your voice, "In this family we hug, kiss, and drink. But, mostly, we drink."

I didn't know what to make of you at first. I had never had anyone call me "sweetheart" before or threaten to kiss me. I am as square as they come, and I tend to be uncomfortable in most social situations. As if putting a down payment on your promise of alcohol, you opened your backpack and pulled out a bottle of rum. I went to my dresser, where I kept paper cups and snacks.

Taking a big gulp straight out of the bottle, you exclaimed loudly, "Cups are for pussies! In this family we drink from the bottle and, when we are drunk, we screw the maid."

At this point I broke out in laughter, grabbed the bottle, and took a big drink. This was our first meeting, and I will never forget how you seemed to laugh with your whole body; slapped you thigh with your hand as if to provide a sound track for your laughter; and drank straight from the bottle, like this would be your last drink on earth and you had to make the best of it.

Before I get too lost in my memories of "The Oaks," let me pick up where I left off. I was at your wake and your friend, Cesar, the expert on all things that don't belong to sets, wanted to know who I was and how I had met you.

I answered him, "I met him at 'The Oaks.' We were friends for almost a year."

Cesar seemed surprised to hear this. It became clear

to me that your parents had kept your priestly aspirations a secret from family and friends. Perhaps they believed this was just a phase and, eventually, you would see the error of your ways and join the family business. As I understood it, your father owned Steerco, the country's largest producer of deli meats. His specialty was Colombian "Chorizo," summer sausage, sliced ham, pepperoni, and cured bacon. His products were the choice of discerning palates across our nation, Venezuela, Peru, and Ecuador. At the time of your death, he was about to enter the Chilean and Bolivian markets.

"Isn't that a place for monks?" Cesar asked dismissively.

"It is a conference center for kids who are thinking about becoming priests. Some go on to seminary, but most just go to university or find jobs after high school." I replied, unsure of how much to tell him.

"He wanted to be a priest?" He asked incredulous.

"He was fourteen years old. I don't think he really knew what he wanted to be. But he loved being there." I said, wanting the conversation to be over.

It was getting late and it had begun to rain outside. If I left now, I would be home by 10:00 pm, sleep a few hours, and wake up early enough to return the next morning for the funeral. The trip home would require a long walk, two buses, and another long walk from the terminal to my home in Bello. As it was, I would be lucky if I got home before midnight.

Cesar was not done yet, however. He stated, "This whole thing has been hell for all of us. If you know anything that could help us make sense of this, you better tell us."

I detected once again that subtle threat I had noticed before. "You better," he had said. I may have looked like the runt of the litter, but I wasn't going to let this rich prick intimidate me into disclosing information that I swore to you I would keep quiet until the right time presented itself. I wasn't ready and no amount of intimidation would make me speak. I also felt that there was something menacing about Cesar, something beyond grief over losing his friend. There was a darkness hiding just below the surface, obscured by Cesar's blue eyes and the refinements of his class.

"I've told you all I know. Now, if you don't mind, I have a bus to catch." I said as I made my way to the door.

I looked for your parents around the building for a few minutes, but I couldn't find them. The funeral director looked so busy putting out fires throughout the busy wake, that I didn't want to interrupt him to leave them a message. I decided to leave without saying my good byes, even though this seemed rude and inconsiderate on my part.

Chapter 4

My plans for the funeral the next day were to arrive after the service had started, sit in the back of the church, and leave right after communion. I had a suspicion that you had left the next set of instructions at "The Oaks." I intended to go straight to the Center right after the funeral, to look for clues, but also to grieve without the distractions of your family's questions or crazy Cesar's intimidation. In a strange act of generosity, my parents had agreed to let me return after having just come back from spending six weeks at the Center. They were convinced that a few days with Fr. Garcia would help me feel better about losing my "special friend."

I know you must be laughing in heaven. God, I hope you are in heaven. Although, come to think of it, if you are in the other place, I know you are surrounded by the excellent company of many of the distinguished people we used to know during our childhood. You would be laughing because, as you once suspected, I think my family believed I was gay, and you were my special friend. Of course, they never said it. In our family we seldom spoke about things that really mattered. I wish they would have asked me, rather than assuming behind closed doors that my priestly vocation was an attempt to hide my latent homosexuality.

The rain had stopped by the time I left your wake. The night was cold and windy. As it was often the case, I was underdressed in my jeans and polo shirt, both of which were damped by the lingering humidity. The streets were extremely dark on that cloudy moonless night. I walked alone to the bus station, which was about a mile from your home. The deserted streets provided the proper background for the emptiness I felt. The only friend who cared about me had chosen to take the last train out of town, leaving behind a pile of shit for me to clean up.

I felt alone, angry, and exhausted all at once. Now, in all fairness, feeling lonely was not unusual for me at the time, as you may remember. I was an anomaly in many respects, both within and outside of my family. There were kids who were born with incredible physical talents and exceled at sports naturally. In our days, we all had soccer gods we worshipped and some of them were our friends. Other kids were born with insane artistic talents and outdid the best painter or sculptor with ease. Some, like you, were born with the social gene and were able to make friends naturally. You felt as comfortable with the aristocracy as you did with street beggars, and you were always impeccably dressed for every situation, whether it was a "Casas Unidas" project, our version of Habitat for Humanity, or a mid-afternoon coffee with a senator or president.

I had none of those talents, but I was a ferocious reader, who preferred the quietness of a favorite spot over the craziness of your thrill-seeking behaviors or my family's overly dramatic ways of relating with each other. At home, I was often quiet, pensive, and withdrawn, which was the exact opposite of my brothers and sisters.

They all spoke at the same time, shouted over each other, ate with the television on and at high volume, preferred put downs and name-calling to any other form of communication, and intermixed dinner conversations with the most heated arguments about almost everything. Other than my younger brother, I didn't seem to have anything in common with them.

Talking about your thrill-seeking behaviors, do you remember the chapel episode? Well, if you don't, let me summarize it for you:

> ***You***: *"I'm going to do it."*
> ***Me***: *"You are drunk, just go to sleep."*
> ***You***: *"I only had one."*
> ***Me***: *"bottle."*
> ***You***: *"Don't be histrionic."*
> ***Me***: *"Don't be an asshole. You'll get us both expelled."*
> ***You***: *"Don't be a wuss. The staff will never know."*
> ***Me***: *"What do you mean? Their building is barely thirty feet from the chapel."*
> ***You***: *"Today is Thursday, moron. Look at the time."*

Fr. Garcia used to spend Thursdays and Fridays at the seminary, about fifteen miles away, mentoring, counseling, and teaching the freshman class at the school. This was part of his duties as the Vocations Director. Rather than coming to "The Oaks" late at night, he stayed at his apartment on the grounds of the seminary. Every Thursday, at 8:00 pm, however, the staff would gather in a windowless conference room to give the day's report to the priest, via a speaker phone strategically located at the center of the table. The conference call never took less than an hour and, in fact, it would often take longer as the priest always ended the meeting with Evening Prayer.

Me: "If you do it, I will tell on you."

You: "No you wouldn't."

Me: "It's stupid. He wouldn't see it anyway. He is assigned to the quads."

You: "I've taken care of that."

The quads were a set of four two-story buildings located on the south side of the campus, next to the soccer field. Arranged as four sides of a square, the buildings shared a common inside courtyard, used for various sports, community parties, and assemblies. Three of the buildings were residential dormitories with space for thirty-six rooms, twelve rooms and six bathrooms in each building. Each room had four bunkbeds and shared a set of toilets and showers with the room next to it. The fourth building had six two-people dormitories with private bathrooms, used for special guests and for the counselors assigned to each dormitory. The counselors remained with the students in each building until lights out, after which they would retreat to their private dormitories. One of the counselors would be assigned to do regular walk-throughs of the buildings until midnight, after which, he too would return to the "Quads Administration Building." This building also housed classrooms, arts and crafts rooms, a large television lounge, and a small kitchen used to prepare snacks for the kids assigned to those dormitories.

Me: "This is the dumbest thing I've ever heard. Please don't do this."

You: "Don't come if you don't want to, but I'm doing this thing."

Suddenly, you ran out of our room in the Gamma building, made a left, and sprinted to the chapel, down the walkway that connected buildings 1, 2, and 3, on the north-side of campus, also known as Alpha, Beta, and Gamma because they were the first dormitories constructed after the chapel, administration, and cafeteria buildings were finished. I gave chase, trying to get your attention without success. The scene unfolded so rapidly that by the time I caught up with you, you were halfway up the ancient oak tree, one of a dozen live oaks for which the conference center was named. The chapel had been built on a clearing next to this, the oldest of the oaks, and several of its branches reached out and hovered several feet above the roof of the chapel.

You: *taking hold of the swing rope, frayed by many years of use by thousands of visitors and students, feet on the trunk of the tree, climbing slowly to the first branch.*
Me: *thinking that if you were caught, we both would be expelled because I was supposed to be your mentor and your behavior would reflect poorly on my ability to enforce the rules and inspire you to be a morally upright future leader of our Church.*
You: *laughing maniacally as you climbed.*
Me: *aggressively whispering for you to grow up and get down.*

By the time you climbed onto the first branch, I had been joined by a group of seven students, all of whom were whispering at the same time, wondering why you were doing this, asking if you were drunk, and guessing what would happen if you fell to your death below or, worse, if the counselors decided to end their conference call early. Undisturbed by the aggressive gesturing of your peers to come down, you grabbed hold of the first branch and the second, and the third. This one branch would lead you to the roof of the chapel. You still had to travel from the trunk of the tree, down the long branch, before you could jump or hoist yourself down onto the roof. We all knew this would be the most dangerous part of the journey. We became very silent as we held our breath. Someone in the group began to pray silently, as we were joined by more kids. By now, we had a group of at least twenty gathered at the base of the tree or in front of the chapel.

You: on your hands and knees, making your way to the edge of the branch

The crowd: becoming louder, some cheering, some placing bets as to whether you would make it to the end.

Me: getting more and more angry with you and wishing I had been given a less stupid pupil to mentor.

Ivan: one of our friends, and the object of your eccentric gesture, angrily running from the quads to the chapel, climbing the steep steps of the long cement staircase that connected the south and north sections of the campus, two and three at a time.

Ivan: out of breath, "What the hell is going on, Joe? I thought you had this shit under control."

Me: defensively, "Do you think that asshole can ever be

controlled?"

About halfway down the branch of the tree, your legs slipped out and you almost fell, grabbing hold of the branch with both hands, at the last possible second. At the ground all of us made a loud gasp, as though the air had been punched out of our lungs. You looked at us and gave us a smile.

You shouted, "Oh, the things we do for love." You climbed back on the branch and continued your slow walk to the edge.

Ivan, was one of those boys, called by girls in my town, a "TDH," Tall, dark, and handsome. At fifteen, he was a year older than you and was in his second year of Leadership School, just as I was. The two of you had become good friends, early on, aided by the fact that you lived in neighboring towns and could see each other in between weekends and during long holidays.

A soccer genius, Ivan traveled with his club for part of the year, which meant that he didn't always join us on weekends at the Center. You had traveled with him to away games often and enjoyed watching him demolish the competition. And, lest we forget, you had a crush on him. He had gently ignored you for months because, in addition to a busy life of soccer, Ivan also had a girlfriend he had been seeing in his home town since he was thirteen.

The reason for your "romantic" gesture was a conversation we had in our room after dinner, the same evening of the chapel incident. You and I had been smoking a cigarette, while Ivan was standing by the open door of our bedroom, trying to prevent cancer from second-hand smoke.

You decided then to start picking on Ivan, the way only you could: "Ivan, why don't you love me? Is it because I am prettier than you?" You asked him in a whinny, sing-songy voice.

We all knew that voice. We all loved that voice.

"You are not prettier than me, and you are right, I hate your guts. Don't start with your bullshit," said Ivan, without much conviction, a smile on his lips.

"But I have dreams about you every night, cupcake. You don't realize how much I suffer without your love." You protested, breaking into the most exaggerate fake cry I had ever heard, you added, "In my dreams, you and I live in a small cottage by the sea, surrounded by beautiful gardens. You coach the local soccer team, and I bake cookies for the PTA. It is so romantic."

Ivan and I started laughing. The idea that a still conservative and homophobic culture, like Colombia in the 1980's, would allow an openly gay couple to join the PTA was comical. Not to mention the fact that, to join the PTA, you needed to have children enrolled at the local school.

Notwithstanding the impossibility of the dream, Ivan asked, "Tell me more about our cottage, Alex."

"Oh, it is the most beautiful little place you have ever seen. It has three bedrooms, one for us and one for Joe and all the friends who will visit us for one of our famous parties. The third room will be for our parents when they are in town. They of course, will bring us house warming plants, and your mother will insist on helping us decorate the spacious living room and the kitchen. My mother will bake us brownies and our dads will play golf together at the local club on Friday afternoons. I have it all figured out." He responded.

Our laughter could be heard down the hallway and several of our peers joined us. They too began to ask questions about the parties you intended to throw, the foods you would serve, and the drinks you would prepare. Before long, half of the students in our building were crammed into our room, laughing, drinking, and egging you on to continue. After about half an hour of heavy drinking and laughing, Ivan announced he had quad-duty.

You protested, "But, I am just getting to the best part, lover."

"One of these days I'm going to kick the shit out of you, pig. I am not and never will be your lover. Now, cut this shit out and go to sleep. We have a big day tomorrow."

Ivan looked at me and said, "Get this under control, Joe, or I swear to God I will rat on all of you."

With that, Ivan left for the quads and the students returned to their rooms. After everyone left, you and I continued drinking and spoke about sports and the next day's lectures, as we had a large group of students arriving in the early afternoon. We all knew that your "housewife" persona was one of the many characters in the theater troupe you carried in your brain. We all enjoyed when she came out to play because her effeminate voice, her mannerisms, and her expressions were the opposite of your normal self. You were a rugged, athletic, and deep-voiced individual, who could be guarded with your emotions, aggressive in the soccer field, and confident about your masculinity whether you were hanging out with a group of boys or dancing with a beautiful girl.

You: *inching your way to the edge of the branch.*

Me: *trying to avoid Ivan's wrath. I knew he blamed me for your craziness.*

The crowd: *cheering you on, as quiet as they could be under the circumstances.*

You: *at the end of the branch, letting go of your feet, dangling from the branch, jumping to safety on the roof of the chapel below.*

The crowd: *holding our breath.*

You: *walking to the middle of the roof, holding on to the wall of the bell tower, like a mime, placing his hands on an invisible wall.*

The wall of the bell tower was built of rustic adobe, rough on the surface. You arrived at the center of the bell tower wall, where a long and narrow window had been installed for ventilation purposes. The window had a small mechanism that allowed it to be opened from inside the chapel on hot summer days. There was a metal ladder next to the window, which workers used when they needed to replace broken tiles on the roof. You started climbing the ladder and took your time, not taking unnecessary risks, while those below held our breath, not knowing what you intended to do once you got to the roof.

The bell tower was a hollow, square structure, with two windows on the north and south sides, and arched openings in the brick at the east and west walls, which allowed those looking up the opportunity to see the giant bell hanging from the ceiling. The bell's pendulum was attached to a heavy rope which dropped into a small sacristy in the chapel below. The bell was completely manual, and it was the tradition of the Center to have a sacristan ring the bell, by pulling on the heavy rope, at least ten minutes before morning and evening prayer, and at least half an hour before Sunday mass. This was the alert system to let all students know another session of prayer was about to begin.

You: on the roof of the bell tower, making your way to the front of the chapel.

The crowd: anxiously awaiting what you would do.

Me: beginning to feel dread at the bottom of my stomach because I knew exactly what you were about to do and I had no way to stop you.

You walked to the very edge of the roof and stretched your arms out, like the statue of Christ the Redeemer in Rio de Janeiro. You looked much smaller from the ground, but in the moonlight reflecting on your arms, you look like the angel in the annunciation scene of a popular Christian movie about the birth of Christ. Then, without further delays, your show began.

You screamed at the top of your lungs, "Ivan, my love, I will jump from this roof unless you tell me you love me."

Although you screamed loudly, we could barely hear you. This was good news because, if we couldn't hear you, neither could have heard the staff.

Undeterred by our lack of response, you yelled,

"Ivan, my love, tell me you love me." It was the voice of your "Housewife" character.

"You are an asshole." Ivan responded back.

"You break my heart, love. Why must you be so cruel?" You retorted.

"Get the hell down from there before you break your neck." Ivan demanded.

"I will not come down until you tell me you love me." You screamed and, as if to show us that you were serious, you let your left foot hang in midair, while pretending you were about to lose your balance. Like a plane with wings flapping before a crash, you pretended your life was in imminent danger.

At the ground, we all screamed, loud enough for the staff to hear us. Thankfully, no one came out of the Administration Building. By now, some of our peers were on the verge of a nervous breakdown and began to put pressure on Ivan to "Tell that ass-wipe -whatever you need to tell him- but get him down from there."

Reluctantly, Ivan cleared his throat to get everyone's attention and said, "Fine, you jerk. I love you. Are you happy now?"

"Tell me you will marry me some day." You shouted back.

"I will marry you and give you three children. Now, get the hell down from there." Ivan responded, not as upset as he was at first.

In fact, the laughter and colorful commentary of those around us, forced him to get fully into the scene. Everyone knew this was high stakes drama and Ivan was a good sport. He played his part well.

"You make me so happy, lover." You said and broke out in rip roaring laughter.

Then, as if this was something you had done many times before, you jumped the eight feet from the roof of the tower to the roof of the chapel, jumped up and grabbed hold of the tree branch, crawled back to the trunk of the oak, and in less than two minutes were back down on the ground to the cheers of all your fans.

Chapter 5

Lost in this story, on my way to the bus stop after your wake, I failed to realize that the scenery had changed dramatically. Over a space of a few blocks, I went from one of the most prestigious and expensive areas of the city to a desolate and dilapidated area, frequented by prostitutes, homeless junkies, and drunk people coming out of local bars. It was obvious that I had made a wrong turn at some point in my walk. I wasn't necessarily afraid, but I found myself more hyper-vigilant than usual.

Lost in my story, I could almost hear your mocking voice, "A penny for your thoughts, buttercup."

"Fuck off" I murmured to myself, crying tears of rage.

I must have said this louder than I thought because a voice yelled back from a pile of carton boxes, on the side of a garbage dumpster, "What did you say to me, you son-of-a-bitch?"

Startled and afraid, I looked at the figure of an emaciated man, dressed all in black, getting up from the temporary shelter where he had been laying down.

Frozen in place, I screamed back, "I wasn't talking to you, buddy."

"I ain't your fucking buddy, okay?" Then, walking towards me, he added, "I am tired of people just calling me names and telling me I'm no good. I have feelings too, you know."

I stood my ground because I didn't know the area well and the man looked like a frequent visitor to these parts. If I ran, he could have taken a short cut I didn't know about, hide in the shadows, and jump me when I least expected it. Even though he was wearing a black hoodie, I noticed the man had a scar that began right outside the outer edge of his left eye and ended a bit south of his mouth. However, that scar had happened, he was lucky it didn't take his eye out. His teeth were covered in black plaque, from years of not brushing. His dirty hair was coiled in dreadlocks and it looked like it had not been washed since the man was a boy. His eyes seemed to look in all directions at once, like a predator scanning for threats before he pounced on his victim.

In the distance a dog barked. Nearby an ambulance siren was wailing its customary sound on its way to a local hospital. A few blocks away, I saw the lights of a car headed in our direction. I prayed silently that the car would not make a left or a right but continue straight to where I was. Perhaps the presence of a witness would stop the would-be attacker in his tracks. About a block away, the car stopped on the left shoulder of the street, turned its engine off, and killed the only lights available to us.

"Black Hoodie" kept coming in my direction, yelling incoherent and paranoid words about the government conspiracy against good men like him, the cartels experimenting on the poor to see how strong to make their drugs, rich assholes who thought they owned the city and sent their goons to kick him out of places he had lived in for years.

I interrupted the man's rant, trying hard not to offend him, but, at the same time, trying to sound more threatening and forceful than I was. "Listen, man. I am not from the government, I don't work for the cartels, and I don't want any trouble. I am just walking to the bus station. So, please, relax. I am not here to hurt you, but I can defend myself if you want trouble."

"You are just a wee little mouse. You ain't no threat to me." He answered, getting closer. "Now, give me all your money. That's the toll. You interrupt my sleep; you pay the toll." He reached into one of the pockets of his hoodie and pulled out a small knife and opened it to reveal a three-inch blade.

Six years of living in this city and I had never been mugged. I knew it was a common practice, as many of my friends and members of my family had been mugged, but I had been spared so far. Of course, it is hard to find muggers in most libraries, churches, and conference centers. To be mugged, you needed to venture outside, and, by this, I don't mean right outside your home's front door, where I played street soccer with my friends.

You used to accuse me of being boring and afraid of risk. You were right, of course. I never got in trouble at home or school and I had never been in a fight with anyone outside of my brothers. You used to call me an "altar boy" and that's what I was.

To say this doesn't mean I didn't know how to defend myself. There are people who train for years at local rings to become boxers and street fighters. There are other people, like me, who are unfortunate enough to be the younger brothers of bullies. Our training is less structured, and it is free. We don't need to make appointments; we don't have to schedule ring time in advance; we don't pay for trainers to help condition us; we don't have to balance our diets in a way that maximizes energy production and develops lean muscle; and we don't have to buy expensive uniforms and boxing gloves.

Our training happens quite casually when the bully in our lives gets caught smoking pot at home, receives a belting from your parents, is grounded until he turns forty, and is forced to do a long list of chores. It was customary at those times that said bully would want to unleash all his rage on his unsuspecting brother, who just happened to be in the wrong place at the wrong time. After several nose bleeds, countless bruises, and many episodes of the Colombian equivalent to "say uncle," you learn to expect the attacks, prepare for them, and use whatever is at your disposal to defend yourself.

After a few courageous stands against the bully, who lost two of his front teeth and received several unexpected black eyes, the younger brother was finally left alone. Soon after, the younger brother decided that self-defense lessons exchanged for math tutoring may be a good idea after all. He may never use the lessons, but one never knows.

I held my ground against "Black Hoodie" and searched the area around me for any weapons. Lying less than six inches to my left I saw a rusted piece of metal pipe, the remnants of some demolished structure that used to stand nearby. The blight in this part of the city was well known and even the Cartel boys, with all their weaponry, avoided this area. In fact, had I not been lost in thought on my way to the bus stop, I would have chosen a different route. But there was no use thinking about "what ifs" now.

I reached down and grabbed the piece of pipe as I said to "Black Hoodie," "I only have enough money for the bus. I don't want to fight you, but I will not be giving you any money today. So, just back off and let me pass."

Most street people can gage when their chosen victims intend to offer any level of resistance to their attacks. Having the survival instinct of people who have suffered great depravation, daily humiliation, and many street fights, they learn to pay attention and don't push their luck unnecessarily. They choose to live another day by backing off from dangerous situations.

"Black Hoodie," however, had not received the memorandum about not underestimating small little mice, who looked emaciated and defenseless but carried around cataclysmic rage because their best friend had just died, their lives no longer made any sense, and they were sick and tired of feeling afraid, insecure, and out of place.

"Black Hoodie" continued yelling about him, needing to collect his toll, life not being free, people needing to mind the places where people live, and little mice needing to be taught a lesson about respect. I started backing away slowly, but when I knew the attack was immanent, I planted my feet firmly on the ground and grabbed the pipe with both hands.

Arm outstretched towards me, "Black Hoodie" charged, trying hard to remain standing on his two feet. He seemed to be either drunk or coming down from something he had smoked. I backed off slightly and moved quickly to the left, easily avoiding the knife. As he missed his target, "Black Hoodie" lost his balance and stumbled past me. I turned around, faced him, and backed off a foot or two. Blinded with rage, the man regained his composure briefly and charged again, this time coming at me from the opposite direction. He was panting, driven by pure adrenaline and raw anger.

I moved quickly to the right this time, as he attempted to stab me for a second time. As the arm with the knife missed its target again, I moved a foot or two to the right, raised the piece of pipe, grabbed it with both hands, and struck "Black Hoodie" with great force across the mid-section of his body. The unexpected impact sent the man flying backwards in the same direction he had come from. His knife fled from his arm and landed a few feet from me. I reached for the folding knife, closed it, and put it in the front pocket of my jeans.

Lying on the ground, holding his belly, "Black Hoodie"

began to yell, "I am going to kill you, motherfucker. I will fucking kill you."

The incoherent attacker grabbed a mid-size rock from the ground and attempted to stand when I struck him on the head with the pipe one last time, releasing all at once years of pent up anger. The man flew backwards one more time and didn't get up again. Nervously, I reached out to examine him. He was unconscious and bleeding from a cut on his forehead, but he was still breathing. I knew he would have a mighty headache the next day, but I also knew that I had acted in self-defense. I uttered a silent prayer that the man would not die, but I had no way to alert the authorities or to call for an ambulance. Even if the authorities would have cared anyway, most cops had no sympathy for street people and would have gladly put them away in cages and thrown away the keys.

Chapter 6

As I started walking towards the bus stop, the lights of a car about a block behind me flooded the street once again. I heard an engine start and the car begin to drive slowly towards me. I didn't turn to face it, but I knew it was the same car that had parked a block away as I was facing "Black Hoodie." My family didn't own a car, but one of my best friends growing up had lived above a garage owned by his father. Over the years, I had learned to identify the sound of various engines worked on downstairs. The sound I was hearing was definitely the sound of the car I had noticed before. Had the driver just watched the scene unfold from the parked car? If so, why had he or she not assisted me? Would this person go to the authorities and file a complaint against me? How long had the driver followed me? And, why?

Fear is the body's alert system and I grew up trusting the system. There was something wrong here and I could imagine all sorts of scenarios. Me, rotting in a Colombian prison, separated from everything and anyone I had ever cared about.

Me, struck by a car and left to die on a deserted street, like so many faceless victims across the city. Me, kidnapped by a hapless criminal who had no idea my family could not pay a ransom, regardless of how small it might be. Me, taken by a rapist with a predilection for under-nourished, bookworms, with no sense of fashion, and too stupid to realize the dangers of walking alone at night in a city like Medellin.

Me, unable to fulfill the promises I made to you a few days before, when you called me in a crisis in the middle of the night. "I am going away for a while, buddy. I need you to do something for me when I am gone...."

This is what you had said, you, asshole. Now, here I was, about to face untold dangers and preparing myself to fight off whatever weirdo was driving the black sedan. Instinctively, I increased my pace, almost breaking into a run. I could see the bus stop about a half a block away. I knew I would be safe if I made it to the area. There were lots of people and cops hanging out at bus stops, stations and train terminals.

Perhaps, this was a policing strategy a few of us knew about. I could almost imagine the police manual saying, "By all means, let us not assign cops to the streets, where things can become dangerous for them. Let us, instead, put all of them in police stations, bus stops and terminals, train depots, banks, and malls. This way, they will be closer to favorite coffee shops and bakeries. This will keep all of us in Medellin much safer. Let the streets take care of themselves."

I wondered if such a manual existed, but, as things presently went, I was glad this was the practice. All I needed to do was reach the area and I would be safe. In the distance, I heard the car accelerate.

I broke into a run and within a few seconds I made it to the bus shelter, where other would be passengers waited for taxis and buses. As I was about to sit on the bench, I heard someone call my name from the car. I turned, while assessing escape routes. The plan was simple: In case of danger, run into the park behind. The driver could not give chase unless he left the car in the middle of the street and chased me on foot. Of course, I knew that no one in his right mind would leave a new car unattended in this part of town, at this time of night. The car was a late model black Mercedes Benz, with tinted glass and a reinforced steel frame. I recognized the car because I had seen it before. This was the car that used to drop you off at "The Oaks." Only, on those occasions, it was your family's chauffeur at the driver's seat.

Your father lowered the window of the passenger's door and called for me one more time. "Hey, you. Come here."

He was alone in the car and it was apparent that he had been drinking. In the Colombia of the 1980's "drinking" and "driving" were not opposite concepts. These two concepts were very comfortable with each other. In fact, "drinking while driving" was a common practice, as were, "driving while smoking dope," "driving while shooting someone out of the window," and the ever famous, "driving while sexually harassing girls walking on the sidewalks."

Your father tried to get my attention one more time, "You are Joseph, right? You were Alex's friend."

"Close enough." I responded. "The name is Joe and yes, I am your son's friend."

You need to know that I meant every word I said. I didn't answer, "I was" but "I am." I knew then, what I had known since the day I met you that I would be your friend forever and even death could not break our bond. I still feel the same way. It is getting harder now to remember some of our conversations, but I remember vividly those that really mattered. I especially remember the intensity in our voices, the fervor of our faith, the depth of our convictions, and the resolve of our actions. I don't feel that passion and fervor in the same way anymore. Mostly, I feel a sense of dread and fear of the unknow. I am overwhelmed with an emptiness that threatens to consume me and drive me insane.

But, barely two years ago, everything seemed so urgent and so important. It was as though we were boys marked for death, with just days or months to accomplish all our dreams. Everything was intense and urgent. Of course, I now believe that you lived your life under the shadow of death. At such a young age, you were fully convinced you had been old enough to die since the day you took your first breath on planet earth. Life seemed so ephemeral and so transitory back then.

All of us knew young people who died incomprehensibly violent deaths, and, secretly, we all expected to be next. This is still the case now. In fact, life has gotten even more dangerous over the last two years. We all expect to be the next victim, not because we are involved in a life of crime and not because we associate with the cartels, but, rather, because we know well that most victims of street violence are innocent bystanders. It is just a matter of time before any of us become "collateral" damage. I walk around this city as one with a contract on his head, waiting for a Sicario to end my miserable life. Somehow, death doesn't terrify me anymore, however. I am more worried about this ever-growing darkness in my soul. The emptiness I feel in my heart.

You were always very comfortable voicing the palpable hopelessness and pessimism in our culture. It was as though you had chosen to be the spokesperson for the collective depression of the city and you had an abundance of facts to illustrate your philosophical arguments about life: Car bombs in shopping malls; heart-wrenching television appeals by families begging kidnappers for mercy and patience; a growing body count as the cartel death squads held the city and the nation hostage; guerrilla mobs killing hundreds of peasants believed to be government collaborators; army thugs killing hundreds of peasants believed to be guerrilla collaborators; preachers obsessed with sexual ethics while remaining silent to the human rights atrocities taking place all around them; government corruption at all levels and in all sectors; out-of-control inflation; unemployment; inadequate infrastructure made worse by increasing street violence and homelessness, etc.

There is a song by the folk music duo "Los Relicarios" which you were obsessed with. This song is an emotional, somewhat histrionic and depressive piece about love lost and the death of a relationship. The first verse fully captures how you saw life and the futility of it all. Loosely translated the verse reads like this,

> *"I feel that my death is very close,*
> *I ask you not to cry for me when I die,*
> *because crying does not raise the dead,*
> *and you should cry for the one left behind.*
> *This world is a lie, it is a deception.*
> *Why would I want to keep on living?*
> *It is the same thing to die young than to die old."*

I know now what ley at the heart of your obsession with death, but, back then, I accepted the premise by Miguel de Unamuno that most Latin Americans have a tragic sense of life. For us, "A man does not die of love or his liver or even of old age; he dies of being a man." He also put it another way, "Life is a tragic disease with a very poor prognosis for recovery."

Now, I know that your risk taking, drinking, and corny humor were attempts to escape that sense of powerlessness we all felt. Life has cheap in Colombia for many years and, like sand escaping in between our fingers, there is nothing a bunch of naive children like us can do. Death is everywhere, all at once, and the stench it produces travels through the crevices of the adobe facades, window frames, door gaps, and gardens of the homes of even the most apathetic, disconnected, and self-deluded aristocrats in the bloated city.

Sadly, that grim reality has become even worse as the Cartels become stronger, the authorities more corrupt, the military more inefficient, and politicians more compromised. Life in the city has become untenable and many of our friends have begun a massive exodus to places like Venezuela and the United States.

We have been first row witnesses of a tragedy many years in the making, a tragedy we can't stop. So, most of us did what we could: We drank, smoked, told jokes, laughed, and engaged in free love, priests be damned.

You were the master of the corny joke. Here is one you may remember, "Hey Joe" You would start, "Have I ever told you the story of the lady who had two baby chickens?"

At this point you would stop and refuse to continue until I took the bait. Exasperated, I would say, "No, Alex, why don't you tell me."

"I will, my midget friend." You would say and then complete your stupid joke. "There was a lady who had two young chickens. One of them got sick one day, so the lady, quite concerned, killed the other chick to make her some chicken soup."

The joke itself wasn't that funny, but one could not resist your infectious laugh, your tapping your leg with your hand as you rocked your body back and forth, and the snorting sounds you would make along the way. There was no one I remember who was immune to your laughter.

By the end, all of us would be laughing with the same intensity, and we would forget, even if it was just for a few seconds, about the decomposing bodies in the garbage hills outside the city limits. Your laughter was medicine at a time when all of us were trying to find our way in the world, and when I was feeling the most disconnected from my family and friends.

Chapter 7

Now, let me get back to the story. Your father was yelling from his car, rain was beginning to fall all around me, and my bus was about to arrive.

"You live in Bello, right?" It was your father again. "Come I'll drive you."

The prospect of riding in the same car with your drunk father was terrifying, but I didn't want to offend the man, especially on the day of his only son's wake. I looked at my watch and found the perfect way to avoid riding with him,

"The bus will be here in five minutes. There is no need for you to drive all the way to Bello." I replied.

"It is no trouble at all." He replied. "I know the way well. I've been there many times."

It had begun to rain again, and I was getting wet by the water bouncing off the ground, as I was standing in the crowded shelter talking to your drunk father. Driven by deep curiosity about the reasons your father had followed me, what he knew about "Black Hoodie," and why he was volunteering to drive an hour out of his way, I made a hasty, perhaps unwise, decision and got into his car. I also wanted to know how much danger I was in. Obviously, he had witnessed the pathetic encounter with the homeless man, and he could choose to do something about it. I wanted to know if I faced any legal trouble.

I sat on the passenger seat and put on my seatbelt. Your dad rolled the passenger window up and drove away. For someone who most likely had been drinking all day, he seemed in perfect control of the vehicle and of his emotions. I remember being very impressed by this because I was barely holding on. Of course, a high tolerance for alcohol was one of the first gifts Colombians received from their creator.

I can almost imagine how God assigned specific talents to different cultures: "Americans, I am going to give you a puritan work ethic, an industrious and self-reliant spirit, and enough ingenuity to make you the most powerful empire in the history of the world." Then, "Italians, I am going to give you a passion for the arts, the best food in the world, and an impeccable fashion sense." Then, at some point, way down the line, "Colombians, I am going to give you a high tolerance for alcohol, the purest cocaine the world has ever seen, and a generally pessimistic view of life, which you will mask with your lively music and numerous festivals."

"I am Arturo Cuevas," your father said extending his right hand.

I found it strange that after hundreds of hours of conversations, dozens of cartons of cigarettes, and gallons of rum, you had never told me your parents' first names. Come to think of it, I never told you my parents' names either. Isn't it amazing that the ability to compartmentalize develops so early in our lives? By the age of fourteen, there were many different worlds to which we could claim citizenship, each with a different cast of characters, a language, a unique set of rules, and a peculiar way of doing things. Some of these worlds would often interact with each other, as in the case of home and school. Some never interacted with each other, as in the case of home and "camp."

Other than signing an original consent allowing their sons to enroll, parents were not expected to be a part of the discernment process. They were almost never invited to functions, were not solicited for funds, were not expected at graduations, and were seldom allowed to interfere with the way the Center ran. It was as though Fr. Garcia had received a heavenly revelation informing him that families could be detrimental to a discernment process for the ministry. The home and camp lives unfolded in parallel narratives, like train tracks, each undisturbed by the presence of the other.

Of course, this is not to say that some families didn't choose to become involved. Some baked cookies for the weekend retreats, contributed financially, attended community masses, and took the time to get to know the staff. Your family and mine chose to keep their distance and allow us the space to scratch our ministry itch, convinced that it was just a phase. Eventually, we would return home and take our place in the family's narrative, assume socially determined roles, and continue to advance the family's dysfunction.

And this is exactly what many seminarians have done over the years. After dropping out of seminary, they have returned home, found homely wives, had a brood of children, worked in respectable jobs, became professional drinkers, danced to the same depressing tangos their forefathers danced to, and assumed their pre-determined roles.

All of this, while promising themselves they would be different from their parents, they would accomplish what generations had failed to accomplish, and they would find the ephemeral happiness and success their parents never found. Unaware that the deck had been stacked against them centuries before, they played the game and went all in, eventually settling for a life of disquietude and silent desperation.

For me, there were just two worlds that really mattered, the home world and "the Oaks." The home world had a cast of characters composed of parents, brothers, sisters, cousins, and, what my father used to call, "the others." The others were distant family members and friends who fell on hard times and would appear at our doorstep with a small, antiquated suitcase and a story of heartache. Sometimes they would stay for two to three days and sometimes they would stay for three to four months.

You could be certain that a census of those living in my home, at any point in history, could yield at least four different last names, if not more, age brackets from zero to eighty, and a combination of married, divorced, widowed, and single people. The place is always busy, loud, and fun, if you were raised in a zoo and are accustomed to this form of crazy.

The rules of the home world are very simple: "Do what your mother tells you." It is ironic that our culture has a reputation for "Machismo," when it is our mothers who run the home, do most of the parenting, and instill in the children any values that really matter. In my case, the boss is a barely five feet tall force of nature no one dares contradict, talk back to, or criticize. Irascible, opinionated and stubborn, my mother is also a woman endowed with great generosity, courage and faith. She is indomitable and fearless, and her faith could be summarized in just one sentence: "God will provide somehow."

This is my mother's preferred mantra and the only belief my father can't never argue against or dispute. It is under this premise that we always find room for one more "other," even when we are already full. And, it is because of this promise of

God's provision that we always find ways to help the poor in our neighborhood, even when at times our provisions run low.

This premise guides the cooks to always prepare two to three extra portions because you never knew who would be joining us for supper. There are always bedrolls hiding in closets, in case someone needs a warm place to spend the night. Clothes are never discarded, but passed down to younger generations, repurposed, reused, or simply given away to needy people. And all of this is possible because "God will provide somehow."

Then, there is the Church world. We belong to this world by choice and we can choose not to belong simply by dropping out of the program. There is something powerful and magical about having choices in a world where grownups make all the decisions, and where unforeseen dark forces have plunged our entire society into a chaotic, almost phantasmagorical reality where nothing is as it seems. Life can be taken from us in an instant and the magical realism of Garcia Marquez is never just a clever literary device but life as we know it. Knowing that we have a choice makes us all want to belong. We hold on to our citizenship at "The Oaks" as drowning people hold on to the remains of their capsized boats.

You and I used to talk about how every group, system, club, or community has a "town's fool." Someone who is so different from everyone else that they always seem to be dancing to the sound of their own drums and to be playing by their own rules. These people don't quite fit in and, as a result, they often feel isolated and strange. I believe I was the town's fool of my family and I know you felt like the fool in your own home.

Did I ever tell you that I knew the town's fool by name growing up? He slept in the local cemetery, begged for food in town, walked the streets from one edge of town to the other every day, kept his head down as he talked to himself in nonsensical phrases, and was often seen engaged in full conversation with stray dogs and other animals.

He was always lonely and sad. I was one of a few people who brought him a meal from time to time, gave him a peso to buy a cup of coffee, and protected him from the harassment of other kids. I knew very little about him, but I felt drawn to his loneliness and sadness.

I often wondered if perhaps he knew something none of us knew and, rather than being the town's fool, he was in fact the wisest of us all. This could have been true, but, sadly, I lost contact with him when I was nine years old and my family moved to the city. I never did find out if he was a wise man pretending to be a fool or a fool who seemed very wise to an equally lonely child.

"The Oaks" is an egalitarian society where students share a common faith and language. We are a true community of weirdos, but we are comfortable being who we are, and we celebrate our weirdness. Just like you were, most of us are the town's fools of our families and small communities. In a nominally Catholic world, we attend mass regularly, participate in prayer groups, are involved in youth ministry, and prefer the quietness of a small chapel over the noise and fanfare of a street carnival.

We are seen as overly religious and even fanatical. We have prayer books and read Bibles at a time when most good Catholic homes still do not own a Bible. We spend our free time in spiritual retreats and local missions, are involved in the charismatic renewal movement, talk about a "preferential option for the poor," and read Liberation Theology books in secret for fear of our pastors and teachers.

We even try harder than our friends to listen to priests and nuns about sexual ethics and Christian morality. We are weirdos and "The Oaks" is the only place in which we truly belong. We are the confraternity of the strange, and we love the fact that we have a place where we can be ourselves.

"I am Joe," I said to your father, shaking his extended hand.

Beyond giving him my name, I didn't know what else to say. I was a kid and my experience talking to barons of industry was very limited. I guess I could have said, "I was your son's roommate and best friend. I was there when he climbed to the roof of the bell tower, half drunk, and threatened to jump unless one of our friends declared his undying love for him. I was there when he broke up with his first boyfriend and officially declared he was going back to having illicit sex with the maid. I was there when he broke up with his first girlfriend and officially declared that he was going to be a priest anyway. I was there when his grandfather died, and I was there when he met his true love, cocaine, and began his veritable descent to hell."

Somehow, I don't think your father would have appreciated any of these details of your life. I have discovered that parents often choose to believe their children are beyond reproach, especially when those children are dead. For some, death is like a purifying bath that takes away all defects, sins, proclivities, and shortcomings. I remember a priest at school joking that he had never buried a bad man. Even the most awful people are celebrated as heroes and saints at their funerals.

Your father broke the oppressive silence in the car, "How old are you?"

"Fifteen," I replied.

"You handle yourself pretty well for someone so young. You beat the shit out of that bum." Your father stated.

I said nothing.

He continued, "Do you have any brothers and sisters?" He asked, perhaps as a way of lowering my anxiety.

"I'm the seventh out of eight siblings." I responded, wondering where this conversation was headed.

"How Catholic of your parents. Procreating lots of good boys and girls for Mother Church." He said sarcastically.

I reminded myself that he was drunk and had just lost a son. "I guess." I replied uncomfortably.

"So, you want to be a priest, right?" He added, more like a statement than a question.

"I want to, but I am still trying to make up my mind," I said.

"I believe all priests are crooks and pedophiles. You can do better being a decent business man." He responded louder than necessary.

I didn't argue with him. Your father was not alone in his beliefs about the priesthood. The truth is that in a homophobic and repressive culture like ours, the Catholic seminary offers a safe place for young men to figure out their identity in a supportive environment. It is also true that many of those young men choose a homosexual lifestyle, become ordained, and engage in behaviors that are scandalous and drive many away from the Church. Furthermore, it is also true that some of them abuse minors entrusted to their care. I have heard all these arguments and stories before and I choose neither to defend these predatory men, nor the Church that provides them coverage and protection.

"I'm not like them and I don't care about money," I said more defensively than I felt inside.

"Bullshit." He said. "Everybody cares about money."

Your father was correct of course. We all care about money in our own way. In our culture money offers instantaneous respectability and honor and, I must confess, that I have done my share of longing to have the things many in your hometown have.

What I meant was that at fifteen I wanted to change the world. I didn't want to spend whatever little life I had left worrying about amassing wealth. Building empires is best left to those who live in countries where human life is respected and allowed to thrive. Ours is not such a place. Besides, I have always felt an immediate need to help those in the gutters and shanty towns around the city. I want to spend whatever life God gives me helping those in need.

We drove in silence, making our way to Bello. Your father seemed lost in thought. He looked exhausted and fragile, not just because he hadn't slept in days. His lostness seemed deeper than that. I sensed a void in his heart that could swallow the entire world and he seemed to be struggling to come up with the right words to continue the conversation. At some point he began to shake his head from left to right, slowly and deliberately, as though trying to shake his thoughts loose of impurities.

"He was a faggot, you know." He spoke in a whisper, almost to himself.

"No, I didn't know." I stated, trying to hide the anger in my voice because I knew you well enough to know that this label was unfair and, in any case, only partially true.

Chapter 8

Your father's question made me remember our first big fight. Early in the summer before your death, my mother demanded that I stay home for the weekend, which meant that you would have to cover my responsibilities at the Center for several days. The reason for the unusual family demand was my older sister's visit from the United States. She and her family were coming on vacation and planned to stay at our home for several days before leaving for the family farm. My mother wanted all of us accounted for, ready for entertainment, and as well behaved as we could possibly be. I complied with her wishes and stayed home that Friday night and half of Saturday, but, by mid-afternoon on Saturday, an explosive argument broke out and I was the cause of it.

Imagine a multi-part operetta, where all the characters sing at once, gesture frantically at the same person or object, and scream and wail in synchronized distress. This is exactly what happened that fateful day in our house. Ten tenors and twenty sopranos engaged in a fight to the death to make themselves heard and to punish in unison the offender who, wanting to be swallowed up alive by some invisible monster, cowered in a corner of the house's living room.

The argument started over a pair of sneakers. Of course, you probably wouldn't understand this because you had a pair of shoes for every day and for every occasion. I was not so lucky. Anyway, as it was customary, my sister had brought each of us several gifts from America. One of my gifts was a new pair of sneakers, which I immediately put on and went outside to play street soccer with my friends. After several hours of rough play, the sole of one of my sneakers came loose and I ran home to fix it before anyone found out. Of course, I wasn't so lucky, and everyone found out as soon as I walked inside the house.

My sister became enraged, yelling that we didn't know the sacrifices she had to make, working a factory job in Rhode Island to send our parents money for our education. We thought money grew on trees and life was easy for her. We didn't appreciate anything she did for us, and we didn't take care of anything she bought us. Such disrespect was too much for her to take. I had offended her to her core, and blah, blah, blah.

Joining the disgruntled chorus, other voices blamed my careless behavior for the worry lines and premature aging of our poor martyr of a sister, who wanted nothing more than for us to be happy and have all the things she never had. Other voices jumped in demanding an immediate punishment, which needed to be strong enough for this snot-nosed ingrate to realize that earning money requires hard work and sacrifice. Yet, other voices demanded an immediate apology that was both heartfelt and contrite enough to pacify my sister's anger. Other voices jumped in all at once, but in all the histrionic yelling,

I could not identify one single voice that advocated for me or sought to offer me any comfort.

I was familiar with these resentments because by the age of fifteen I had two sisters and a brother in Rhode Island, and they all felt taken advantage off. In fact, two more of my siblings, my mother and my father have all gone to Rhode Island during the last nine months. My brother Juan and I have been left to the care of a sister who is in her third year of university. The house feels so empty now, but we still have an eternal parade of "others," and my sister cares for them with the same love my mother always did. I know it's just a matter of time before the three of us will have to leave for the United States. I feel very conflicted about this prospect because, on the one hand, I want to serve my people, here in my city. On the other hand, this city belongs to the cartel now. They are just gracious enough to let us walk the streets, if we don't interfere with their business.

Back to the argument at home. When I had taken enough abuse from all, I quietly walked passed the chorus of voices, went to my room, changed shoes, grabbed by backpack, and left the house without apologizing and without asking for permission. Much to my surprise, nobody gave chase, no body blocked my way, and nobody asked any questions.

I arrived at "The Oaks" after dinner, but I wasn't hungry anyway. Still smarting from my sister's tongue-lashing, I walked into our room unannounced. You and Ivan were in bed together, naked as could be, and engaged in extreme physical activity. Embarrassed, I quickly closed the door, and started walking outside our building towards a sitting bench on the other side of the walkway.

"Just give us a second, cupcake." I heard you yelling, followed by rip roaring laughter.

I was both angry and confused. I had never seen another human naked, and I was completely ignorant about all things related to sex. Even masturbation was a great taboo, which according to the nuns at my school was a mortal sin punishable by hell. I still remember Sister Maria's sex education classes. I had been warned by one of my brothers to sit in the back of the class and avoid eye contact, which is exactly what I did.

On this one occasion, the good Irish nun called for a volunteer to help her teach the lesson. A young boy on the front row volunteered and she had him face the class. She came alongside him, asked him to extend his right hand out, palm down. She then grabbed his wrist in a death grip with her right hand and took out a cigarette lighter out of her apron with the left. She lit the small tube and placed it directly underneath the boy's extended hand, not close enough to burn him, but close enough for the heat to cause some distress.

The Sister looked at her pupils with great intensity and said, "Now, boys and girls, imagine this flame over your entire body, minute after minute, hour after hour, day after day, for eternity. This is what awaits you in hell if you engage in masturbation."

Only she pronounced every syllable, as the boy began to squirm, and big tears came down his face. "Mas-tur-ba-tion." The big irony was that we were only twelve years old and none of us knew the word. After such great display, however, we all left class, resolved to find out what it was and determined to do it as often as possible because, if the good nun was so scared of it, it must be good. This was the extent of my sexual education in a family and a town where all matters of sex were seen as a great mystery, not to be revealed to children under any circumstance.

An embarrassed Ivan left the room a few minutes later, quietly, head down, and trying hard to avoid my anger and recriminations. I still waited a few minutes on the bench before I entered the room. When I did, I walked quietly to my side of the room to place my clothes in my dresser. The tension in the room was palpable and both of us were uncomfortably silent.

You spoke first, "Listen, Joe, you saw what you saw, and you can't un-see what you saw." You started in typical deflection mode. "But, in this family you can screw whoever you like, just as long as we don't talk about it."

I knew you dealt with stress through humor and I knew you were trying to make me laugh, but I didn't take the bait this time.

Undeterred you asked, "Hey, Joe. Have I ever told you the story of the boy who thought his grandmother was an auto-mechanic?"

"Fuck off." I responded.

Somehow, I felt as though the sanctity of our common space had been defiled and some form of exorcism or sacrifice needed to be offered. I wanted you to feel guilty, claim extreme duress, or beg for forgiveness. Of course, I should have known you wouldn't do any of those things. You were one of those people for whom sex was just a physical experience, void of any moral value or lasting significance. This is not to say that you were immoral or uncaring. In fact, you were one of the most compassionate, generous, kind, and self-giving people I had ever known. But, when it came to sex, you didn't have the same hang-ups the rest of us had.

"Ok, I will tell you, if you insist," you continued mockingly, just as I knew you would. "A boy of about ten years of age asked his dad, 'Dad, does grandma know how to fix cars?' The dad responded, 'You know she is seventy years old, right? Why do you want to know if grandma can fix cars?' The boy quickly added, 'because I just saw her under a bus, Dad.'"

"You are one sick bastard." I said angrily as I stormed out of the room.

I must confess, however, that I ran to the chapel, sat in complete darkness, and laughed until I started crying. You had that effect on people. I hated what you did that night and I hated your tendency to avoid difficult issues by using humor. The tears of frustration also had an element of concern. I worried about your salvation. I could hear the voices of dozens of teachers and preachers throughout my childhood who would describe your actions as a mortal sin, would find you guilty as charged, and would sentence you to the eternal flames of hell.

Alone in that chapel, I earnestly prayed that God might forgive you of a sin you would never call sin and offer you the grace you would never think you needed. To you sex was anything but a sin from which you needed to repent.

We made up soon after this event and to your credit, you became a model of decency at camp. Of course, this was aided by the fact that Ivan withdrew from the program soon after this event, choosing to be a heterosexual soccer prodigy, over a confused and guilt-ridden future priest. You grieved his loss for weeks, calling him a closeted idiot and refusing to accept his calls. I learned soon after your death that you and Ivan had made up several months later and had remained friends until your death.

Of course, in typical fashion, you placed Ivan into the "home" world and narrative and refused to mention his name at camp again. Within six months of your death, Ivan ascended to national prominence, was drafted by a soccer team from the coast, and is playing in the majors. It is so weird to see his face on the cover of magazines, but I always knew he was going places. He has written me two brief notes, but we haven't spoken in a while.

Chapter 9

Your father's statement, "He was a faggot, you know." surprised me because of the raw anger in his voice.

I had answered him, "No, I didn't know."

He looked at me intently and asked, "How could you be his friend and not know? Everybody knows."

I remember thinking to myself, "If he knows about this part of Alex's life, I wonder what else he might know?" Could you have been wrong when you said your dad didn't know shit? In either case I gave nothing away. I didn't know yet if I could trust the man. In fact, I didn't trust anyone I had met at the wake, crazy Cesar and your parents included.

"I guess he chose not to share this with me." I said weakly.

"Bullshit." He sputtered. "He was proud of it. He never hid it from anyone. I think he enjoyed shaming the family. It was as if he was punishing us for something we did."

Your dad became silent for a while and I said nothing. Then he added, almost to himself, "Maybe it was something we didn't do!"

I remained as still as I could be, and we drove in silence for about five miles. "Maybe it was something we didn't do!" How could your father have uttered those words and not know your secret? I was confused and that uncomfortable feeling at the pit of my stomach was returning. I was cold, I was hungry, and now I was terrified. What would I say if your father suddenly asked me about your story? How would I respond? Would I be able to lie convincingly about something this serious? And, If I answered truthfully, what would this do to your expressed request that I wait until further instructions before I acted?

"Doing the right thing at the right time is crucial here. Do you think you can do this?" You had asked, and I had given you my word that I would wait for your instructions.

Of course, I had no idea your trip had a destination from which you would never be able to return. I had agreed because I though the instructions would come when you returned from your trip. How naive had I been. How stupid. My naiveté didn't matter at this point, however. I had given you my word and I was determined to honor my promise at any cost. Personally, I wanted to see this thing through. I owed you this much.

After a few minutes of driving in silence, your dad asked me, "Do you mind if we take a small detour? There is something I want to show you."

I was about to protest that it was late, I was hungry, and I really needed to get home as my parents would be worried. When I looked at your dad, however, I noticed that he was crying an endless stream of quiet tears, freely falling on his expensive suit.

"Sure," I said, worrying about the time and remembering that the funeral was scheduled for ten the next morning.

I don't remember how we got there, but after ten minutes of silent driving, your dad pulled into a look-out spot from which the entire city could be seen. Medellin looked beautiful from this altitude. Peaceful, quiet, almost idyllic. Of course, the view obscured the real Medellin, the one boiling like a grotesque and malodorous stew about to overflow.

The city was like a majestic animal grazing on a beautiful valley, surrounded by mountains. From the lookout point the beast was graceful, strong, full of vigor and strength. A perfect picture of health and grace. But, hiding on the belly of the beast were thousands of infectious larvae, sucking the animal's blood, feeding without remorse on the animal's life force, entering the animal's body and infecting every major organ, weakening the beast's health, and, eventually, causing irreparable damage. But, on this evening, from this look-out point, all we could see was the seductive beauty of the city.

"Alex loved this city." Your father said absentmindedly. "He was such a happy and loving boy for so long, but we could barely see that inner goodness these last few years." He breathed deeply, held his breath, and exhaled all at once, as though expelling all his rage in one giant motion. "Our boy became a stranger to us." He continued. "We couldn't reach him."

There was something eating at him deep inside. He carried the weight of the world on his shoulders, and he seemed unable to understand the magnitude of his grief and loneliness. I can only imagine how the loss of his only son would feel to him. I once heard that empires are built not for us but for our descendants.

How empty his world must have looked, knowing that there was no heir left to inherit his company. All the sacrifice that went into building his empire had been for naught. The sleepless nights worrying about contracts and bottom lines had proven worthless. The endless meetings with government bureaucrats to secure permits and licenses now seemed wasted time. The multitude of small decisions about personnel, facilities, expansions, transportation routes, quality assurance, acquisitions, and investment opportunities had not meant a damn thing at the end.

He was a middle-aged man without an heir.

"Please tell me something, anything. You knew him better than we did. What was he going through?" He implored.

"I know he loved you very much." I said, trying to stop my own tears and trying hard to comfort him.

"He loved me, but he thought I was weak." Your father added. I waited for him to continue. "He used to accuse me of being afraid of his mother. 'You have no backbone,' he would say. But I was so busy building a future for him that, when it came to domestic matters, I let his mother make all the decisions. A man has no business choosing curtains or bossing the maids around. That's a woman's job."

He became lost in thought for a while, then he blurted out a question, "Was Alex a cokehead?"

I became immediately uncomfortable, but I made a choice to answer his question honestly. The truth of the matter is that since the advent of the Medellin cartel a few years ago, many in the Medellin aristocracy have discovered cocaine. They can afford the pure product the Americans use, and they take to it like a lost man in the dessert takes to newly found water. There is no escaping it. Cocaine is a staple of every high society party, gala, banquet, or fundraiser.

For the rest of us in the middle class, the cartels have developed a hybrid product called "bazuko." The drug was introduced to Colombian blue-collar towns at the same time its more refined cousin was making its way to American markets. Bazuko began when Colombian cocaine traffickers had difficulties refining some of the local production of coca leaves.

After "The boys from Medellin" found ways to

harvest coca leaves that could be refined into the pure product the American markets wanted, they used the less refined paste for domestic consumption. Bazuko can be rolled into cigarettes and smoked, but it is highly addictive, and produces serious side-effects that include hallucinations, paranoia, feelings of grandiosity, violent outbursts, and extreme risk-taking.

"He started using cocaine about three months ago, but lately he had been smoking bazuko. He kept it from us at 'The Oaks,' but his behavior changed a lot these last few months." I responded.

"My boy. My poor, sweet boy!" Your father cried out in a heart-wrenching sob.

He climbed on the trunk of his car and planted both feet on the hood, his sight fixed somewhere in the distance. He brought his knees to his chest, cupped his face with both hands, and sobbed angrily. I walked to the edge of the look-out point and started crying once again, without sounds, biting my lower lip with my teeth, and swaying back and forth, as a mother rocking a colicky baby.

At some point, your father raised his head and said, "I better take you home now. Your parents must be worried."

Gratefully, I smiled at him as I entered the car. Your father continued crying as he drove, but he had left the guttural sobs at the mountain top. After several minutes of quiet driving, your father reached inside the right lining pocket of his jacket and pulled out a small envelope.

He handed it over to me, saying, "The police found this letter on Alex's desk. It is addressed to you." At this point he looked intently at me and confessed, "I opened it. I shouldn't have, but I did. I was looking for clues, I wanted to understand. Anyway, I put it back in the original envelope and closed it with tape. I didn't show it to anyone. I didn't see a point."

My heart skipped a beat as I held the letter. I stared at it for a few minutes, not knowing what to do. I wanted desperately to tear it open and read it at that moment, but I was concerned

I would react poorly to something in the letter and your father would realize that I knew more than I had let out so far. Finally, I folded the small envelope and put it in my pocket.

Much to my surprise, your father gave me a sad smile and said, "We were all Alex's accomplices, weren't we?"

I didn't know what he was talking about, so I said nothing.

Soon enough, he continued, "I would cover for him often, you know? With his mother, I mean." He then continued as if narrating an old movie, hidden somewhere in his memory vaults. "I found him in one of the pantries, screwing the maid's daughter when he was just thirteen. Julia was her name. The daughter, not the maid. She was nineteen and already in her second year of college. The girl had grown up in the house since she was a young teenager. Her school bus dropped her off near our house and, every afternoon, she would help her mother in the kitchen, do homework in the living room, and help my wife with any chores that were needed. We loved the girl and would often ask her to babysit Alex when he was a little boy.

At some point, when the boy was twelve, he developed a crush on her. Obviously, his love would not be denied and by thirteen they were having sex in every room of the house, out of my wife's view. Of course, I didn't know until much later."

At this point he smiled briefly almost unconsciously and then continued, "I never told his mother. I spoke to Maria, the maid, and gave her a year's salary to tell my wife she was moving out of town for health reasons. She and the girl moved to Rio Negro, where I helped Maria find a job at a friend's house. Alex was furious. He called me a wimp. 'Who cares if mom knows I'm screwing the help? It's none of her damn business.' I am convinced he continued to see the girl for a while because we had friends in Rio Negro who spoiled him just as much as I did."

I thought about this and wondered how he could call you "A faggot" and still acknowledge you were having regular sex with the maid's daughter. In either case, the sad reality was that in affluent Latin American homes "The Help" and their children had been seen for generations as the play toys of hormonal teenage boys, sowing their wild oats. Most of the encounters are con-sensual and the affection between both parties genuine, but, in some cases, forceable rape takes place. These episodes often lead to sophisticated cover-ups that include buying victims off, silencing them through intimidation or violence, and termination of employment.

Chapter 10

"He was screwing Cesar too." Stated your father to my surprise. He continued, "I suspected that relationship had become romantic for a long while. Alex and Cesar had become very close friends when Cesar's family moved to the city from England. Cesar was nine and Alex was eight. I don't remember a time since then when Cesar was not in our house: sleepovers, playdates, joint vacations, birthdays, homework dates, you name it. He was always at the house and, when he wasn't, Alex was at his house. This, of course, is natural in young children, but from around the time Alex turned twelve, the relationship changed. Cesar became possessive of Alex. He was insanely jealous when Alex started spending more time at his church's youth group, when Alex made new friends, and, especially, when Alex was chosen to join the Leadership School and started going to 'The Oaks' almost every weekend."

Your father paused for a few seconds and then

continued, "Missy was embarrassed to acknowledge that Alex was thinking about the priesthood, so she made up a story about an equestrian camp outside of the city. Alex, didn't care one way or the other, so he started calling the Center, "My Camp." Anyway, there were times Cesar was outright miserable without Alex. He would call the house on Friday afternoons every couple of hours, asking my wife if she had heard from Alex, when he was coming back, whether he could call Alex at the camp, and how long he would be gone this time."

Your father paused briefly, as we approached the edge of Bello, then he picked up the story, "On one of the sleepovers at our house, close to Alex's fourteenth birthday, one of the new maid's children walked in on Cesar and Alex. Scared and confused, the young boy ran out, leaving the door of the room wide open. I was coming down the hallway when I saw the boy running out of the guest room. At first, I thought he was lost because he didn't know the large house well enough and we had a row of guest rooms on this hallway.

I approached the room, ready to close the door, when Alex was running from inside of the room, on his way to close the door. He was completely naked, as was Cesar, who ley on the bed, on top of the covers. They had not even bothered to undo the bed. Alex looked at me, with fright in his eyes. I simply walked into the room and said, 'Cesar, I think it's time to go home.' The terrified boy responded, 'yes, sir.' And that's exactly what he did. Both boys got dressed, while I waited outside the room. Cesar went home, and I said to Alex. 'We will not speak about this. And, we will not tell your mother.' With that, I left the house."

"In this house we can screw anyone we like, as long as we don't talk about it!"

This story explained well Cesar's reaction at the funeral home, just a few hours earlier. He had just lost a childhood friend, who also happened to be someone he was in love with. And knowing the effect you had on those who loved you, I could picture the boy's misery on those long weekends. At the very same time you and I were drinking rum, smoking and laughing without a care in the world, Cesar was at home crying in absolute desolation, feeling abandoned, unable to understand why you had left him. In many ways, this describes you.

You had the intensity of a tornado. You changed every environment you walked into, with furious energy, intoxicating charm, and a raw power most of us had never seen in someone so young. But, when you left the room, without a care in the world and without a hint of sorrow, you always left a mountain of debris for those left behind to clean up.

And, yet, almost no one resented you for it. In fact, your victims often prayed the tornado made its way back to them soon enough, even if they would have to pay the consequences later. This is who you were with almost everyone you knew. Raw power and strength.

I was not one of those people. In fact, you were drawn to me because I could call your bullshit out, and I could set boundaries no one else in your life had ever been able to set. I learned a few months later that this was the reason Fr. Garcia chose me as your mentor. As insecure as I was about many things, I was unwavering about where I stood on various issues. This, of course, was the result of years of self-righteous piety and fear of the terrors of hell, as described in detail by the nuns of my school.

On the one hand, I could accept you and love you as you were. On the other, I would have rather died a violent death at the hands of the likes of "Black Hoodie" than to behave the way you did. To be fair, I envied your freedom, your charm, your comfort in all social situations, and your very liberated views about sex and drugs. But, for better or for worse, I was the product of a very conservative and repressive home and there was only so much I was willing to do. I was an acolyte. You were right about this and, these many months later, I have come to value the sheltered life I had at home and school when I met you.

"I should have been tougher with him." Your father continued. "But, as I said before, I assumed his mother was dealing with these things. Parenting wasn't my strongest quality. I grew up in a home where my dad had absolutely no power, either because he was a passive and uninspiring little man, or because he just didn't care enough about anyone or anything to assert his authority at home. Like me, he was a business man. He was a provider and that's how he saw his duty as a husband and father. He was an oligarch of the old order with a dualism almost unknown today. Outside the home he was irascible, unbending, conservative, and always in control. He was obviously a despotic boss used to get his way through fear and intimidation. But, at home, he was quiet, pensive, reserved, and almost passive. My mother ruled the house with an iron fist, fussing over every detail, whether it was laundry or cooking, homework or church attendance, work or play. I guess, I just learned to parent how my old man parented. I know it sounds like bullshit and I wish I could go back in time. But, it's too late."

I didn't want to contradict your dad or stop his monologue. But I doubted what you would have needed at home was more discipline. I think you needed what your mother and father were unable or unwilling to provide, which was time. There was a deep loneliness in your heart few people saw, precisely because you were such an expert at hiding it, but you and I talked about it often. Raised with a silver spoon, you would have gladly traded all your wealth for a decent conversation with your father. It was somewhat ironic that in a home filled with parents, servants, and friends, you could have felt as alone and disconnected as you did.

You once said to me, "There is only one default setting for my father. He talks, and I listen. Better yet, he teaches, and pontificates, and I'm supposed to learn, absorb, and act grateful for his wisdom. He's never interested in hearing what I have to say."

Your father's confession and the honesty in his voice cut me to the core. He was wrestling with demons he had carried in his heart for many years and those demons now convinced him that your death was his fault. He didn't do enough: he had failed as a father, he wasn't strong enough to parent and discipline you, and he had missed his chance and now it was too late. I am often amazed by the rich vocabulary guilt uses to torture its victims, and guilt was doing a great job tormenting your father this wet, cold night, in December of the year 1981.

He was miserable and he wasn't alone. I was feeling just as guilty. I had missed something, I had failed to ask enough questions, I wasn't as in tune with your anguish as I thought I was, I should have known what you meant by "going away for a while," I shouldn't have assumed those were the usual rantings of 'coke-head Alex' or 'drunk Alex' or 'overly dramatic Alex.' I shouldn't have assumed that you would feel better when you slept it off and that you would explain your cryptic rantings the next day.

Wanting to comfort your father, I said, "Alex loved you so much. We talked just about everything, and he almost never complained about you. He admired you so much. This wasn't your fault."

"Almost?" Your father asked and at first, I didn't know what he meant. "You said, he almost never complained about me, which means he sometimes did. What did he say?"

"He never complained about you. I'm sorry. I'm tired and hungry." I said evasively. But he was too smart for my amateurish back-peddling.

"Bullshit." He said, without much anger. "Just tell me."

"He didn't seem to like his mother much." I said, unsure of how to proceed.

"Go on," He insisted.

"There is not much to say. He just thought she wasn't a nice person, especially to you. I swear that's all I know." I said miserably.

If I could use the image of a large house to describe the hundreds of hours of conversations you and I had about your life at home, your mother would occupy the living room, dining room, kitchen, most bedrooms, the patios, the bathrooms, and most of the closets. The stories about your sexual conquests would occupy one or two of the guest rooms. Your home friends would fit into less than one quarter of the available space in the smallest drawer in your pantry, and your father would be relegated to his favorite Lazy-boy recliner in front of his beloved television set.

"He was right, of course." Your father continued. "You know, I am quite good at putting puzzles together, building stuff, tinkering with appliances and machines, and figuring out how things work. I think, Missy, is the only puzzle I have never figured out in almost 18 years of marriage."

Your father slowed the car as we entered the one-way street where my house was located. He parked in front of the house I pointed to, and continued talking, "I think Alex always knew her better than I. They were inseparable until he was about nine years old. She fussed over him like a mother fusses over a handicapped child. She went as far as cutting his steak into perfect little squares until he was almost ten, when they began to drift apart. Missy became involved in local politics and Alex started spending more time with Cesar and other school friends." He paused his story, taking time to compose himself.

I noticed that the lights in my house were still on, even though it was almost 11:00 pm. This was unusual because my parents' bedroom was in the back of the house and, except for the light emanating from their television set, the home was usually dark by lights out, which was 10:30 at night. As your father was talking, I saw my mother's face peeking through the blinds on one of the windows in the living room.

The contrast between your home and mine is incredibly pronounced. Your home sits on a single lot with almost a half an acre of front yard and a half an acre of backyard, which is rare for homes in the area. The home itself is over nine thousand square feet of space, spread over three floors, twelve bedrooms, nine bathrooms, a spacious sitting room on every floor, a huge kitchen on the first floor, and an entire row of rooms on the second floor dedicated exclusively for guests.

At the back of your house, in a detached single-story building next to the garage, the staff's rooms occupy an additional two thousand square feet of space and have four bedrooms, a large kitchen, an office-library, and a comfortably furnished living room.

My house is one of eighteen houses on the left side of the street, which faces eighteen on the opposite side of the street. All homes share a common wall, and some have second floors, but the majority are single floor structures. Ours is the third house from the corner, which means that we have two neighbors before us and fifteen after us, all the way to the corner.

All homes are painted in bright colors, the first four feet from the ground up a dark color, and the rest of the wall a lighter shade of the same color. The largest home of the block is approximately 1900 square feet, but ours is an incredibly 1450 square feet. This sounds extremely small for the sheer number of people who live there but growing up it always looked spacious and comfortable. All siblings share beds, bedrooms and one bathroom, and we all must wait our turn to use the cold-water shower. Yet, we make it work and no one goes without bathing for more than a day or two, unless they choose to do so.

Our neighbors get along for the most part and the daily parade of children knocking on doors borrowing a cup of sugar, rice, or flour is a tradition in which all neighbors on both sides of the street participate. On Christmas seasons, the children make Paper Mache chains which we hang between the roof of both sides of the street. Block parties are common, and we spend the holidays dancing and drinking together. Food is shared with all, especially the Christmas delicacies of Natilla, Bunuelos, and pig roasted on a spit, which are as plentiful as rum and aguardiente.

I have been happy living on this block, and I know everyone and feel proud of our communal life. Yet, sitting in your father's elegant car, I felt immediately embarrassed by our humble home. Of course, I said nothing.

Before I let your father go, there was a question that I still wanted to ask. "Your wife is in politics?"

This was an honest question, since you hadn't shared with me this factoid about your mother.

"You didn't know that Alex's uncle is the State's Secretary of Education?" He asked incredulously.

"I had no idea." I answered truthfully.

He continued, "Yes, Manuel Escobar Estrada is Alex's uncle and Missy's older brother. Several years ago, Missy helped Manuel elect the current governor of the State and, as soon as he was elected, Governor Mejia, appointed Manuel as his Secretary of Education. He oversees the thousands of schools, both public and private, across the state. He's a big deal."

"I'm impressed." I said, surprised you had never mentioned this.

My mother, dressed in a nightgown that had seen better days, opened the front door of the house and waved at me. I looked at your father apologetically, and he gave me a weak smile.

"It was really nice finally meeting you, Joe. I now know why Alex liked you so much. You are a wise old soul for someone so young. Are you coming to the funeral tomorrow?" He asked.

"I am. I wouldn't miss it for anything in the world." I replied more emphatically than I intended.

"That's great." He said. "I will see you tomorrow then. And, Joe, thanks for being Alex's friend." A new wave of tears began to fall quietly down his face.

"It was my pleasure, sir. I will never forget Alex. Never in a million years." I said as I exited his car.

Chapter 11

I too was fighting fresh tears, when I exited you father's car, but I quickly dried my face off with the back of my hand before I entered the house in silence, followed by my concerned mother.

She seemed as tired as I felt and, surprisingly, she wasn't angry about my being late. She said, "Are you hungry?"

"Starving." I replied

"I made you a plate, but it's cold now. Come, I'll reheat it for you." She added.

"Thanks," I said gratefully.

I followed my mother into the kitchen, sat at the small dining room table, and waited in silence. She looked at me with that concerned look only a mother can manage to pull off. She asked, "You look wet, are you?"

"Soaked to the bone," I replied.

"Go shower and change while I heat up your food, and please don't go into your bedroom. Irene is back and I didn't know where to put her." She warned.

I paled at the sound of the news that Aunt Irene was back. She was my Uncle Pedro's wife and she had a severe mental illness. Pedro was my mother's youngest brother and Irene was barely thirty years old. The young family lived in a small town about four hours away by car from my home. The town was so isolated that it didn't even have a doctor. Once a month, a medical resident from the university would make their rounds at the town's clinic, located in a small backroom of the parish house.

On their visits, the residents would conduct physicals, tooth extractions, vaccinations, and eye care exams, in addition to checking those who were sick. Loaded with a bag full of antibiotics, anti-inflammatories, and first aid meds donated by the school, the residents treated all conditions with the same basic formula: "Take daily showers, wash your hands often, take these pills, and, if the condition gets worse, go to the State's hospital or one of the many doctors in the city."

I remember telling you once how the residents had successfully treated Irene's schizophrenia with the same baby aspirin, antibiotics, and herbal teas with which they had treated blood disorders, heart disease, and constipation. Unfortunately, about three years before, Aunt Irene began to hear voices telling her that Padre Tomas, the local Roman Catholic priest, was a dark angel sent by Satan to eat the town's infant children, snatching them from their cribs at night while their parents slept. The voices also convinced her that only she could save the village by getting rid of the old cleric.

Armed with a kitchen knife, Aunt Irene had chased the rotund priest around the town's square, screaming obscenities and threatening to kill him if she caught up with him. Can you imagine the scene? Terrified, the priest sought shelter at the local police station, threatening to leave the parish alone and return to the city, unless the crazy woman was taken to a state hospital. Not knowing what to do, Uncle Pedro had shown up at our doorstep with a small suitcase and his sick wife. Back then, as it was the case this evening, Aunt Irene and Uncle Pedro had been given the bedroom I shared with my youngest brother, Juan.

"Where is Juan?" I asked concerned.

"In my bed," my mother answered. "Your dad had to go back to the farm, so I thought both of you could sleep with me tonight."

"But I need clothes," I protested.

"I put your pajamas in the shower already, and I have your suit pressed and ready for the funeral tomorrow." She added.

As you may remember, this is just like my mother, anticipating every need at least three moves ahead. Although I wasn't thrilled about the situation, I was grateful I didn't have to enter my room while Aunt Irene was there. Since her first visit three years before, when I was just twelve, Aunt Irene had thought that I was Jesus. Let me make this clear. She didn't think I looked like a teenage version of Jesus of Nazareth. She was convinced that I was the returned Son of God, who one day would lead the heavenly armies into a glorious battle against the armies of Satan, led by Padre Tomas. After the victory, which, of course, would be televised by both national television stations, I would gather the sons and daughters of light in the Valley of Consolation, where we would live happily ever after.

I believe the delusion started because of a small picture of me on my First Communion outfit which hung on one of my bedroom walls when Aunt Irene first came to stay with us. After she was taken by ambulance to the state's psychiatric hospital, several days after their first visit, I noticed the picture was missing. About a week later, when I accompanied my mother to the hospital, I saw the small framed picture on the top of a heavy institutional dresser, surrounded by small glass candles, and draped with a Rosary over it, like one of those Hawaiian leis given to tourists when they arrive on Fantasy Island.

The day Aunt Irene was taken to the hospital will remain etched in my mind forever. She and Uncle Pedro had been in my home all weekend by the time I returned from a sleepover at my friend Julian's house. As soon as I entered the house, I came face to face with a tall, skinny, rather beautiful mulatto young woman, who looked impossibly young for her age.

As soon she saw me, she dropped to her knees, gathered both hands in a prayer gesture under her chin, and exclaimed, "Don't smite me, Holy Avenger. I belong to the children of light."

Startled and not knowing what to make of the young woman, I looked at my mother in utter confusion. Standing behind Irene, my mother raised her index finger to the side of her head and began to make circular motions, letting me know that the young woman was mentally ill. Even then, I knew the gesture for "crazy," "deranged," "coo-coo," and about one-hundred other pejorative words used to describe mentally ill people in my hometown.

"I am Joe, nice to meet you." I told Irene.

She cried out, "No, you are not. You are Jesus of Nazareth, Son of the Most Holy God. You are God's avenger!"

Behind her, my mother mouthed the words "Play along," followed by the same circular gesture by her left ear. Unsure as to what to say, I channeled my local Catholic priest and exclaimed,

"You are right, my daughter." I started. "But I need you to keep this a secret for a while longer. My time has not yet come."

"Forgive me, Lord." Irene cried out. "I know how tricky the evil spirits are. I know their dark archangel, Padre Tomas. He is a snake."

"Arise, my daughter, I want you to go to your room and rest." I ordered Irene.

She stood up and began to back away, walking backwards, with her face hanging low and frantically making the sign of the cross over her forehead and chest. Once inside the room, she closed the door and started praying in front of the small picture.

Terrified, I looked at my mother and Uncle Pedro and said, "What the hell was that?"

The question took both by surprise because I was just a child, I was terrified of my mother, and I had never cursed in public before. Rather than being angry, however, they both broke out in hysterical laughter.

"I met her about a year ago. Her name is Irene," Uncle Pedro stated, apologetically. "I didn't know she was ill. When I met her, she was fine. A little eccentric, but I kind of liked that."

"She will be okay." My mother reassured her favorite brother. "God will provide somehow."

My brother and I had slept on bedrolls on the floor of my parents' room for three full days by the time Irene received her divine vision that God had given her the ability to fly like one of his angels. I remember this was a Wednesday, a little before 3:00 o'clock in the morning. A desperate Uncle Pedro woke us up, loudly knocking on all the doors of the house, frantically looking for his wife.

Within minutes the entire household was up, looking for Aunt Irene on the street, in startled neighbors' houses, and even on the terraces and roofs of all the homes in the block. By 5:00 am, Uncle Pedro was beside himself with worry; my sisters were busy in the kitchen, making empanadas and black coffee for the search party; the neighbors had started a rosary chain to Our Lady of Perpetual Help, believed to be the patron saint of those in desperate need; and the children were getting ready for the day because even the excitement of the search could not interfere with school.

At around 5:15 that morning, Sofia Rodriguez, perhaps the nosiest of all our neighbors, ran into our kitchen still wearing hair curlers, an old nightgown and sandals. She lived directly across from our house and was the best source of news and gossip in town. Speaking to Mrs. Rodriguez for five minutes was more productive than watching the evening news for an hour.

Excitedly, Mrs. Rodriguez announced that she had found Aunt Irene. Rather, her son Nicolas, a truck driver who lived three streets south of our block, had found a strange woman wrapped on a white sheet, running back and forth on the roof of his eighteen-wheeler. Nicolas worked for a cooperative of small farms carrying fresh produce to the largest markets in the region. On occasion, he could take the truck home, which he parked on an empty lot across from his three-story house.

On this morning, as he was getting ready to go to work, he had heard a strange noise from the lot across the street. From the third-floor window of his bedroom, he could see a young woman about to jump from the truck. He opened the window and heard the woman asking an invisible person to give her a sign before she set out in flight. Terrified by the huge liability the woman posed, Nicolas ran to his truck, still dressed in his pajamas.

My mother and Uncle Pedro ran after Mrs. Rodriguez to her son's house, while my siblings and I stayed behind, packing our lunches for school. Lunch usually consisted of mortadella sandwiches with sliced cheese, a piece of fruit, and a bottle of water or soft drink. On occasion, some of us were courageous enough to bring dinner leftovers packed in lunchboxes.

About twenty minutes later, however, an excited Mrs. Rodriguez ran back into our kitchen and breathlessly said, "Joe, come with me. Your mother needs you to get Irene down from Nicolas' truck. He is running late to go to work and the woman is refusing to come down. Hurry up, boy!"

Without asking any questions, I followed the woman,

who by now was speed-walking, to her son's house. From a distance I could see Aunt Irene, wrapped in one of my mother's white sheets, running to the front of the truck. On the ground, a small army of onlookers where trying to cajole the young woman to come down.

I thought Irene looked radiantly beautiful that morning. The rising sun reflecting off the white sheet made her look like a veritable angel. Her dark hair, tossed by the cool morning breeze, gave the scene a surreal and seductive look. Feeling a mixture of sadness and pity, I approached the truck.

As soon as she saw me, Aunt Irene dropped to her knees and screamed loudly, "Blessed is he who comes in the name of the Lord. Blessed be God's avenger."

Somewhat embarrassed and fearing the town's gossip, I called back to her, "And blessed are you, my helper. Can I come up and speak to you, my daughter?"

By now, the crowds were in complete silence watching attentively this impromptu "Shakespeare in the park" performance. Some were probably wondering if this was some extravagant play and others must have wondered if I was as out of touch with reality as the young woman on the roof of the truck obviously was. Some were laughing and whispering amongst themselves. Not knowing exactly what was going on, Nicolas refused to allow me to climb the side ladder to the roof of his truck.

Exasperated, I said to him, "If you have a better way to get her down, go for it. Otherwise, let me do this quickly because I have school in a few minutes, and I have a test today."

"He knows what he's doing," my mother jumped in.

Reluctantly, Nicolas lowered the ladder and I climbed up the side of the truck all the way to the roof.

Irene remained kneeling and praying to God's anointed. As soon as she saw me, she started weeping loudly, "Don't get near me, Lord. My sins are too heavy upon my soul."

In the distance I heard the sirens of an ambulance

approaching. Apparently, a neighbor had called them when she first saw the young woman on the truck. On the ground the crowd was growing, as children on the way to school became curious about the scene unfolding on their usually quiet street.

"What are you doing up here, my daughter?" I asked in the most serious tone I could muster.

"Your angel," she cried out. "He appeared to me in a dream and gave me the gift of flight. He asked me to wait for a signal before I flew to him in heaven."

"You will fly to heaven soon, my daughter," I started. "But not today. I still need your help preparing for our final victory. After we win the last battle, you will fly to heaven." I intoned, channeling what I imagined a Baptist preacher would have sounded like.

"You mean I can help you defeat that snake, Padre Tomas?" She asked somewhat incredulous.

"Yes, my daughter, but I am only a child. The battle will not commence until I am eighteen years old. In the meantime, I need you to start preparing this very day. A special car will arrive very soon. I need you to go with your husband to a special place I have set up for all my helpers. You will receive further instructions when you get there. Will you do that for me?" I asked, praying silently that she would buy my story. As if on cue, the ambulance made a right turn on Nicolas' block, driving towards us. The crowds parted leaving enough space for the ambulance to park next to the truck.

"Yes, Lord. I will be your servant." Irene responded.

As she had done at home several days before, Aunt Irene walked backwards to the edge of the truck and without giving her back to me, started coming down the narrow ladder, to the relief of everyone. I remained on the roof, shaken, but grateful. I wondered how many other twelve-year old boys had helped a relative walk off the ledge of a precipice before going to school that morning. Once Irene, Pedro, and my mother left in the ambulance, I came down the truck to the cheers and questions of all who wanted to know what I had told the woman to get her down.

"I told her that either she came down or Nicolas would have to drive to work with her on the roof," I lied. This answer seemed to satisfy the curiosity of most bystanders, some of whom went back to their homes or proceeded to walk to school. Mrs. Rodriguez, however, wanted to know the full story.

"What's wrong with her?" She asked.

"She just has more faith than all of us." I responded, leaving the scene behind as I walked to school with my brother Juan in toe.

Chapter 12

Now, three whole years later, Aunt Irene was back, and her timing could not have been worse. Of course, this was hardly her fault. Patients don't schedule their mental breakdowns when it's convenient for their relatives. The demons in our heads have minds of their own, and they come out to play when we least expect them. And, I do mean it when I compare hallucinations with demons in our heads. Of course, these demons are not spiritual entities as much as they are the result of organic, genetic conditions we inherit at birth and experience at some point in our lives. In fact, I believe most of the demoniacs we meet in the Bible were people who suffered from undiagnosed mental illness. Not being in full possession of your faculties must, indeed, be hell.

Quietly, I walked into the bathroom, took a long, hot shower, changed into the pajamas my mother had left for me, and started walking back towards my mother, as the sweet aromas of the fried plantains wafted from the kitchen. I instinctively knew that the plantains would be accompanied by pinto beans slow-cooked in garlic and cilantro, with large pieces of smoked bacon thrown in for flavor. Completing the holy trifecta, my mother's Spanish yellow rice would add a perfect canvas for the beans, which always went on top. On the side of the rice and beans, occupying the place of honor, would be a pan-friend skirt steak covered in lime juice and more cilantro.

I ate in silence as my mother drank a hot cup of strong black coffee and smoked an unfiltered cigarette.

At some point I asked, "What's wrong with Irene now?"

"She is pregnant and can't take her pills until the baby is born. She's beginning to hear voices again. We have an appointment at the hospital on Monday." She replied.

"I'm going to 'The Oaks' after the service tomorrow." I reminded my mother.

"I know," she said empathically.

"Thanks for everything, mom." I said as an unexpected shower of tears fell down my cheeks.

"You're welcome," She said. Then she added, "God will give you the strength you need."

"I know." I said.

"Go on to bed before we wake up Irene." She said with a grin on her face. I smiled back.

I stood up and went to the bathroom to brush my teeth. I removed your letter from my jean's pocket and went to my parents' room. The small room is located at the end of the hallway, after the kitchen and bathroom, on the right side of the house. The room is sparsely decorated, but it has the best bed in the house.

Entering the room, I noticed two things at once. First, my Confirmation suit, neatly pressed, was hanging from the door of my parent's tall dresser. Second, my brother Juan was lying on a bedroll by the foot of the bed, which means I could have half of the large bed all to myself. Grateful for my brother's generous gesture, I laid on the bed while my mom cleaned the dishes in the kitchen. I opened your letter, hoping to find an explanation for your death, some new revelation, a set of instructions, or, even, one of your corny jokes. I missed you so much already that I craved just a bit of normalcy. "Hey, Joe, have I ever told you..."

What I found in the neatly folded piece of paper surprised me, not so much for what it said, but for what it didn't say. The note did not offer any clarity, clues, or instructions. In fact, the note wasn't even a letter in the classical sense. I could recognize your neat penmanship, small letters perfectly aligned, all in small caps, and all in cursive. The note was a well-known poem by the "best poet in the world in any language" as Garcia Marquez had once called Pablo Neruda. You and I had once read this very same poem, spending half a night trying to decipher its meaning. The note read,

> *The Light Wraps You by PN*
> *The light wraps you in its mortal flame.*
> *Abstracted pale mourner, standing that way*
> *against the old propellers of the twilight*
> *that revolves around you.*
>
> *Speechless, my friend,*
> *alone in the loneliness of this hour of the dead*
> *and filled with the lives of fire,*
> *pure heir of the ruined day.*
> *A bough of fruit falls from the sun on your dark garment.*
>
> *The great roots of night*
> *grow suddenly from your soul,*
> *and the things that hide in you come out again*
> *so that a blue and palled people*

your newly born, takes nourishment.
Oh, magnificent and fecund and magnetic slave
of the circle that moves in turn through black and gold:
rise, lead and possess a creation
so rich in life that its flowers perish
and it is full of sadness.

That's it! That was your note. Your final words to me. You made me the "pure heir of the ruined day." Like a day ending in twilight, your life was over way too soon, and I was destined to outlive you, to survive you, to mourn you. You made me your "fecund and magnetic slave." Was this note an apology? Was this an acknowledgement that your decision would make the "great roots of night grow suddenly from my soul?" Was this a reminder that even while gripped by anger and sorrow, I still needed to "rise, lead and possess a creation so rich... that it is full of sadness?" Was there a clue hidden in these familiar phrases? I would have to figure that out later, as I heard my mother's footsteps approaching the room and I wanted to avoid worrying her any more than I already had.

I got up from the bed, placed your note in its envelope, put it inside the lining pocket of my Confirmation jacket, lay back down on the bed, and pretended to be asleep when my mother walked in. As it turned out, I didn't have to pretend long, as I quickly passed out and slept until 7:00 am when my mother woke me up.

Chapter 13

"Did you sleep well?" My mother asked.

"Soundly," I responded, stretching and yawning.

"Go to the living room and look out the window." She commanded smiling.

Curious, I got up from the bed and went to the living room. I peeked through the window and saw a beautiful four-door limousine parked in front of our house. Standing by the passenger side window there was an elegantly dressed chauffeur, wearing a perfectly tailored black suit and an Irish flat cap. Confused, I looked at my mother, who was standing right behind me.

She said, "He arrived a few minutes ago, politely knocked on the door, and asked me to let you sleep as long as you needed to. He said he didn't mind waiting for you. Mr. Cuevas sent him to take you to the funeral."

"He didn't have to do this." I said, almost apologetically.

"He wanted to, honey. Now go get dressed. Do you want some coffee?" She offered.

"Yes, please." I said, while still trying to shake myself awake.

"You can use your room to get dressed if you want to. Pedro took Irene to morning mass a few minutes ago. He didn't want her to bother you on a day like this." She added, as I was walking to her room to get my suit.

My brother was still asleep on the floor and I tip-toed around him not to wake him up. It was customary for all my siblings to sleep late on Saturdays. This was our day to catch up on much needed rest. Our lives tended to be busy during the week and Saturday morning cartoons and sleeping late were two of the perks of the weekend. I often chose the cartoons, quietly in the living room, while Juan always chose to sleep late. I brought my suit to my bedroom and dressed quickly. Somehow, I felt awkward letting the driver wait outside. My mother had invited him in, but he had refused. She brought him a cup of strong, black coffee, which he had gratefully accepted.

Reading my mind, my mother was waiting right outside my room, holding a Styrofoam cup filled with the hot beverage. She stated, "You better go now, there is no need to keep him waiting."

Propped on one of the dining room chairs was my backpack and, knowing my mother as well as I do, I knew instantaneously that it would be filled with clean clothes, underwear, my favorite towel, and hygiene supplies for three days to a week. This is just how she is, three moves ahead.

Grateful, I gave her a smile, and said, "How do you always know what I need before I ask?"

She smiled and replied, "Mothers always know."

"Thanks." I said, avoiding her eye contact, mainly because I didn't want her to see how sad and empty I was feeling inside.

"You are welcome. Call me from 'The Oaks' when you

get there." She requested, not as an order, but, rather, as a customary reminder.

"I will." I said, as I walked out.

The limousine was the most elegant vehicle I had ever seen in my life. Four-door sedan, American, leather seats, mini-bar, and a small magazine rack, located behind the driver's seat. The driver was wearing a name tag on the lapel of his jacket. William Jaramillo. Underneath the name the words "Steerco Corporate Driver," announcing to the world his role in the company. He was not your family's chauffeur, but, rather, your father's personal driver at his company. It was his duty to drive your father to meetings, while he reviewed contracts and spreadsheets in the back seat. William opened the back door of the driver's side of the limousine for me.

I asked, "Do you mind if I drive up front with you? I would feel very uncomfortable in the back all by myself."

"Absolutely." He said. "Hop on."

I came around the front of the limousine to the passenger's side and was about to get in when a familiar voice called me from across the street. It was Mrs. Rodriguez standing outside the front door of her house.

She asked, "Everything okay, Joe?"

"Everything is fine, Mrs. Rodriguez." I responded. Then, knowing that this bit of news would travel across town before the car left Bello, I added, "Just my driver and I going to market."

I could hear William laughing inside the car and I could also see my mother peeking through the windows. I entered the car and closed the door. William drove away, leaving a confused Mrs. Rodriguez, scratching her head.

"You are a smart ass." William said smiling and extending his right hand to me. "I'm William, like the ID tag says."

"Nice meeting you, William." I said. "I'm Joe. Thanks for picking me up and for waiting."

"No problem. I live close by. Mr. Cuevas let me take the car home last night on condition that I pick you up at 7:00." He responded.

"It's a bit early," I said, looking at my watch. "The service doesn't start until 10:00 am."

"How right you are." He said, grinning. "I have instructions to bring you to Mr. Cuevas' country club for breakfast before I take you both to church. He'll be waiting for us there."

"It'll be my first time at a country club." I commented, mostly to myself.

"It's just like a fancy restaurant where everybody fusses over you and you don't have to pay the bill." He answered.

"It's free?" I asked surprised.

"Nothing in life is free." He answered with a laugh. "You pay dues every year. All meals, drinks, golf, and all the other perks are included in your membership fees. You don't even tip the servers. Once a year you write an additional check at Christmas time and the money is divided among all the service staff. I know because I used to work there before Mr. Cuevas asked me to come and drive for him almost five years ago. Rather, Alex hired me when he was ten years old."

A sad smile on his lips, let me know that William, who was approximately thirty-five, short, stout, and had the distinctive red nose of those who enjoy their whiskey or aguardiente every night, knew you well and liked you. Perhaps he too was your, "Magnificent and fecund and magnetic slave."

I begged him, "Please tell me the story."

"It happened a while ago, during the last race for Governor. Mrs. Cuevas was so busy running the Mejia's campaign that she forgot to order a 'Ponque Maria Luisa,' which had been Alex's only request for his tenth birthday. The family had made reservations for fifty of the biggest movers and shakers in the city and the country club had been in frenzied preparations for the lunch for almost a week. The chefs had prepared an incredible meal with all the families favorites: Shrimp, Argentinian stakes, the best meats Steerco could provide, salads, and a large chocolate sheet-cake decorated with marzipan flowers and balloons.

This wasn't just Alex's birthday. It was also a fundraiser event for Governor Alfonso Mejia, then Candidate Mejia. There were beautiful flowers everywhere; an army of perfectly dressed ushers, responsible for parking all the fancy cars in the lots; beautiful waitresses in brand new uniforms, purchased for the occasion, carrying trays with champagne cocktails; photographers from both of the city's papers, carefully documenting the event for their social pages; and the Cuevas family dressed in impeccable outfits made specially by Cesar's father and designed by well-known Parisian fashion gods. It was, by far, one of the fanciest parties I had ever worked in my seven years with the club."

He took a pause, drank a gulp of water from a bottle, and continued, "Everything was going according to plan. The guests were arriving, everyone was as picture perfect as the occasion demanded, and the staff was like a well-oiled machine. All this changed when Alex realized that the birthday cake was not a Maria Luisa. He stormed from the restaurant to one of the rooms where his mother was entertaining a distinguished guest. He planted himself in front of her, both fisted hands on the sides of his body, and demanded to know what had happened with his cake.

I remember Alex yelling angrily, 'What happened with my birthday cake? Where is it?'

Mrs. Cuevas, obviously embarrassed by the child's tantrum, answered him, 'Honey, the bakers made you a wonderful cake. It is chocolate.'

Not impressed, Alex yelled, 'I don't want a stupid chocolate cake. You promised me a Strawberry Maria Luisa!'

Mrs. Cuevas, flustered in anger, tried to help the boy calm down, 'I promise you, we will get a Maria Luisa tonight, honey. Now go play, while I talk to this nice gentleman.'

Alex, held his place, unwilling to move. He yelled, 'I didn't even want this stupid party.'

Mrs. Cuevas, excused herself from the guest, took the child to a private bathroom, and yelled at him in measured, teeth-grinding sounds, 'Now, you calm down, you little shit! This party is important to the family and you will not ruin it. Now, stop this!'

Alex started crying tears of rage. He said, 'I hate you and I hate your stupid party.'

Mrs. Cuevas, without a warning, slapped Alex on his face, ice-cold stare on her eyes. She repeated her warning: 'Either you control yourself or I promise you I will give you a belting in front of all these people.'

Alex, ran to the entrance of the closed room, turned back to face his mother and yelled loud enough for anyone in the city to hear him, 'Fuck you. I hate you!'"

William stopped his tale for a few seconds, lost in thought, took another sip of his water and continued. "I was right outside the room when the boy stormed out and I saw Mrs. Cuevas frozen in the middle of the room. Like nothing happened, she composed herself, gave me one of those 'what can a mother do?' looks, powdered her nose with a small compact in her purse, and returned to her guests, as calm and collected as she could be.

I ran after the boy, caught up with him and said, 'Hey, Alex. Do you want me to get you a Maria Luisa?'

The boy stopped on his tracks, turned around and faced me. He asked, 'Can you?'

'I don't see why not.' I answered him."

Another sip of water, another faint smile, and a few seconds of silence. Then the tale continued, "Now, you need to know that this behavior was not like Alex. He had never been a spoiled brat. In fact, he was always a sweet, funny, gregarious boy, who treated the help with great respect, and was always chasing us around, telling us his corny jokes. We all loved the boy and he loved coming to the club with his mother when he was a little boy. Obviously, something was wrong on this occasion and I wanted to make the boy happy on his birthday. All kids deserve to be happy on their birthdays.

I made a few mistakes that day, however. First, I didn't tell my boss I was going to the bakery, about a ten-minute drive from the club. Second, I didn't punch out, which was an immediate cause for termination in my case because this had become a common way for some employees to pad up their hours. And, my third mistake was that I invited the boy to come with me to the store."

We had just left Bello and William was entering the deserted highway. Perhaps it was the hour of the morning or the day of the week, but I found it strange that the usually congested highway that led to the city was this empty. It was as though all traffic had been diverted to allow us safe passage.

William continued his story, "There were lots of people at the bakery that day, which means we had to wait. By the time we got the Maria Luisa and started to head back to the club, almost an hour had passed. Knowing that I was in trouble, I drove my crappy 1972 Simca car like a demon, switching lanes frantically, running through stop signs, and almost doubling the speed limit. In the meantime, the boy was having a great time. This was an awesome adventure for him. His laughter and 'go, go, go' encouragement were sufficient motivation for my irresponsible behaviors. No excuses, but I was much younger and carefree then. Anyway, by the time we arrived back at the club, Mrs. Wilomina Gomez, the Iron Madden herself, who was my boss at the time, was waiting for us at the club's valet parking."

William gave me a furtive smile, indicating that I was getting to the best part of the story, "Furious, Mrs. Gomez said, 'Alex, your father is looking for you. Go along.' To me, she said, 'William, empty your locker and leave immediately. We will mail you your last check.' Seven years working for them and she fired me just like that. Alex started begging Mrs. Gomez to reconsider, saying that it was all his fault, that he made me drive him, and that she was being unfair. The Iron Madden, unmoved by the child's pleas, walked past him and returned to the party." One more sip of water and another smile.

I was engrossed by the tale and I dared not ask any questions. I could picture you, the lover of all things dangerous, enjoying the crazy ride and encouraging William to break the law for your enjoyment. Even at ten, you seemed to have a death wish. I was also impressed that this grown man loved you enough to risk his job to make you happy on your birthday. Even then you seemed to have your way with people.

I looked at William appreciatively and encouraged him to continue. "What happened then?"

"Mr. Cuevas was waiting for me outside the employee lockers after I gathered all my stuff. A contented Alex, standing to his left, was holding a second piece of Ponque Maria Luisa in his hands, crumbs and refined sugar all over his white shirt. Mr. Cuevas stated, 'I understand you are a pretty good driver.' I said nothing, so he continued, 'How would you like to work for Steerco? I'm in need of a corporate driver.' At that point Alex, interjected, answering for me, 'He'll love it. Right, William? And you will pay him twice as much as he makes here, right, Dad?' He said, looking at Mr. Cuevas. The old man smiled and said, 'I guess it has been decided. I will see you Monday morning.' And that's it. That's how I started working for Steerco. God, I loved that boy."

"We have something in common there." I said, awkwardly.

"I know. He talked about you sometimes. The first time

he came back from 'The Oaks' he said to me, 'I may have just met the coolest kid ever.' I asked him, 'What makes him so cool?' To which he answered, 'He knows what he believes in and he is not ashamed of it.' I think this was a great compliment to you." William stated.

That may have been the nicest compliment I had ever heard. You respected my beliefs, even after picking on me mercilessly, calling me an "altar boy" and a "Boy Scout." I wish you would have said this to me because I often felt very self-righteous and arrogant when I was around you. I often wished I would have been more spontaneous, more carefree, better able to mold my beliefs to suit specific situations. I think I would have been a better companion, instead of being your "Jiminy Cricket," the sometimes-unwelcome voice of your conscience.

I said nothing for a long while, but as soon as we entered the imposing gates of the "Poblado Country Club," I decided to ask William a question that had been circulating in the back of my head. I asked, "What do you make of the Cuevas?"

"Do you mean, do I like them? If this is your question, then, yes, I like them. He is an amazingly generous man who is well loved by his workers and business associates. He works too hard and can be aloof sometimes, but his heart is in the right place. Mrs. Cuevas, on the other hand, is a complete mystery to me. Alex and she had a very difficult relationship over the last four years or so. He used to tell me that he hated her, which was hard for me to hear, you know? I grew up thinking my mother walked on water. I could have never said about my mother the things Alex said about his. Anyway, I feel like I'm gossiping, and gossip is for women." He ended the conversation abruptly.

"I can appreciate that." I said quickly, but then I pressed on, "What kinds of things did he say about her?"

"That she wasn't a nice person. He thought she was having an affair. He had found a love letter from a suitor in her room, during one of Mr. Cuevas' long business trips to Venezuela. One night he and Cesar were playing ball in the hallway and their ball rolled into his parents' room, which had been left open. As luck would have it, the ball stopped right under Mrs. Cuevas' nightstand. The boy reached down to pick up the ball and, on his way up, he saw the red stationery, which smelled like talc powder and perfume. Curious, he picked up the note and read it. It was a love letter written by someone with the initials Y. M. According to Alex, it was a rather intimate and sexual note. He also noticed that neither the handwriting nor the initials belonged to his father." William paused for a few seconds while he parked the limousine in one of the reserved spots in front of the club's restaurant.

I said quickly, "Wow! Did you ever suspect anything?"

"I wasn't her driver, but Mr. Cuevas once complained that his wife favored the company of certain politicians and real estate moguls, over the company of her own husband and son. He said it in passing and perhaps as a joke, but I never forgot the comment." William got out of the car, came to my side and opened the door for me.

I said, "Thanks again William. It was an honor meeting you. Do you mind if I call you sometimes? I really want to learn more about Alex's home life. This side of him is a mystery to me."

"Call me any time, little man. A friend of Alex is a friend of mine." He said as we walked into the luxurious restaurant.

Chapter 14

Everything about the giant hall spoke of wealth and elegance. Red mahogany and leather everywhere, marble floors with very light layers of pink perfectly formed in the limestone, impeccably made tables with white linens and fresh flower vases at their center, perfectly uniformed staff, giant European chandeliers hanging from the ceilings, original Botero and Picasso paintings displayed throughout the imposing walls, a replica of the famous Roman Trevi fountain in a center courtyard that could be seen from every window of the room, and elegant menus in Spanish, French, and English.

Arturo Cuevas, dressed in a double-breasted black suit with a red carnation protruding from a buttonhole near the top of the jacket, and the corner of a small red silk tie showing from the jacket's breast pocket, was seated near the entrance of the restaurant. As soon as he saw me, he waved me to sit across from him, which I did.

"Good morning, Joe. Thanks for joining me this morning." He said in a business tone.

Gone from him were the raw emotions and tears of the night before. He was back in control, sober, and ready for his son's funeral, which means he was resigned to what was about to happen and he felt he needed to be strong for his wife's sake.

After shaking hands for a brief second, he asked, "So, what did you make of Alex's note?"

"It is a poem by Pablo Neruda. It was one of our favorites," I responded honestly.

"I thought it was pretty sad. Why that poem?" He asked.

We were interrupted by a young waitress who took our breakfast order. I wasn't very hungry, so I just ordered black coffee and toast. Your dad ordered poached eggs, bacon, coffee, and croissants. He grabbed the jar of fresh orange juice the waitress left behind and served us both a glass of juice. After drinking about half of the juice, I answered your father's question,

"Both Alex and I believed the poem was about the bittersweet ending of a perfect day. The twilight announces the coming of the night, and we mourn the fading light. The poet then welcomes the moon, which circles and turns around the earth. He invites her to rise, lead, and possess a creation filled with death and life, light and shadows, past and future, joy and sadness. Of course, the poem can also be a metaphor for death. Someone dies and their death fills us with darkness and sadness. It forces us to become mourners and survivors who must rise to lead and possess a creation in which they no longer live. It works both ways." I said.

"Thank you for the lesson, professor." Your dad said in a fake gesture of admiration, but in good humor. "I meant, why did he leave you that particular poem? Alex loved most of Neruda's poems. Why that one?"

Your father made an excellent point. Why this poem? Better yet, why a poem at all? Why not just write a note about what I had meant to you, or about the reasons you were about to take your own life, or a list of specific instructions of what you wanted me to do next? Perhaps, there was a clue in the poem I had missed. Perhaps this was your way of telling me something without raising suspicions with the police or the family who would eventually find the note. If this was the case, then it had worked. Your father thought the poem was so innocent that he hadn't even told your mother about the note.

Of course, the message would only work if I figured out the clue. Several questions came to mind: Had you substituted any word of the original poem with a different word? I didn't know because I had not memorized the poem. Had you switched a phrase or two around, revealing something in the new order of sentences? Again, I didn't know.

Almost by instinct I touched my jacket, feeling if the note was still there. I panicked when I didn't feel the note, but then I realized I had put it in the opposite pocket. I couldn't wait until I had some quiet time and a Neruda book to compare the original poem to the one in the note.

"I have no idea." I told your dad, lost in thought.

"Well, if you figure it out, please call me and let me know." He said, quite causally, as though it didn't matter either way.

I promised I would, finishing my orange juice, just as the waitress was approaching our table with the food. We ate in silence and your dad refilled my orange juice glass twice before breakfast was over. The orange juice at the club was 100% freshly squeezed every morning by the kitchen staff. It was then filtered of any impurities or seeds and refrigerated until perfectly chilled.

I never knew oranges could taste this good. After enjoying one more glass, I asked, "Is Cesar's dad in politics as well?"

“Michael? No, he is a foreigner. His wife is a big supporter of Governor Mejia, as is Missy, but neither Michael nor Linda are in politics. Why do you ask?”

“Somehow I thought he was a diplomat, in addition to being in business.” I fished.

“No, he is not a diplomat. In fact, he doesn’t have a political bone in his body. You know he was chased out of London for labor issues he could have easily solved if he had been a bit more tactful. Some people are arrogant and believe they can treat people any way they like. Michael is just like that. I don’t much care for the man, but Linda and Missy are best friends, and Cesar and Alex grew up together. I had no choice but to tolerate the son-of-a-bitch.” Your dad stated quite honestly and showing a fair amount of resentment towards Michael Walters. Could he be the mysterious lover whose note Alex found?

“Is Cesar a foreigner too?” I asked, knowing the answer already

“Have you taken civics yet, Joe?” He asked, somewhat surprised by the ridiculous question. “Children of foreigners who are born in Colombia are always Colombians. They may have another citizenship, but they never lose their Colombian citizenship. Cesar was born here in Medellin. In fact, this is where Michael and Linda first met. Here, in this very club. Her family have been members here since the club first opened back in the 1940’s. Michael’s family owned textile mills in the States since the turn of the century and had vast interests in Latin American cotton gins, including here in Colombia.

It was during one of the many trips Michael made to Colombia that the family accepted an invitation to vacation here in Medellin with one of their biggest suppliers, who was a member of this club. After meeting Linda, Michael made several trips to our fair city, began to invest in local real estate, married Linda, and settled here permanently.”

“So, why move to London?” I asked.

"That would be because of Linda," your dad answered. One more glass of orange juice later, he continued, "One of the things Linda and Michael had in common was the fact that Linda spoke perfect English. In fact, she spoke the Queen's English, having gone to Monmouth School for Girls in England when she was just thirteen. After five years in England she had fallen in love with London, where her parents had a flat, used for inter-term vacations. The parents would fly in, pick up the girl up in Monmouth and travel to London for the break.

Michael had been to London often and had business partners in the area. So, one thing led to another and the family left Medellin when Cesar was less than a year old. When they returned, eight years later, they decided to move all the company's manufacturing to Medellin, where labor was cheap, and Linda's family was considered royalty." Your father answered.

"Did your wife know Linda growing up?" I asked, already imagining what the answer would be.

"Missy? Hell no!" He laughed dismissively. "Let's say that Missy and her family traveled in different circles. Much, much humbler circles. Missy's father left the family when she was just three and her brother was four. Her mother had to work two jobs to provide for them. They lived in rental property, went to public schools, and had full-time jobs when they were barely fourteen. Missy and Linda became friends when the Walters, that's their last name, moved next door to our home in Envigado."

I looked at my watch and realized it was almost 9:30 am. Your dad noticed me, smiled, and stated, as if answering a question beginning to form in the back of my mind, "The church is literally five minutes away and William is waiting outside. We are not late."

"Sorry, I have a bad habit of looking at my watch. I don't know why. It's not like I have a busy life and need to be anywhere at any time. It's just something I do." I said apologetically.

"No need to apologize." He said standing up.

He walked out to his car and I followed silently behind.

Chapter 15

We left the club without talking to anyone, signing any bills, or bothering to thank the waitress for her service. I don't know exactly why, but this made me feel quite guilty. I believed the young woman had done an excellent job serving us and deserved a "thank you," at the very least. Not seeing her around, I followed your dad.

William was waiting by the driver's side of the car. He quickly opened the back door for your dad with great reverence. Without thinking, I sat on the passenger's side, next to William, as I had done before.

Your father said, "Come, sit back here with me, Joe."

Embarrassed, I moved to the back seat, and said, "I'm sorry, I'm not used to riding in limousines."

Your dad said, smiling, "Stop apologizing. Why don't you ask me the question you want to ask me, Joe?"

"I don't know what you mean." I lied, defensively.

"You want to know how I met Missy, especially

because I just told you she didn't travel in our circles." He started. "Well, my little friend, I will tell you. But only If you ask."

I had no choice but to laugh at this comment. It was like being in the car with you. From the title, "Little friend," to your refusal to continue stories until I took the bait and asked you to continue, and the playful tone in his voice.

"You sound just like him." I said. "Okay, I will take the bait. Mr. Cuevas, Sir. Could you, please, tell me how you met your beautiful wife?"

In the front seat, William, let out a guttural laugh. "I told you he was a smart ass."

"You told me." Your dad told his driver. He then added, "I will tell you, Joe. But first you need to answer one of my questions. Do you know why Alex often said he loved you as much as a blind man loves his monkey?"

Both were laughing now. Of course, I had never figured out your stupid saying, and, honestly, I had never paid much attention to it. Knowing you, it was probably something sexual or disgusting.

"I have no idea. I never tried to understand much of what he said anyway." I lied, smiling.

"Bullshit!" He said. "You loved that boy and you tried harder than any of us to understand every silly thing that came out of his mouth."

He was right again. Your dad was hitting on all cylinders that morning. It was as though he was training for one of the most difficult things he would ever have to do by flexing his humor muscles. I realized then where you got your tendency to deflect pain, conflict, and stress by using humor. You were more like your old man than you were able or willing to acknowledge. Chip off the old block, if you ask me.

"William, please tell our bespectacled friend the story of the monkey." Your dad ordered.

"We are almost by the church, but it goes like this. I used

to read Alex a story when I first met him at the club. He was maybe three or four years old, and he and I were good buddies. I watched after him while Mr. Cuevas took his tennis lessons. Anyway, in the story, a man rescued a small monkey when he was just days old and had trained him to do house chores, fetch him a beer, and alert him when any intruders entered the property in the middle of the night.

The monkey learned to love the man and the man learned to love his monkey as the son he never had. At some point in the story, the man had a freak accident and went blind. The monkey began to take care of him, becoming a great caregiver over time, until, one day, the man died of old age. At this point, the distraught monkey sat at the gravesite of the blindman, refusing to eat for days, until he died, days later, remaining faithful to his owner in death as he had been in life. It was a cute story of loyalty and friendship.

The funny part of the story is that when Alex was barely five years old, he announced at a dinner party that if he ever went blind, he would want me to be his monkey. Everybody around the table started laughing, but I thought it was the best compliment I had ever gotten. About six months ago, Alex was riding in this same car with the two of us when he said, 'No offense, William, but if I ever go blind, I want Joe to be my monkey!' We all laughed, but I knew then that you had replaced me as the favorite."

As William was telling his story, a big lump was forming in my throat. Somehow, I knew where the story was headed, and big tears were making their way upwards from my heart to my eyes. I didn't want to cry at this moment, but the story moved me greatly. Suddenly, I found myself loving that cryptic phrase. "I love you as a blind man loves his monkey." I would be honored to be your monkey, Alex Cuevas. I wish you would have given me the opportunity to take care of you. I wish you would have lived to a ripe old age with those who loved you surrounding you with their care and affection.

As the car pulled into the church's parking lot, your dad stated, somberly, "Thank you, William. Now, a promise is a promise. I didn't know Missy until she was eighteen and her mother, who worked for my father at Steerco, died in an auto accident. I was nineteenth then and in college. I accompanied my dad to the funeral because, Mrs. Betty, as she was known, had always been very nice to me growing up. She loved my father and was a dutiful secretary to the end, even when he could be a horse's ass to her sometimes. Or, rather, most of the time.

I met Missy at the wake, and I fell in love with her the moment I saw her. She was the most beautiful woman I had ever seen. And by this, I don't mean that she had a beautiful heart, or a nice personality, I mean she was gorgeous. Dark brown eyes, perfect breasts, long dark brown hair, impossibly long legs, an awesome ass, and I could go on and on. The girl was a goddess. Plus, she had the inner strength of one who has suffered greatly and still managed to come out okay. Her sad smile could melt ice, and to watch her walk through a room was enough to make you want to praise God for having made her. I knew she would be mine, the second I laid eyes on her, but she was a clever girl and there was no way to make her mine without making her my wife. Now, let's get inside and say good bye to my boy. The best gift Missy has ever given me and the only person I have truly loved."

Shocked by the revelations, I walked in silence towards the church. As I entered the imposing building, your dad placed his hand on my shoulder and said, "I think the boys are listening to the service from the sacristy. William will show you the way. And, Joe, please call William if you ever need a ride to 'The Oaks.' He lives about ten minutes from your house and he wouldn't mind it. Would you, William?"

Placing a business card in the front pocket of my jacket, William responded, "It would be an honor, Joe. I mean it."

Chapter 16

I shook your dad's hand and followed William to the sacristy. It was about five minutes to 10:00 and the other four boys were already in the sacristy. On the way in I came face to face with my mentor and favorite priest in the world. Fr. Wilbert Garcia had come from "The Oaks" to the funeral because he too had loved you. In fact, he had brought the entire staff, and they were sitting in the congregation.

He gave me a big hug and reminded me, "I will see you tonight, right?"

"Yes, Father. I will be there. Thanks for speaking to my mom and Fr. Gaviria," I said tears beginning to form in my eyes.

He looked at me with great sadness in his eyes and said, "I know what this means to you. We'll get through this together."

"Thanks, Father. God will give us strength." I said, meaning every word.

"He will." He said, leaving the sacristy as the service was about to start.

Behind him Fr. Bedoya, the Rector of the church, welcomed me with a hug, as though we were old friends, even though this was the first time I ever met the man. It occurred to me then that you must have talked about me with him because he was your rector and he had sponsored you to join the leadership school at "The Oaks."

Fr. Bedoya said, "You were special to him. Thank you for being his friend." With that he left the sacristy after Fr. Garcia, fully vested in religious attire.

As soon as Fr. Bedoya entered the church, the service began with the sound of the organ playing "Happy Holy Morning." The five of us in the sacristy found places to sit and no one paid much attention to the others. Sitting in the sacristy was akin to having the chef of a famous restaurant invite you to sit in the kitchen or private table with him to enjoy the meal.

Whereas everyone in the pews were constrained by the people to the left and right of them to remain in place, we had space to roam, could use the restroom, get a glass of water, and cry loudly without distracting others. I was glad they had invited me to sit with them in this small, but comfortable space.

Sitting by that old filling cabinet, I became lost in thought about the fact that three different grown-ups had thanked me for being your friend in the last two days, as though this had been a huge sacrifice on my part. I believed at the time, as I do now, that I was the lucky one.

Your friendship and your death defined who I am, and I will never forget the lessons you taught me. I know that I will live my life trying to honor your love for the undesirables and the outcast. You have made me more accepting of those who are different and don't fit in. Anyway, sitting on that floor, head resting on my knees and tears freely flowing on my Confirmation suit, I replayed in my head our last conversation, the memories still fresh and raw.

Your call took place on the early hours of Wednesday,

December 9, 1981, but in a way, your last goodbye began several days early at "The Oaks."

Sunday, December 6, 1981 was the end of our Christmas term at the Center. We had been there since early November and we were about to be deployed to our home parishes to help with Christmas pageants, youth group functions, and Christmas services. For most of us this would be a busy time of church work, but, for others, this would be an opportunity to get a vacation from the intensity of camp before the new school year started. I belonged to the first group and my parish priest, Fr. Gaviria, was anxiously waiting for the help. I still help him every time I come home.

You were planning on a long vacation with your parents to San Andres islands, which was scheduled to start on Saturday, December 12. For the staff at "The Oaks" the break from the leadership school and the weekend retreats was an opportunity to stay at the Center in spiritual retreat and annual debriefing for two weeks before their break. The Center closed from December 23 to January 6, which was the official staff's vacation.

The day before the end-of-session, the Center always celebrates a traditional good-bye party, which is followed by the official closing Eucharist the next day. The party includes a gift exchange among all the members of the school and the staff and, since handmade gifts are preferred, many of us spend weeks, working on carvings, paintings, calligraphy projects, poetry-writing, and pottery trinkets to gift our favorite staff and each other.

You were an accomplished pencil artist and had already completed several beautiful works by the time I started working on my crude and unrefined calligraphy posters. I did notice about two weeks before the party that your usually lively drawings had taken a dark, almost demented, turn. Animals with multiple heads and tails, devouring their small prey with gleeful gluttony, had replaced the usually placid drawings of forests, rivers, and small cottages nested between beautiful mountains.

You also seemed constantly drunk or high since the beginning of November. You were moody, irritable, rude, and impatient with me and others. You complained more than usual about the "shitty state of affairs" in the city, and you skipped most morning and evening prayers. Fr. Garcia was beginning to worry about you, but you convinced the old man that you were just grieving the loss of your paternal grandfather who had just died in early October.

We all knew you loved the old man and visited him almost every week at the rehabilitation facility where he had been treated since a massive stroke about six months before. So, your story of grief made sense to us, and we often prayed for you at chapel. Your friends visited you daily in our room and, under some duress, you agreed to join us at soccer matches and social functions, although you only stayed for part of the time.

The Friday before the end of the session, I could barely get you up from bed. I made excuses for you, telling everybody that you were under the weather. At around 3:00 that afternoon, I excused myself from all afternoon sessions to take care of you. I found you sitting on the side of the bed, smoking and crying. I approached the bed, sat next to you, and gave you a side hug.

I then asked you, "What's wrong, Alex? Please talk to me."

"My life is shit, bro. That's what's wrong with me," you responded, a combination of anger and sadness across your frowning mouth.

"What's making your life shit? Is it your grandfather?" I prodded.

"I miss the old guy. But no, my funk has nothing to do him." You whispered.

"Is it the drugs? Too much vino?" I pushed in a gentle

voice. I didn't want to upset you any more or sound overly judgmental. I often came across as self-righteous to you.

"The drugs are bullshit, Joe. I can stop this shit whenever I want to. The drugs are something I do to deal with the crap in my life, not the other way around." You said, irritated.

"Then tell me about your crap." I demanded.

"You would hate me. Everyone would hate me. And you wouldn't believe me!" You screamed louder than you intended to.

Startled by your own anger, you continued, "Sorry, I didn't mean to bark at you. I know you are the only one who gives a shit. Anyway, I am just a little blue today, buddy. I will feel better in the morning."

You tried to avoid the conversation. I protested, "Don't do this, man. Don't shut me out. I deserve better than this. Give me some credit. I promise I won't judge you."

"I know," you said. You offered me a drag of your joint, which I quickly refused. You looked at me, smiled, and said, "It's not that shit. I would never corrupt your upstanding morals with bazuko. It's just pot."

"Fuck you!" I said taking a drag of the Mexican pot, the highest quality in the market and a pricy affair only the rich could afford. Then, I begged you, "Come on, tell me what's wrong."

"I'm not the person you know. All the jokes, the partying, the crazy stunts, the funny little sayings, the risk-taking, all of it is just bullshit. It's all just crap I do to hide the truth about me. I'm not a good person, I don't even think I believe in God, and I'm just hiding here, so I don't have to face the garbage heap my life has become. I'm not me, which means that you don't know me. I've been lying to you all this time. I've been lying to myself." You paused, tears of rage falling down your face.

I waited for almost an interminable minute and decided to break the silence, "Let's play the poetry game. If you are not Alex Cuevas, the biggest asshole I have ever known, then who are you?"

"I've taught you well, my son." You said smiling, "Using humor to reduce the tension in this decrepit little room. Well done. I shall play your poetry game, my astute little midget."

I smiled at your insult and you started the familiar game.

"I am darkness and I am shadows. I am a puppet on a string. I am tribute to the gods of misery. I am an object of desire. Wealth has made me hungry and I am as parched as a dessert. I am silence and regrets. I am the guilt that darkens a perfectly sunny day. I am walking shame. I am breathing death. I am nothing."

"Have you always been these things, Alex?" I asked, beginning to identify a pattern in your poetic self-descriptions.

"I died when I was still nine and not yet ten, or perhaps it's the other way around. Perhaps, I woke up from a bullshit dream when I was nine and now, I must contend with the fact that I am awake, and there is no way to go back to my dreams." You said.

Ironically enough, I knew how to play this game well. We had done it many times before. The rules were rather simple. The questioner would ask a general question that could not be answered with a simple "yes" or "no." The speaker would then speak in poetic terms that answered the question, while hiding embarrassing details. The questioner then would ask clarifying questions until he was pretty sure he knew what the answer was, but the speaker would always have the cover of poetry, images, and metaphors.

If the questioner arrived at the wrong conclusion, it would be his own fault and not the speaker's. If, on the other hand, the questioner arrived at the right answer, the speaker could always claim that he was speaking in poetic language, which was open to several interpretations, the questioner's interpretation being just one of the many possibilities.

"Did you wake up from your dream, or did someone else wake you?" I asked, suspecting an answer I wouldn't like.

"The puppet master, the deceiver, the angel with dragon teeth, the hyena in sheep's clothing, the destroyer of dreams, and the lord of shadows who pretends to be light. He woke me up in the wee hours of the morning."

Your head was down, and I had to strain to hear your whisper. But I knew well were you were heading, and I had no choice but to press on. I said, "Had you known this deceiver before he woke you up, or was this the first time you met him?"

"He was everywhere and nowhere all at once, present where he shouldn't have been and absent from where he should have been. Familiar yet unknown. Always present yet filled with absence. A destroyer who could have built. A builder of destruction. Pure darkness and void of life. Filled with a life that kills," you whispered.

Chapter 17

By now, I was beginning to get a picture. Something tragic had happened to you right before you turned ten years old. This tragedy involved someone you knew. You had somehow been able to live with the trauma, finding coping mechanisms like humor, risk taking, and sexual conquests. This worked for the last three to four years, but something had happened a few months back that rendered all coping mechanisms insufficient.

At that point you had turned to drugs, starting with cocaine and graduating to bazuko. Now, you felt your life was spiraling out of control and the memories of the trauma were haunting you day and night. You felt guilty for what happened to you and walked in shame, not trusting anyone, feeling like a liar and an impostor. You felt dead inside and filled with a life that kills because it destroys everything in its path: your self-confidence, your joy, your carefree spirit, and even your faith.

Whatever happened a few months back was the key to how you were feeling. This was the key to finding out what happened to you four years ago. The death of your grandfather may have been a breaking point, but somehow, I doubted this was the case. I believed there was something more sinister lurking in the background.

I placed my hand on your shoulder and asked you, "Something happened a few months back that made you remember what happen to you when you were almost ten years old. What happened to you?"

"One's loss is another's gain. Or rather one's gain is another's freedom. Sometimes freedom can feel like death. One pain replaces another. One string breaks and a new one is formed. One puppet dies the painful death of neglect, while a new one takes its place. Twilight comes and the light suddenly dies out. A new light comes and bathes creation with sorrow. A love once hot dies in the ice of winter. Spring creates new lovers, soon to replace the skeletal remains of lovers of yesteryear." You responded, covering your face to hide your tears.

The picture was getting clearer. I guessed, "You were the old puppet that was replaced by a new puppet. You lost someone you loved, and that person has replaced you with a new love?

"It is a sad thing to be replaced, to be retired at fourteen. It is a sad thing to feel so old and so useless. The puppet master offered freedom, but I wanted captivity. He offered light, but I wanted shadows. I rebelled and he offered death. I cried out and he threatened vengeance. I imploded and he mocked my pain. I begged for love and he threw me into the wilderness of discontent. It was not to be, he said. He said, it was not to be," you said, imitating the rhythm of a popular song we knew.

The words you had used filled me with dread. You had been replaced at fourteen. This is easy enough to understand. Relationships break at any age. But what you said after could only mean one thing. You said you were retired at fourteen. Did this mean your lover preferred someone younger? If so, could you have been in love with an older person who somehow thought you had aged out? Could you have been the victim of sexual abuse at the age of ten by someone you knew, who then used you until he thought you were too old?

"Alex, were you molested or raped as a little boy?" I asked trembling, fearing your answer.

"Soon, my friend. Soon all things will become clear. Be patient for now and rest knowing that you have helped me tonight more than anyone could. I'm tired now and I will rest soundly tonight. Tomorrow we will celebrate our work here. Sunday we will worship together in thanksgiving for our friendship and brotherhood. And then, I will reach out to you and you will know the truth. Thanks for now. We will talk tomorrow." You said with a tired voice and lay down on your bed.

It was as though our poetry game had exhausted you beyond measure. You felt so empty and vulnerable and I didn't want to press any further. I covered you with your blankets and then I did something extremely uncharacteristic. I reached down and kissed you on the forehead.

I whispered softly in your ear, "Rest, sweet boy, rest. And I will be here when you wake up in the morning."

Chapter 18

Since it was only about 5:30 pm, I went to Evening Prayer and dinner. After dinner I went to the chapel and prayed for you for what seemed like an eternity. Your story had saddened me deeply and I felt overwhelmed. I also had no one to talk to about this. Fr. Garcia hadn't returned from seminary, and I didn't want to share my suspicions with staff because I didn't want to "out" you in any way. Additionally, although I had a pretty good idea what your problem was, I knew how the poetry game was played. All poetry is open to interpretation, and I still needed information before I went to our superiors for additional help.

Alone in that chapel, I allowed myself to cry my sadness away. I also felt an emotion that was uncommon for me to have back then, rage. I wanted to find the son-of-a-bitch who hurt you and I wanted to castrate him without anesthetics. I knew you to be a man of your word, and, as you had promised, you would eventually tell me what happened to you. Until then, I had no choice but to wait, even though I hated waiting.

You were still fast asleep when I returned to my room at 9:30 that night. I slipped into my bed quietly. The exhaustion of the day came crashing down on me like a mighty tree falling in a field. There was an indescribable heaviness in my soul and my mind. I closed my eyes and I fell asleep, almost instantaneously, until the next morning.

I thought I was dreaming when your beautiful baritone voice woke me up the next morning. You were singing a popular funeral song that was well known to us at the time, but you were not in your bed or in the building. Concerned, I followed the sound of the music until I arrived at the chapel.

A choir of eight students and two priests were practicing the music for next day's liturgy. For some reason I couldn't understand, they were practicing the 1967 popular song by Alberto Cortez, ***Cuando Un Amigo Se Va,*** or, "When a friend goes away." Even though this song started its life as a secular popular ballad, it had become an often-played funeral song in Catholic churches.

An amateur translation of the song may go like this,

When a friend goes away,
there is an empty space
that can never be filled
by the arrival of another friend.

When a friend goes away,
there is a burning fire left
that cannot be extinguished
even with the waters of a river.

When a friend goes away,
a star has been lost-
the one that illuminates the place
where there is a child asleep.

When a friend goes away,
All roads suddenly stop
And you start to discover
The tame ghosts of wine.

When a friend goes away,
All that is left is a wasteland
That only time can fill
with the stones of boredom.

When a friend goes away,
a fallen tree is left
which will never come back
because it has been overcome by wind.

When a friend goes away,
there is an empty space
that can never be filled
by the arrival of another friend

Your clear, beautiful, voice sounded sad and full of nostalgia that bright Saturday morning. I was so glad you were out and about that I didn't make much of the lyrics of the song. You were radiant all-day Saturday: Clean, sober, impeccably dressed, and full of laughter, jokes, and compliments. I thought it was a miraculous recovery and the answer to my prayers.

You participated in rehearsal to the end, attended prayers, finished a full game of soccer, put the last touches on your artwork for the evening, helped set up the courtyard for the party, were appreciative for all that the staff was doing, hugged students and staff alike throughout the day, and passed out a few gifts you wanted people to have.

At the party you stuck to soda and Marlboro Lights, danced with the female staff to the sound of salsa music, participated in the games the staff organized for the occasion, and volunteered to lead the prayer service of Compline.

Once in our room, you took out a bottle of Ron Medellin you had saved for a special occasion, and you and I drank until late at night, listening to Bob Dylan, Simon and Garfunkel, Mercedes Sosa, and a few Folk Colombian singers.

When I had tried to speak about the night before, you brushed me aside and said, "Yesterday is for the dead, today is for the living." With that we finished an extremely enjoyable day and got ready for bed.

Right before we went to bed, you looked at me in the eye and said, "You know I love you as much as a blind man loves his monkey, right?"

"Yes, Alex. You have said this once or twice before," I responded smiling.

"Good night, little buddy." You said,

"Good night, Giraffe." I responded.

The close-out ceremony at the end of each term was always a bittersweet event. We always had tears, hugged interminably, promised calls and visits during the break, hugged some more, shed more tears and, one by one, left in the Center's cars, the cars of relatives who came to pick us up, or by foot. I always walked, which explains why I never packed more than a backpack when I went to "The Oaks." You were picked up by your family's driver, a tall, skinny, humorless old man, who barely spoke to anyone and who always seemed put upon when he came to the Center to drop you off or pick you up.

Before you entered the car, we hugged for several minutes,

you hunched over to reach me, and I strained upwards to reach you. You had a hard time letting go of me, and we shed a few more tears. Then you entered the car, waved at me, and left. That was the last time I saw you alive, and the last time I hugged you. That was our last goodbye.

Chapter 19

I returned to my boring, uneventful life at home, but I spent most of Monday and Tuesday at the church, helping the children's ministry coordinator plan for the children's pageant on Christmas Eve. I did morning prayer with Fr. Gaviria, my parish priest, mentor, and friend. And I went back to my old afternoon job selling popcorn at the stall of a local vendor and neighbor at Bello's Central Park. I had worked this job off and on for several years, and the money always came in when I needed it the most.

I woke up several times during the early hours of that Tuesday. I was restless and could not shake the feeling of impending tragedy. In the morning, I inquired about everyone's health and forced my mother to call my dad at the farm to find out if he was well. I called Fr. Garcia with a pretext of looking for a book I had left behind at "The Oaks," but, mostly, I wanted to hear the old man's voice to make sure he was fine. I went to morning prayer, just to check on Fr. Gaviria.

I called you at home around 10:00 am and left a message with the maid for you to call me back.

I called my boss, pretending I had forgotten my work schedule and was somewhat relieved when he told me he had the flu and wasn't going to work that day. I wished him a speedy recovery and convinced myself that I was probably worried about him all along since I noticed he wasn't feeling well the day before. That must have been it. Yet, I was excitable and anxious all day and went to bed early, exhausted of all the worrying and checking up on people during the day.

Early on Wednesday, around 3:00 am, my mother woke me up with a tone of urgency in her voice. She said, "Joe, wake up. It's Alex. He sounds upset. I think he's drunk."

I ran to the living room, followed by my worried mother. I grabbed the phone and said, "Alex, this is Joe. Are you okay?"

"Joe, sorry I didn't call before. I was out of the house all day." You said,

"Don't worry about that. Are you okay?" I demanded.

"No, Joe. I'm not okay. In fact, I think I may need to go on a trip for a while. I wanted to call you before I left." You said, obviously upset.

"What kind of trouble are you into? Why are you not okay? Does this have anything to do with what you told me last Friday?" I asked in rapid-fire style, quite afraid of the answers.

"You were right, Joe, you usually are. I was raped when I was almost ten. I learned this week that someone had taken pictures of the event and I broke into an office building and stole those pictures. I didn't know it when I went in, but there were guards on duty. They saw me leave the building with the stuff I stole. They know I took the evidence and they may come after my family." You then repeated yourself, "I am going away for a while, buddy. I need you to do something for me when I am gone."

"I will, but first tell me. Does your old man know what you did or why you did it?" I asked.

"My dad doesn't know shit," you answered.

"Does your mom?" I asked intrigued.

"I think the bitch knows more than she pretends to know. Don't trust her, Joe. Will you do me the favor I am going to ask or not? I don't have a lot of time." You repeated.

"Tell me what you want, Alex." I said, registering the anxiety in your voice.

"I will send you a clue very soon, I can't tell you what yet because I think they are listening to my calls. When you get the clue, please do what the clue demands. But, Joe, doing the right thing at the right time is crucial here. Do you think you can do this?" you insisted.

"Trust me, Alex. I can do this." I reassured you.

Then you said, "Joe? Don't trust anybody until you are fully convinced you can trust them. Do you understand what I'm saying?"

"Yes, Alex, I will be careful. Now, please go somewhere and find help. If you are in danger, please don't wait until it's too late. You hear me? Please go now and call me in the morning," I pleaded with you.

"Don't worry about me. I'll be okay. You know I love you, right?" you asked one last time.

"I know, Alex. Me too. Now, go somewhere where you can get some rest." I demanded.

"Good night, Joe. I'll see you when I wake!" These were your last words to me,

"I'll see you when you wake, Alex!" These were my last words to you.

Chapter 20

With the excitement of the conversation, I had forgotten that my mother was standing right behind me. I sat on the couch in the living room and covered my face with both hands. Her voice startled me, and I jumped. She said, "I didn't mean to startle you. Is he okay?"

"I don't know, Mom. I really don't know. He sounds drunk and paranoid. He says he is in trouble, but he has been acting strange for the last few weeks. He thinks people are after him. Maybe he will feel better in the morning." I answered her, not wanting to say too much.

"Is he using drugs, Joe? Please tell me the truth." She demanded.

"Yes, I think he is, Mom. I am not sure, but he certainly is acting like he is," I replied.

"I'm sorry to hear this. He is a funny, well-mannered boy." She said, recalling the two times you had come to my home during the last year.

My mother had liked you from the start and was impressed by your distinguished appearance. She once called you "the little prince," although you towered over her by almost a whole foot then. The first time you came to my house was on a weekend when I couldn't be at "The Oaks." After the closing Eucharist, you volunteered to drop off posters announcing the beginning of a new round of exploratory retreats about to start during the summer. I was then to distribute the posters to all the Bello churches, using the opportunity to touch base with all the rectors and encourage them to send their kids to camp.

You had volunteered to make the drive because you had a private driver; you had missed me during the weekend; and you had nothing to do. Even though you had been inside the house for less than five minutes, that was enough time for my mother to form a favorable opinion of you. She thought you were, "beautiful and very refined, like one of those models you see in the magazines."

The second time you came to visit us, you stayed for the overnight, which made my mother a veritable basket case. She fussed over dinner, as though the president of the republic himself was visiting us or the papal nuncio was in town from the Vatican to deliver a papal indulgence to my mother in person.

You thought the whole thing was very comical, although you enjoyed the fact that she was treating you with the deference and respect you often claimed you despised among your maids, gardeners, and drivers. I guess, the fact that we didn't work for you made our hospitality less forced, more spontaneous, and, therefore, more sincere.

We stayed late into the night drinking with two of my older sisters, and my mother took my younger brother to her room, so that you and I would have the bedroom all for ourselves. That night, lying on twin beds, separated by less than three feet of space, you had said,

"Your family is wonderfully provincial."

"Shut up!" I retorted, knowing you were joking.

"I do love spending time with the masses. There is something so refreshing about the simplicity of their lives." You said with a familiar inflection on your voice I recognized immediately.

Your friends called this snooty, over-indulged, nose-up-in-the-air persona of your theater troupe, "The Professor." We imagined him to be an Ivory Tower, opinionated, aristocratic, old man who had grown up in simpler times when there was an order and a pattern to life. A time when social classes behaved in accordance with pre-set expectations and norms.

This persona always had a critical commentary about art, movies, and the characters in the books we read. He also had a strong opinion about the lack of taste and morals of the high classes and tended to speak about the refinements that should naturally belong to them, but which were often denied because of their base nature. You allowed "The Professor" to be a critic of everything that angered you about the shallow and self-directed ways of your own social class.

The Professor would often say things like, "I can't believe these cartel boys are from my hometown. They show such unrefined manners. They settle their disputes with semi-automatic weapons. Can you believe that? How vulgar. What happened to the personal touch of the Italian garrote? What happened to the patient workings of the Russian torture chambers? Are they so busy that they can't take the time to kill someone in the proper way? I tell you, it is a darn shame. This shouldn't be allowed to continue. It dilutes the good morals of our society."

"Tell me more about life among the masses, Professor." I egged you on.

"Oh, it is absolutely charming. They wake up early at dawn to feed their pigs, all of which are given names. It is sad, really, when you come to think of it. The pigs think they are being fed and named because they are loved, but the farmers just want to fatten them up to sell them at the local markets.

Anyway, after feeding the pigs, they wake up their dozen children and feed them a delicious cup of porridge or leftover rice and beans. Have you seen anything cuter than a family of twelve eating rice and beans before the morning chores? It is delightful, absolutely delightful. The gratitude in the children's eyes is awe-inspiring. Who needs fresh orange juice, Mimosas, or Bloody Mary's? Who needs gruyere cheese and French champignons omelets? Who needs Canadian bacon or Steerco sausage? All the poor masses need is a cup of black coffee and the love of family."

"We have no pigs, ass wipe," I protested.

Undeterred, you continued, "But, you do have at least twelve people living in your home. Anyway, after morning chores, the family gathers in the small living room to pray their novenas for the dead. The poor have so many dead people to pray for. And they always feel compelled to pray for each one by name, individually, as though God needs to be reminded which Jose or Manuel belongs to their clan and which does not.

After prayers, they milk the cows and make the cheese. Oh, Joe, you have never seen such display of communal effort. Everyone is involved in this arduous task. God bless the industrious masses of our country. What would we ever do without their efforts?"

As you stopped for a break, I jumped in, "When do we go to school, Professor?"

"Oh, school is not for everybody, child." One more pause for effect, "The parents make the choice early on about who among the brood will be educated, who will join the army, and who will be their tribute to Mother Church. Only those selected as the most likely to improve the family's name are chosen to walk the three miles daily to the local school. The others will spend the rest of their lives caring for the livestock or learning to harvest the fields and cook a decent meal. It is very economical and organized. I fully support this type of thinking. It is cruel to lie to children. Why tell them they can be anything they want to be, when they lack the intelligence and social graces required to succeed?"

The Professor took a brief pause and then continued, "Don't you think making the decisions for them early is the morally upright thing to do, Joe? I believe this is most proper. In fact, I believe the high classes lack morality. I know many rich idiots in school who see themselves as geniuses because their deluded parents have convinced them they are. It is cruel! Even if they have all the money in the world, their servants will probably have to wipe their asses until they die. Absolutely clueless, I tell you. The rich should just accept the fact that they don't need to work and leave school to the striving masses."

I actually had an opinion about this, "This is most generous of you, Professor. If the rich drop out of school, maybe going to college will not feel as difficult as winning the lottery."

"You get my point, exactly. This shows your high intelligence. I definitely believe your parents made the right choice of tribute for Mother Church."

"Fuck you!" I laughed.

"Not tonight, sweetie. It's time for sleep. The masses have schedules that must be followed, you know. Seven hours for sleep, eight hours for work or school, two hours for prayers, one hour daily for procreating, and the rest of the time for house chores. We must not interfere with the natural order of things," you laughed.

"Good night, Professor. I'm glad you came to our humble abode," I said.

"Good night, Joe. I'm glad I chose to spend the night in this charming little cottage." You responded and went to sleep.

Chapter 21

Lost in thought, I failed to hear my mother's question the day of your crisis call to me. She repeated herself in a louder tone, "Joe?"

I turned to face her in an apologetic way. I often had the ability to enter "the zone," that place where I could be alone with my thoughts regardless of where I was and whom I was with. My parents used to complain that one day I would become so lost in my own head that I wouldn't be able to find my way out.

I responded, "Sorry, I didn't hear you, Mom. What did you say?"

"Do you think we should call Alex's parents?" She repeated.

"I don't think that would do any good. He seems to have a pretty bad relationship with his mother, and his dad works long hours and gets home late. I wouldn't know what to tell them, anyway. I don't think they know Alex is using drugs, and he made me swear I wouldn't tell them. He is planning to talk to them soon." I responded more honestly than I felt I needed to be.

"It's hard to know what to do." My mother stated sincerely.

"I know." I said. "He'll probably be okay once he sleeps it off."

"Go on to bed then. You have work tomorrow." She said.

At 6:15 that morning, my mother woke me up again, but this time she did something extremely unusual. As soon as I got up, she gave me a big hug and started crying. I thought something had happened to dad or one of my siblings.

Panic rising inside me, I asked, "What happened? Is it Dad?"

"No, honey, it's Alex!" She whispered, still holding me.

I felt like a rag doll and she had to hold me. It was as though all my bones had evaporated from my body, and my out-of-control muscles had no support left.

My mother sat me on the bed and ordered Juan, who was just waking up because of her frantic calls, "Please get him some water from the kitchen."

He did as she ordered and returned a few seconds later.

My mother said, "Drink some water, Joe."

I couldn't breathe. I felt like a 700-pound gorilla was sitting on my chest. My mother held the cup of water to my lips and I took a sip. I felt extremely cold and I started shivering. She reached down to the bed, grabbed a blanket and wrapped it around my shoulders.

I was in complete shock and could barely speak. I managed to say, "What happened?"

"They don't know yet, but they think he killed himself. One of the maids found him in the garage when she came to work around 5:00 am. The police are at the house." She paused for a second and then continued, "Honey, they want to talk to you. They called a few minutes ago, and I asked them to give me half an hour to wake you up."

"Why?" I asked, beginning to feel nauseated.

"They did a call-return, honey. You were the last person to talk to him. They want to know what he told you, whether you heard anything strange in the background, stuff like that," she reassured me.

"How?" I asked, feeling sick.

Before my mother had a chance to answer, I ran to the bathroom and threw up. Sitting on the floor with my head leaning towards the toilet, I felt like my whole world was collapsing around me. I kept telling myself over and over, "It's my fault. It's my fault. I should have known better."

My mother and brother, standing outside the bathroom, were keeping guard, letting my other siblings know what was happening and why I was sick. After a long while, my mother entered the bathroom and, without saying a word, set up a shower for me.

Once the shower was running, she gently said, "Jump in and take a shower. I will get you some clean clothes. I suspect this will be a pretty long day for you."

I got undressed and jumped in the shower, simply because I didn't know what else to do. I was in a fog and the nausea was making me light-headed. I held on to the walls of the shower and I let the water wash over me. At some point, the full realization of what was happening hit me all at once. I sat on the floor, rested my head on my knees, and started crying, softly at first, and then louder and louder. At some point, my mother walked into the bathroom, sat on the floor outside the shower, and began to caress my back softly.

She whispered as I cried, "Cry it out, Son. Let it all out

now because you may need to be strong for the Cuevas later. They want to talk to you. Let it all out."

I felt so angry at you, so betrayed, so manipulated. Had you mentioned what kind of "trip" you were taking, I would have called your parents, the police, the goddamn National Guard, your crazy neighbor Pablo Escobar, or the pope himself. I would have taken a taxi to your house. Hell, I would have tried to make it on my bicycle. But, of course, that was the point, wasn't it? You knew I would have tried to stop you, didn't you?

"Mom, the police are here," Juan said from outside the bathroom.

My mother responded, "Have them sit in the living room. We'll be with them in five minutes. Offer them some of the coffee I just made."

My mother stood up and held a towel for me to dry off. On the counter she had placed a clean set of clothes: Underwear, blue jeans, polo shirt, socks, and sneakers. Grateful for her concern, I smiled weakly. I got out of the shower, got dressed, brushed my teeth, and came out of the bathroom.

My brother was holding a steamy cup of coffee for me. I looked at him appreciatively and mouthed the words, "Thank you," as I walked to the living room.

The first thing I noticed was that the two young policemen, dressed in green uniforms, had refused to sit down or accept the coffee my brother offered them. They had long rifles hanging from the side of their shoulders, and they looked like they were twins. I don't just mean they were similarly dressed. They looked identical in all respects.

My mother made the introductions and the twin on the left said, "Our Colonel, would like to have a word with you, young man."

"Well, have him come in then," my mother interjected.

"He is not here, ma'am," said the twin on the right. "He has asked us to bring your son to the police station in Medellin. We are locals, but, since the death took place in Envigado, they will conduct all interviews at the Central Police Station in Medellin. You can come with him if you want, but he is not in any trouble. It would be just a few questions and we will bring him right back."

"I will get ready in five minutes. Are you sure you don't want to sit down and have some coffee?" My mother asked.

"We are sure, ma'am," said the twin on the right.

As if waking up from a bad dream, I said, "It's okay, Mom. I will go by myself. You have a house full of people to take care of. I will be back as soon as I am done."

"You need an adult with you," my mother protested.

"Please, Mom." I begged. "I would feel more comfortable by myself. I will be safe. I'll call you as soon as I get there, and I'll call you as soon as I'm about to leave."

"He will be safe ma'am. We will remain with him the entire time and we will bring him right back," the left twin added.

"Fine, but if you need me, call me and I'll take a taxi right over," my mother acquiesced.

She knew well that in the Colombia of the 1980's adults don't need to be present when police interviewed minors. Police can do whatever they want to do and even her presence would in no way offer any protection in case I needed it. I, on the other hand, knew that I might have to lie about things my mother would know to be lies. Having to deal with her after the interview would have been more painful than going to the interview alone.

"I will," I promised, grabbing my backpack and following the twins out to a patrol car parked in front of my house.

Standing by the side of the patrol car, a concerned and overly excited Mrs. Rodriguez asked the police men, "Why are you arresting him?"

"This is police business, ma'am. Please move away from the car," one of the twins ordered.

Reluctantly, Mrs. Rodriguez moved away from the car and crossed the street, back to the front door of her house.

She then turned around to face us and asked me, "Are you okay, Joe? Is there anything I can do?"

"They finally caught up with me, Mrs. Rodriguez. Tell your children goodbye for me. I will write you soon to explain." I yelled back, a mental smile beginning to form in my mind.

Both police officers were laughing when I finally closed the back door of the patrol car. One of them said, "There is always one chismosa (gossip) in every street."

"She means well. I shouldn't mess with her." I replied.

"Everyone will think you are the biggest criminal in town by the time she is done calling all her friends," the second twin offered.

"Well, at least this will not be a boring day for her." I said. Then, trying to avoid mindless chit-chat, I asked, "Hey, I have some work to do for church. Do you mind if I read while you drive?"

"Go right ahead. This will only take about twenty minutes," the driver said, blasting his police siren to the complete astonishment of Mrs. Rodriguez.

I opened my backpack, got a small binder with the script for the upcoming Christmas play, and began to familiarize myself with all the characters. This was a multipart play with unlimited possibilities because in addition to the innkeepers, Mary, Joseph, and the three wise men, we could have as many shepherds, sheep, and other animals as we wanted. This was good because we often had an additional two or three kids show up at the last minute, and we always struggled to find parts for them. In fact, the only speaking part of the whole play was the narrator who told the story while the kids processed in down the nave of the church when their roles appeared in the story.

Reading this silly little play, allowed me some distraction from thinking about you, and it calmed my nerves about the upcoming interview. I wondered why they hadn't done this over the phone, what kinds of questions they would ask, who would be asking the questions, and how long it would take.

As promised, we arrived at the Central Police Station in Medellin within twenty minutes. This was possible because the driving twin kept the accelerator to the floor the entire time, driving at speeds of over one-hundred miles per hour, while blasting his siren. The station was busy with phones ringing throughout the building and people seated on rows of desks interviewing people, speaking on the phone, or typing on their manual typewriters.

I followed the policemen to a small interviewing room, which looked nothing like the sweat boxes I had seen on television crime shows. This was a small living room with a desk in one corner and a large sofa against the wall, opposite a large window that showed the main hall of the police station. On the wall opposite to the door, there was a loveseat, and above the door there was an additional window, but it was unclear what the purpose of the space beyond it was. Probably a storage room, I thought.

I sat on the loveseat nervously and waited for the interviewers to come in. Later that day, I learned that the small living room was often used to notify families their loved ones had been killed. This was the "death notice room," which I thought was a very appropriate name, although I believed another phrase needed to be added to the title. From this day forward, the room needed to be known as the, "Death notice and children-without-lawyers interview room."

Chapter 22

I had never met a woman cop before, which is the reason I was confused when a matronly detective walked into the room, lowered the blinds, closed the door, and introduced herself as Detective Morales of the Juvenile Crimes Division. She said, "Sorry for your loss. The family tells me you were friends with the victim?"

This was more a statement that a question, and I automatically resented the word "victim" to describe you, but I said nothing about this. I meekly responded, "Yes, ma'am. Alex and I are friends."

"I understand you both go to the same school, is that correct?" she asked,

"We go to different schools, but we belong to the same church camp. It's called 'The Oaks'." I told her.

"I know that place." The detective stated. "It has one of those Spanish Mission style chapels with a beautiful bell tower. Isn't that the place?"

"Yes, ma'am." I answered, thinking of the statue of Christ the Redeemer and a silly boy threatening to jump from the roof of a bell tower.

"How long have you known the deceased?" Detective Morales asked.

"Alex. His name is Alex," I stated somewhat too forcefully. Then I answered the question, "Eleven months. I met him last January."

"Sorry about that. Force of habit." Then she asked, "When was the last time you saw Alex in person?"

"This last Sunday, when the Center closed to students for the Christmas break." I replied.

"Did he look upset to you?" She asked looking intently at my body language and reaction to her question.

"No, he was the same usual self. He was looking forward to going on vacation to San Andres Islands. I believe the family was flying there for the holidays." I volunteered, knowing that the detective already had this information.

"Did he complain about anything to you?" She pressed on.

"He always complained about the shitty state of affairs in the city, but this wasn't anything new. It was just his way of showing his concern for the violence he saw on TV," I lied.

"I can empathize with that." She stated. "Any particular complaints about anyone in the city?"

Invisible flags beginning to rise in my head, I said, "No, just general complaints. Nothing specific."

"I see." She stated, beginning to formulate another question in her head. "I understand you were the last person to talk to Alex. What did you talk about?"

"He sounded drunk and he apologized for calling late. He just wanted to hear my voice. He missed 'The Oaks' and wanted to reminisce about how much fun we had in the last session. It was a brief call." I lied.

"Oh, we know how long the call was. What we can't figure out is why he would call you so late. Did he have anything pressing to tell you that couldn't wait until the morning?" she asked.

"People like you and I have schedules for when to eat, when to go to school, when to take showers, and when to talk to people. This wasn't Alex. He ate when he wanted, drank when he wanted, and talked to people when he wanted. He used to wake me up at all hours of the night to talk about stuff that could have waited until the morning." I lied again.

"What kinds of stuff?" She wanted to know.

"All kinds of stuff. Let me just give you an example. A few months back our team was scheduled to do a skit of one of the parables during our lesson. After bouncing ideas about which parable to reenact, he woke me up at 3:45 am, excited because he thought we should write our own parable. He wanted us to ask the question, 'How would Jesus react to the plight of street kids in Medellin?' Then compose a narrative where Jesus would address the issue by telling the disciples a parable about street kids. I told him to stop bothering me and to go to sleep, but he went on and on and, by the time I woke up at 6:30, he had written the parable. This was Alex." I had just made up this story, but I knew it sounded plausible enough to the detective.

"That was kind of annoying, don't you think?" she added.

"I didn't mind. This is just who he was," I said.

Not buying my bullshit story, the detective asked, "Did he tell you he got in trouble earlier that day?"

Once again, piercing eyes watching my every move.

"No, ma'am. What kind of trouble?" I asked.

"That's police business. Are you sure he didn't tell you about it?" She insisted.

"No ma'am. I swear he didn't say a thing. Alex never told me much about his life at home. We just talked about camp, sports, and stuff like that." I said innocently.

"When you saw him last, did he give you anything to hold for him?" She asked.

"Yes, ma'am. He gave me this small cross, which had belonged to his grandfather. He said it was an early Christmas gift." I said, opening the top button of my polo shirt.

I showed the detective the small cross, and she asked me to take it off, which I did.

"It's beautiful." She said, inspecting the small cross in detail.

Satisfied that the small cross didn't contain the nuclear codes for some dangerous weapon, she returned it to me, and I put it back on. She asked a second time, "Are you sure he didn't give you anything else?"

"Pretty sure." I said, beginning to be uncomfortable with this line of questioning.

"Joe, what do you make of the Cuevas family?" she asked almost matter of fact, but I knew this was a major reason for the interview.

They wanted to know if you acted afraid of your parents during your call, if you were hiding something from them, or if you had accused them of anything. I found the question very interesting and quickly glanced at the wall opposite to where I was sitting. It was then that I noticed the one-way mirror, framed in the window above the door. There were people watching this interview. Somehow, I had the suspicion that your parents were in that room.

This made perfect sense. For an up-and-coming detective to offer protection to a politically connected family could become a winning bonanza. Promotion in exchange for silence, financial remuneration, private security gigs in the homes of the powerful, recruitment by private security firms, and a hundred other benefits could be obtained. This was a high stakes game, and she wasn't going to leave any stones unturned if she could advance her career in any way because of this high-profile case.

Cautiously, but also honestly, I answered, "I don't know them. I waved at his mother once in the parking lot of 'The Oaks' when she dropped Alex off at camp. I have never met his father. So, I don't have an opinion of them because I don't know them."

"Did Alex talk about them at all? I'm sure you talked about everything. I have a nephew your age and he's a big talker," she pressed on.

"We talked about almost everything, but Alex was always very reserved when it came to his private, home life. Not that I asked, anyway. I never talked about my family either. There is nothing wrong with them, but I had better things to talk about than parents, siblings, or home drama," I lied for a third time.

"Are you telling me everything you know, Joe? I get the sense you are holding back. If you don't tell me the truth, you could get in trouble. You do know this, right?" she threatened.

The obvious attempt at intimidation was a bit comical. But this was a game my cousin, Fernando, who had been a city cop before moving to the coast, had taught me to play well.

"I have told you everything I know, and I have nothing else to say. But, if you think I might be in trouble, maybe I should call my mom. I feel like maybe I need a grown-up or an attorney with me." I feigned fear, which I wasn't really feeling.

"You don't need your mother and you don't need a lawyer. I just want you to know that since you were the last person to speak to Alex, what you tell us is very important to us. You can make the difference in how this case goes." She insisted.

"I thought he killed himself? But now you tell me there is a criminal case open? You don't think he was killed, do you?" I feigned concern, which I wasn't feeling either.

"I'm not saying anything one way or the other. We are still investigating." she answered, somewhat frustrated.

Knowing that I didn't intend to answer the questions she wanted answered and that I wasn't going to give her the ammunition she needed to improve her status in life, she excused herself, told me to stay put, and left the room. I was glad she left because I was done playing games with Detective Morales, from the Juvenile Crimes Division, and with any of the people behind the one-way mirror, including your parents.

About ten minutes later, an older gentleman dressed in full police uniform walked in, identified himself as Colonel Julio Rodriguez, thanked me for my willingness to come all the way to Central Station to answer their questions, and gave me a business card to call him if I remembered anything else.

With that, he called the twins and ordered them to take me home. I never did receive a call from your parents to find out what our last conversation was about, but I wasn't surprised. They knew word by word what I had told the cops.

Three blocks away from my house, I asked the driving twin if he could turn the siren on about a block from my home.

He smiled, looked at his partner, and said, "You remind me of my little brother. He too is a pain in the ass."

"As long as we are exchanging insults. Would you mind doing me another small favor?" I asked tentatively.

"Shoot," he said.

"Will you mind showing me some respect when we get home? I can't let the neighbors believe I'm on probation or awaiting trial. It would be hell for my family to have to answer all their questions later," I asked.

"Let me see if I understand this correctly. You want us to offer you a full police salute, apologize loudly for interrupting your busy morning, and open and close doors for you like you are the highest-ranking police officer in Medellin?" the twin on the passenger seat asked with a grin on his mouth.

"Only if the neighbors are watching," I clarified.

The two officers looked at each other and started laughing in unison. The driver said, "Only because you just lost your friend, and because I kind of like you."

"Thank you, kind sir." I replied as he turned the siren on.

A block later, we arrived at my home, just as Mrs. Rodriguez and her sons were beginning to walk out of their house. A few other neighbors were also now either outside their front doors or peeking through their windows. The twins parked the car, came to the back door of the passenger side, stood at perfect attention with their right hand positioned vertically against their foreheads, and proceeded to open the door for me.

I got out of the car slowly. Stood on the street in front of them and returned the salute by bringing my right hand to my forehead in a swift, well-choreographed motion. Then, to my surprise, one of the twins stretched out his right hand and, as soon as I shook it, he proceeded to wrap it with his left hand, in an act of great reverence. He said loudly for most to hear,

"We apologize for the interruption, Sir. Please convey our deepest regrets to your mother."

"You are too kind," I stated in response to his reverend salute.

Both twins entered their car slowly and drove away, sirens off. I looked at Mrs. Rodriguez briefly, smiled, and went inside my house. By 4:00 pm that afternoon it was well-known in town that I had helped the Metropolitan police crack a difficult case, and I was soon to receive a commendation from the Governor himself.

To my delight, the family did nothing to correct or change the story. When asked about it, all my mother said was, "He is a very special boy."

Chapter 23

Several days later, I was sharing a small space with four of your friends and Fr. Bedoya was eulogizing you in the great church attached to the sacristy. The church was packed with hundreds of mourners, and members of the media had been covering the event for the local stations. Most of what Fr. Bedoya was saying in his sermon I already knew. You were a natural born leader, you loved the poor with intense passion, you were very involved in the youth group and everyone loved you....

Once again, the words I had once heard came to mind, "I have never buried a bad person." I began to think about how unfair undeserved praise can be. Yes, you were an amazing human being, but by no means were you perfect. To deny your imperfections was to deny your humanity, your full complexity, your shades of grey. You were an amazing person precisely because you were fully human, and not because you were so good that God himself chose to bring you home to him. I saw this line of thinking as such crap, not to mention bad theology.

None the less, Fr. Bedoya was extolling your virtues, your friends were weeping loudly, and all I could think about were your last words. "Joe, I'll see you when I wake."

I also couldn't wait to get to "The Oaks" to read your note again. Fr. Garcia had called my mother and had offered the Center as a place where I could come and grieve in the company of mentors and priests who loved me. They all knew how close you and I had been. It was the priest's idea that I should miss a few days of work to be "on retreat" with the staff. He volunteered to call Fr. Gaviria, my parish priest, to explain the situation. I couldn't wait to be there, alone to grieve. Alone to search for clues.

Leaving the church without being noticed was easier than I had expected. The five boys left the sacristy at communion, came down one side of the church, turned to our left at the center aisle, and joined the communion line, walking once again towards the front of the church. However, I made a right at the center aisle and left the church, instead of joining the communion line. I was tempted to stay and spend some time with the staff of the camp, but I knew I would see them that evening. It had occurred to me that "The Oaks" may not have a complete collection of Neruda's poems and I wanted to search your note in detail.

Neither your mother nor your father noticed that I had left, until much later. On the street, I was surprised to find a ready line of taxis waiting for passengers. Although I was nearly broke, I knew I had enough to get me where I was going and to "The Oaks." I climbed into the first taxi and asked to go to the Medellin Public Library. Ten minutes later, I arrived at the library. It was almost 11:00 am, but the cavernous building was almost empty.

I approached the circulation desk and asked the attendant where I could find Neruda's works. Rather than pointing me in the right direction, the young college student, stood from her desk and asked me to follow her. She took me to a section of bookshelves dedicated to Latin American poetry and literature.

She pointed to the third shelf from the top of a book case and said, "You can find all his works there, unless they have been checked out."

Grateful for the help, I decided to push my luck just a bit further. I took out the poem from my jacket pocket and asked the young lady, "Do you know what collection of poems this one belongs to?"

She took the poem in her hands, read it and said, "This is one of the sad ones. I much prefer his poems of love."

The young woman knelt on one knee, reached in the middle of the bookshelf and took out a tome entitled, *"Twenty Poems of Love and a Song of Despair."* She opened the book to the second poem in the collection. There, in its full glory was "Light Wraps You." I thanked the attendant, sat on a nearby table, and started my search.

After about twenty-five minutes, I realized that there was absolutely no difference in language and sentence order between the published poem and your poem. I cursed silently in my mind, beginning to panic. Perhaps you thought too highly of me. Perhaps I would never be able to decipher your code. Why couldn't you have used ***Sesame Street?*** I could find the item that didn't belong to sets, but that was the extent of my sleuthing abilities. Feeling quite defeated I returned the folded poem to its envelope and, suddenly, the simplicity of the clue struck me like a thunderbolt. The clue was not in the poem, nor was it on the page the poem was written on. The clue had always been on the envelope itself.

The envelope read:

Joe Cardenas
7ʰ Street #42-54, Apartment 6.
Copacabana, Antioquia, 51048

But, of course, I didn't live in Copacabana. I lived in Bello. You never intended to mail the letter, although it was addressed to be mailed. The address was the clue. Whoever resided in this address, in Bello's neighboring town of Copacabana, would most likely have the clue you wanted me to find. Excited, I asked the young attendant if I could use her phone. I made the decision to call the only person I knew who had a car.

One of the telephone numbers on the card was William's office at Steerco. The second was his home number. I looked at my watch and realized it was almost noon. William would most likely still be at the reception the country club was hosting in your honor. I called the number at Steerco, hoping to get a number for the club. I was surprised when a live voice answered the phone. It was William.

I was confused, but quickly identified myself. "William, this is Joe. I thought you would be at the reception?" I asked.

"Hey, Joe. Where are you? I looked for you after the service, but you were gone. The Cuevas wanted to invite you to the reception," he stated.

"I had something pressing to do," I answered. "Why aren't you at the reception?"

"Do you remember Mr. Personality himself, the pompous ass who drives the family? His name is Juan Machado. He took the couple to the reception. I'm strictly a Steerco employee. I was ordered to return to Steerco in case one of the executives needed me to drive them somewhere. Of course, that was a stupid order from my half-witted supervisor because all the executives are at the reception and they all drove themselves," he stated resentfully.

"I thought Mr. Cuevas was your supervisor?" I asked confused.

"He is everyone's supervisor, but, unless he expressly asks for me, I belong to the motor pool. We have twelve company cars, which means I am one of twelve drivers. Our supervisor is a whiny little man who has been with the company for over twenty years. He cuts me some slack sometimes because Mr. Cuevas likes me, but I report to him. If I want a job, I need to do what he wants me to do," he explained.

"I understand. I'm sorry to hear you are not at the club. I called to ask you a favor, but your boss may not let you. I don't want you to get in trouble," I said, hoping he would take the bait.

"What's the favor, little man?" he asked.

"I'm at the Medellin Public Library and I need a ride to Copacabana. After that, I may need a ride to "The Oaks," I stated, hoping he would be available.

"Give me five minutes and call me back. Five minutes, you hear?" He insisted.

"Got it," I said.

Five minutes later I called back, but the phone rang for nearly two minutes before the line went dead. I waited five more minutes and dialed again.

William answered the call on the first ring, "Is that you, Joe?" He answered.

"Yes, it's me. What's the news?" I inquired.

"Could you hang loose until around 1:30 pm? I need to drop off one of the managers in El Poblado, but I will be free after that. You can have me all day, and Mr. Cuevas agreed to pay me for the time. I just spoke to him," William offered.

"That's excellent, man. Thanks. I will wait for you at the main entrance of the library at 1:30 pm. See you, William," I said as I ended the call.

I looked at my watch and realized I had one hour and twenty minutes to kill. I topped my front pocket thinking about lunch, but I knew I had barely enough to get me to camp in case William was unable to drive me. I didn't want to risk it. I reached into my back pocket and took my wallet out. To my great surprise, I found two hundred pesos neatly folded in my billfold.

This could only mean one thing. My mother had put some money in my wallet just in case I needed it. The woman is the most intuitive person I know. She would have made a great chess player. I realized at that moment that as much as her irascible moods drove me crazy, I love the woman like I have never loved anyone. She is often at a loss on how to reach me, especially when I am in my introverted, pensive moods. But she always knows how to anticipate my needs. I love that about her.

Realizing that I was hungry and that my sainted mother had given me enough money for a great lunch, I left the library and walked to the vendors across the street.

Chapter 24

I got two chicken empanadas, an order of fried salted potatoes, and a Coca Cola, and I sat on a park bench, eating as I faced the front entrance to the library. About twenty minutes later, I noticed un unbelievable sight. A dark grey sedan, driven by Juan Machado, Mr. Personality himself, and your family's driver, stopped in front of the library. Two tall men, dressed in black suits, entered through the library's main entrance. I could not recognize the men from where I was seated.

Machado parked on the side street of the building, in front of a delivery truck, kept the engine running, and rolled the windows up. The truck provided perfect cover if anyone looked down the side street from the park. I stood up from the bench, grabbed by backpack, and retreated to a clubhouse that housed several public restrooms. I hid behind one of the walls of the building. I was able to see the front entrance of the library and the car down the street, but there was no way for anyone looking in my direction to see me.

About five minutes after the men in dark suits entered the library, they came back out, looked in both directions, inspected the park across the street, walked to the left and to the right of the entrance looking inside cars, and then walked down the side street, entered the dark gray sedan and drove away. I began to connect my call to William with the sudden need of your family to find me. Somehow, I didn't think William was involved in whatever was going on, but I wasn't sure. He seemed to love you so deeply that I had a hard time thinking he had anything to do with what happened to you.

But, as I began to have doubts about William and your dad, there was a voice buried deep within me, telling me William could be trusted. Of course, I have been wrong before many times and my own powers of deduction needed to be kept in check. Hiding behind that public bathroom building, however, I realized I was outmanned and outgunned. If I was going to follow your instructions, I would have to trust somebody. I decided to wait for William's ride. I also decided to find out as much as I could about how your parents knew I went to the library after your funeral mass.

William arrived on schedule at 1:30 pm. I waited until he stopped in front of the library and then ran from the park, came around the back of the car, and entered the passenger side. I closed the door quickly and ordered, "Drive."

William, startled by my voice tone, started driving straight ahead with no specific direction. I turned and looked out the back window, expecting the grey sedan to be following us.

Relieved at not seeing anyone giving chase, I turned to William and asked, "Whom did you tell I was at the library?"

"No one. What's going on?" He asked, quite concerned.

"I hung up with you, walked across the street to the vendors in the park, got some lunch, and started eating, when, suddenly the driver for the Cuevas family dropped off two men in dark suits at the front entrance. Once they went in, he parked the car down the street, where no one could see him. The men spent five minutes in the library and left, looking everywhere for someone. I think they were looking for me, but I was hiding behind the bathrooms. When they didn't find me, they went back inside the car and drove away. Now, what the hell do you think that was about?" I asked.

"Are you sure it was Machado?" He asked incredulously.

"I'm sure," I said, angrily.

"I honestly have no idea how he knew you were there. I swear." He responded defensively. Then he added, "When I called Mr. Cuevas to ask permission to leave and spend the afternoon with you, I heard voices in the background. I could recognize Missy's voice, among others. It looked like Mr. Cuevas was trying to whisper into the receiver, but, since I couldn't hear him, he had to raise his voice. I think maybe Mrs. Cuevas heard the call. But, why would she send people after you? It makes no sense. What that hell is going on, little dude?"

His answer seemed plausible and I chose not to press the issue any further, but I also chose not to answer his questions in too much detail. I simply said, "I have the impression Alex was in some trouble when he died. Do you know anything about this?"

"I know he seemed angrier at his mother than usual, but he didn't tell me why? The two of them have been fighting for months," he said.

"Do you know what they were fighting about?" I asked, beginning to formulate a theory in the back of my mind.

"I think it had to do with Cesar. I overheard Mrs. Cuevas begging Alex to call the boy. I think they had a fall out and Cesar was miserable without Alex. He could be a needy kid and he was obsessed with Alex, calling him all the time, asking people if they had seen him, and wanting me to drive him to the equestrian camp Alex was in, which, as you know, didn't really exist. Stuff like that. Stoker shit, if you ask me," William added helpfully.

"How long ago was their fall out?" I asked, again, beginning to put the pieces together.

"It must have been three to four months ago, I think," William guessed.

"Do you know what the fall out was about?" I pressed.

William answered, "Little man, I am a simple man. I don't pretend to know everything about people, and I try hard to live and let live. I don't judge and I don't like when people judge me. But Cesar and Alex's relationship often tested the boundaries of what I was willing to tolerate. Cesar had a crush on Alex, plain and simple. I always thought that for Alex the whole thing was a game, but the relationship was painfully serious for Cesar. The boy worshipped the ground Alex walked on. He was possessive and jealous.

Alex thought it was cute at first, but a few months ago they had a big fight when Alex told him to back the hell off. Suddenly, it wasn't funny anymore for Alex. He started avoiding Cesar, not answering his calls, not showing up at family functions, and refusing to talk to him when they happened to find each other at club events. The whole thing was driving Cesar crazy, which means it was driving his parents crazy. I think they were putting pressure on Mrs. Cuevas to bring Alex back into the fold."

At this point, William realized that, although he was driving in the direction of Copacabana, he didn't know exactly where he was heading. He asked, "Now, where are we going?"

"I'll show you in a sec, but first I need to ask you something serious. Can I trust you, William?" I asked, taking a risk.

"You don't know me, little man, but I wish you did. If you knew me, you would know your question is stupid. I'm not the smartest man you will meet. In fact, my family always treated me like I was retarded when I was a kid. But there is one thing you need to know right now. I loved Alex Cuevas, and there is no way in hell I would have done anything to hurt him. I covered up for the boy, and I spoiled him behind his mother's back. Other than you, no one cared for the kid more than I did. So, go ahead and get your doubts out of your system. Ask whatever you want. But, when I'm done answering your questions, you either trust me fully or you don't call me again. Got it?" He seemed wounded, but I had to be sure I could count on him.

"Fair enough!" I said. "I know something happened to Alex and he was in trouble right before he died. I need to find out what that was. Will you help me, without telling the family too much? This can get dangerous, especially if Machado's goons are sniffing around. Can you help me?" I repeated the question, hoping I could appeal to his love and loyalty towards you.

"First, I don't know what's up Machado's ass, and second, hell yea, I will help you." Then he added for my benefit, "From this time on, mum is the word."

"Thanks, William. I really appreciate this." I said, meaning every word.

We arrived at the address I gave him at around 2:25 pm. I realized as soon as we pulled up that the place was a rather elegant apartment building, located right off the main thoroughfare of Copacabana. The complex was a two-story structure, which covered almost the whole block and was home to twelve large, modern apartments, six on the first floor and six on the top floor. All the apartments on the second floor had balconies facing the street, while the apartments on the first floor had two parking spaces for every apartment. It was obvious that the complex had recently been renovated and now included lush greenery spread throughout the grounds, balconies, and selected areas next to the parking spaces. Across from the apartment complex, there was a new shopping center, which housed a diner, several clothing stores, a bakery, and a hair salon.

William and I parked the car in a private lot one block south of our destination and walked to the address. At my request, William left his jacket, tie, and flat cap in the car and now he looked like an average human, rather than a corporate speed demon. We decided to have a cup of coffee at the diner across from the apartment complex to scope out the place before we knocked on Apartment Six, which was the first ground apartment as you turned into the street. I took out a cigarette from my backpack and offered one to William. He turned his nose up in the air with a dismissive sigh and stated, "Never have I been so offended. Cigarettes are for pussies."

"You sound just like him. He was such an ass!" I said, smiling sadly.

"I know. He was the funniest kid I have ever known. I laughed more at his silliness than I should have. I think I encouraged his nonsense. He knew he had a ready audience and I used to egg him on. Did he ever use his housewife persona with you?" he asked smiling.

"Only all the time," I said, missing you greatly. "By the end, I wanted to kill that histrionic bitch."

William broke out in a hysterical laugh that was a bit too loud for an undercover operation like ours. I begged him to quiet down, but he just couldn't stop. Across the street everything was quiet, just the normal pedestrian traffic to be expected on a Saturday afternoon. On our side of the street the shopping center was busy with many shoppers going in and out of the various stores and the bakery. We noticed there were no cars parked in front of Apartment Six, and we hoped we hadn't made the trip in vain.

That changed at 3:05 pm when a lady I knew well, and had grown to love for over a year and a half of my life, parked a late model Mercedes Benz in front of Apartment Six and proceeded to walk in. She didn't notice us staring at her from across the street. I told William to pay the bill and meet me outside the diner, which he did. We walked across the street a few seconds later and knocked on the home of Luisa Santos, my friend Ivan's mother.

Chapter 25

Every sports team, club, school, and church have a "group mother." Mrs. Santos is that mother for us at "The Oaks." A jolly, heavy-set woman from the Pacific North Coast of Colombia, Mrs. Santos contributed the "D" to Ivan's, "Tall, Dark, and Handsome" looks. The daughter of a prominent fisherman and tourism guide in El Chocó, Luisa had grown up leading tourists on whale watching and waterfall hikes, teaching scuba diving lessons, and driving expedition buses from the city to the hot springs for which her home town of Termales was well known.

She had met her husband on a Scuba-diving trip to the coast of Utria National Park and the two had fallen desperately in love from the first moment they met. Alfredo Santos, Ivan's father, was tall, blue-eyed, and as white as his Catalonian ancestors had been. Although he was born in Medellin, both of his parents were Spaniards who had relocated to Colombia in 1947, during the years of Francisco Franco, Spain's famous dictator.

Mrs. Santos never forgot a name, important event, graduation ceremony, or fundraiser at camp. She provided most of the baked goods for our weekend "Exploratory Retreats" and fussed over Fr. Garcia and the staff, like a disappointed mother who thinks her children work too hard, don't take enough breaks, and, will die of a heart attack, if they are not careful.

The students of the leadership school loved her, and she never forgot our names, birthdays, talent shows, or graduations. A moderately well-off woman, she drove in and out of "The Oaks" as frequently as the staff and could be seen on any given day, helping the cooks, making copies for the secretaries, or cleaning up the chapel after services. She loved the Center and she loved me.

My surprise at seeing Mrs. Santos at the apartment complex in Copacabana was palpable because I knew the family lived in El Poblado, an upscale neighborhood about ten minutes away from your home. In fact, this proximity intensified your relationship with Ivan and his family. They adopted you as a second son almost from the first day. Often you traveled with them to watch Ivan play soccer in nearby towns. You even went with them to Bogota on two occasions for intra-state tournaments. As we approached the door of the apartment, I wondered if she knew about your death. If not, I feared the woman would collapse and die on the spot. The question was answered for me as soon as Mrs. Santos opened the door.

"My boy!" She exclaimed and enveloped me in an interminable bear hug. I felt swallowed up by her. She started crying loudly, while rubbing my back with her large maternal hands. Still crying, she spoke to me in an accent similar to Creole, for which some people from El Chocó are known.

"I know you suffer, mon chéri. Come, come. Join an old lady for a cup of coffee."

I introduced William to Mrs. Santos, and she proceed to

give him a big hug as well, exclaiming that "any friend of Alex" would forever share her devotion and respect. William loved the attention and accepted a cup of chicory coffee you could eat with a spoon. I knew Ivan's family loved strong, dark coffee, but I must confess that I could not drink more than a sip of the cup of sludge she gave us.

Still holding the hot beverage in my hand, I asked, "Is Ivan around? I would love to say hello."

"Oh, how forgetful you are, my sweet. My Ivan travels with his team every weekend. He has been in Cali since Wednesday. He will not return until Tuesday next." She answered.

Cali is a city approximately 270 miles south east of Medellin in the center of the country. Known for the high quality of their soccer, Cali hosted many tournaments of national significance. It occurred to me that Ivan's team was beginning to get national recognition, which means that talent scouts would soon start keeping an eye on the sixteen-year-old prodigy. It also occurred to me that since Ivan had left for Cali on Wednesday, he most likely didn't know about your death. Perhaps this was the reason you directed me to this address. I asked next,

"Mrs. Santos, does Ivan know about Alex?"

The woman sighed deeply, took a sip of her coffee, and answered my question. "You must tell no one, my sweet, but Alex and Ivan were together most of the day on Tuesday. Alex spent the night here on Monday and the boys drank a little too much and stayed up a little too late. Around two in the afternoon on Tuesday, Alex asked Ivan if he would drive him to a building in La America. Ivan agreed, and the two boys left soon after that. Ivan told me Alex asked him to wait for him about a block away, which he did. He said Alex was in the building for less than twenty minutes."

La America is a section of the city of Medellin, known

for expensive shopping centers and upscale residential housing. As far as I knew, your family did not have any business interests in the area, so the revelation that the building you may have broken into was located there was a bit surprising to me.

I gave Mrs. Santos a few seconds to take another sip of coffee and then I asked her, "Did they return here after their trip to La America, or did Ivan drop Alex off at his home?"

"They came back here." She sighed. "They walked in around 4:30 pm. They were acting all silly, telling jokes, drinking, and Alex was smoking pot. I told them they had to be in the outside patio." She pointed with her index finger down a long corridor to two French doors that led to an outside patio.

She continued, "I allowed them to hang out until around 7:30 pm, and I fed him dinner. But then I reminded Ivan that he needed to be at the school's parking lot by 4:30 am the next morning. The team bus was driving them to Cali, and they needed to leave pretty early. When it was time to go, I called Alex a taxi and pre-paid it in advance. Then we left to Alfredos' lab. We always eat together, and, since he has been working late, we met him near the plant. He is a chemical engineer at Pro-Chem-Co near Bello."

I knew where the plant was. The woman's story explained why you sounded drunk and high when you called me. You probably had gone home and continued drinking until something spooked you enough to call me. I wondered if you had told Ivan your plans before you left, but I doubted it. He would have told his mother, and she would have done all in her power to stop you.

A more plausible explanation is that you had been planning this move for a while and that, once you made your decision, you were mostly at peace. After spending two days drinking and doping, you came home and carried out a plan no one could prevent because no one was around to stop it. To test my theory I asked Mrs. Santos, "Does Ivan know about Alex's death?"

The woman started crying loudly again, cupping her face with her hands. Instinctively, William stood up, went to the sink, and got her a cup of water, which the woman took gratefully.

In between sobs, the woman stated, "My boy knows nothing. My sweet, sensitive boy will be so mad at me when he comes home. You see, he called me yesterday afternoon. I couldn't tell him over the phone. The men from the national teams were there and he has a shot at being drafted. I couldn't do that to him. It would have broken him. My sweet boy."

She continued to cry, and I gave her a moment to compose herself. She added, "I will tell him on Tuesday. I will. I may have to call you to comfort him. He always loved you and he missed you when he had to stop 'The Oaks.' He was traveling more and he felt guilty when he couldn't go to the Center. So, one day he tells me, 'Momma, I think I need to stop going.' It broke my heart, Cheri, but I agreed. I think God wants him to be a player."

"He's very good," I admitted. Then I asked, "I know this is going to sound strange to you, but did Alex leave anything here for me?"

"It's not strange at all, my sweet. He did. He told me he was going on a long trip and wanted to send you a note, but he didn't remember your address. He said he would leave it here and you would pick it up soon. He said, if you didn't pick it up by Christmas, I should bring it to 'The Oaks' next time I go help the ladies. Let me go get it for you." She said, standing up and heading to her room.

William and I exchanged a glance, and he spoke for the first time in almost an hour, "Nice lady. I like her. I never met Ivan, but Alex used to talk about him. They had a big fight a few months back, but I knew they had made up and used to hang out sometimes."

"They used to be neighbors," I said, just to fill the silence with words.

I was feeling quite anxious about what Mrs. Santos was about to get me, but I had a suspicion that whatever it was, it would explain some of the mystery surrounding what happened to you at the age of ten and, perhaps, the reasons why you chose to end your life. To my surprise, the woman returned with a legal-size letter envelope. Somehow, I thought the package would be bigger. I knew you had said something about pictures, when we last spoke. Not wanting to wait until later, I opened the envelope in everyone's presence, as soon as Mrs. Santos sat back on the chair next to me.

The envelope contained two newspaper articles, both from English papers. The first one was from *The London Bugle* and it had been published in June of 1975. The second was from The *London Daily News* and it dated to January of 1976. Both articles were written in English, which none of us in the room spoke. The articles were held together by a stapled note written in your very characteristic handwriting. The message read,

"Joe, it all started here. More instructions will follow soon. Please be careful. I love you, bro. Alex."

I placed the envelopes in my backpack until we found a translator we could trust.

In the meantime, I still had several questions for Mrs. Santos. I started with the easiest, "Didn't your family use to live in El Poblado?"

Smiling, she answered, "That is an interesting story, but I will tell it to you briefly. Yes, we lived in El Poblado for more than eleven years, but, about six months ago, Alfredo's only brother, Miguel, died of cancer and left us this entire building. Can you believe that, my sweet? We went from middle class to owning all these buildings and the shopping center across the street. The man was never married, and he adored Alfredo. Well, Alfredo and I talked and, since his job is close to here, we decided to rent the place in El Poblado to a nice family, and here we are, my sweet. I take care of the tenants and Alfredo works at the plant."

"Well, I can't think of anyone more deserving, Mrs. Santos. Now, I have just one more question and we will leave you. I am going to 'The Oaks' and I don't want to get there too late," I said. "Did Ivan say whether Alex asked him to mail a package for him or deliver a message to anyone at all?"

"How did you know, my sweet? As a matter of fact, Alex asked Ivan to stop by the post office in city center. He had Ivan wait while he went inside to mail a package. He returned a few minutes later and they drove home." She responded.

The visit to Mrs. Santos' home had been a gold mine of information, and I was grateful she had been so helpful. We said our goodbyes, endured another excruciating hug, promised to keep in touch, and left one of the kindest women I knew to agonize about having to give her only son the worst news he would receive in a long time.

Chapter 26

We drove in silence for a few minutes, trying to digest what we had learned. First, you and Ivan had reconciled; second, the Santos were now a wealthy family; third, you had left me two newspaper articles to translate; fourth, you had mailed someone a packet that contained explosive evidence about what happened to you almost five years ago, evidence you had stolen from a building in La America; and five, I had an idea who the recipients of the packet were, and I knew who could provide me their contact information. On our way to "The Oaks" both William and I knew what we needed to do next. We needed to find a reliable translator who could tell us about the two articles in my backpack.

The logical choice for translator would have been my English teacher at school. Barbara Gomez had grown up in California until the age of sixteen, when she returned home to care for elderly parents, went to college, met a local boy, married, and started teaching English at the parochial school. The problem was that the school was closed for Christmas break, and all the teachers were on vacation until the second week of January. For obvious reasons, I didn't want to wait that long.

Another option would be for me to translate the note using available dictionaries. The problem with that idea is that a rudimentary translation, by someone who doesn't know the language, misses so much of the language's nuances, regionalisms, geographical references, and context that the translation becomes misleading or unusable. This is the reason why the Romans used to say, *"Traduttore, traditore,"* or "every translator is a traitor." Since so much was riding on the proper understanding of these articles, I needed the best translator I could find. I knew Cesar and his parents were fully bilingual, but I had a strong suspicion they were the wrong people for the job.

William was also in deep thought mulling over these issues. He simply didn't know anyone who could help us. As we were approaching Medellin, heading in the opposite direction of Copacabana, I thought of a crazy idea that might work.

I asked William, "Would you mind stopping at the library for a few minutes?"

"The Medellin Public Library?" He asked.

"Yes," I said. "Its 4:40 pm and the library closes at 6:00 pm on Saturdays. I might be able to find the same girl who helped me before. She might know someone who can help us."

"Hey, it's worth the try. Plus, I'm starving. While you snoop, I will eat." He said smiling. Then he asked, "Do you want anything?"

"No, thanks, I'm okay for now." I lied. The truth is that I was uncomfortable with William spending his money on me, and I wanted to save a bit of money in case I needed it for later.

We arrived at the library barely five minutes later.

William dropped me off at the same entrance he had picked me at before. I glanced in all directions before I left the car. Seeing no one suspicious, I left the car and quickly entered the imposing building. I went straight to the same desk I had gone to earlier that day. An older woman was at the reservations and check-out desk. Using my most friendly and charming face, I asked,

"Excuse me, I was here around 11:00 this morning and there was a young woman who helped me find a book on Pablo Neruda. Do you know is she is still around?"

"Was there a problem?" The woman asked concerned.

"No, not at all," I said smiling. "She was so helpful that I wanted to ask her another question. I have this big project that's due when I return to school and I wanted to get a head start."

"That's very good. Kids these days procrastinate about everything. I'm glad you are a responsible young man. Let me call the back and see if she's still here." She offered.

The woman picked up the phone, waited a few seconds, and asked someone on the other line, "Hi, Maria. Is Lucia still here or has she left yet?" A few seconds of silence, then, "Wonderful, could you have her come to the central desk? There is a young boy here who needs her help."

I resented the "young boy" label, but I realized that I had done a good job sounding innocent and helpless. Plus, in the words of my best friend, "Black Hoodie," I was a wee little mouse anyway. About three interminable minutes later, the same college student who helped me earlier that day, arrived at the desk.

She recognized me immediately and said, "I'm glad you returned. I found another Neruda book you might be interested in." Then, walking away from the desk towards the "Latin American Literature" section, she whispered, "Just follow me and don't say anything."

I followed her quietly, until we made it to the Neruda shelf. Then she said, "Are you in trouble? Who were those guys who came looking for you earlier?"

"What guys?" I asked innocently.

"There were two tall guys, dressed in black, who came looking for you after you left. They had a picture of you and asked me if I had seen you. I think they were carrying guns because I could see the bulge underneath their jackets. They were wearing those gun holsters you strap on your body." She said awkwardly, not knowing what terminology to use. I understood perfectly what she was trying to convey, however.

"You mean, they looked like secret police? And they were looking for me?" I asked innocently.

"That's what I am saying. Are you in trouble?" She repeated.

"Not that I know off," I tried to act concerned. Did they leave a number I can call to clarify this? I think they have me confused with someone else."

"As a matter of fact, they left their business card. Let me go get it." A few minutes later she returned with a card for "Castle Ridge Consultants." The card had a very light and serene image of a mountain in the background. In the forefront it read:

Lt. Jaime Castro
Corporate Security
275-4115 ext. 2

There was no address, facsimile number, or name of a town where the company might be located. I took my notebook out of the backpack, wrote the information down, and returned the card to the library attendant. I said, "It's probably nothing. I will have my mother call them later and find out what's going on. By the way, I have a question to ask you. Do you know anyone who speaks and reads English? I have some papers I need to translate, but I don't know anyone who can help me."

"My cousin, Elvia, speaks and reads three languages well. She works for the Inter-American hotel, but she is not working again until Monday. I can call her Monday morning and tell her you're coming. She might be able to help you, but she might charge you. That's her job, you know? She translates documents and charges by the page or by the document. I can ask her to give you a break, but she will have to charge you something," Lucia offered helpfully.

"That would be great. Can I give you the number where I will be for the next few days? Once you speak to her, please ask her to call me. I will pay her whatever she charges," I said, writing my name on a piece of paper and handing it over to her.

I did not know where the money would come from, but I was convinced I could get some money before Monday.

"You have a deal. And, please, stay safe. There's so much craziness going on right now. I would hate for anything to happen to you. You look like a nice kid," Lucia said affectionately.

"Thank you very much. I'll stay in touch," I said and proceeded to leave the building.

William was waiting right in front of the building, food in each hand. The car was parked about fifty feet to our left. As soon as we sat in the car, he handed over a bag of pastries and said, "I know you said you weren't hungry, but these are to die for. You can always eat them later."

In the bag there were three guava pastelitos, which smelled as though they had just come out of the fryer. Although my mouth was watering, I closed the bag and placed the pastries in my backpack.

I looked at William appreciatively and said, "Thanks. By the way, we have a translator. She works for the Inter-American hotel as a translator. I will be able to see her on Monday. Do you know where I can get some money? There will be a charge for her work."

"First, Monday is no good for me. It happens to be the

busiest day for me this week. But I'm off on Tuesday. Second, I don't have a lot of money, but I have some. I'll spot you for the translation, but if this detective shit gets expensive, we may have to get old man Cuevas on board," William stated.

I had already thought about this, but I wasn't sure if I could trust your father yet. I said, "I'll see if I can schedule for early Tuesday. Let's hold off on involving Mr. Cuevas yet, although we may have to at some point. Thanks William. You are awesome."

"Don't I know it. I have a weakness for little shits like you and your deceased comrade, may he rest in peace," William added solemnly.

"Indeed." I said.

Chapter 27

William and I drove in silence to "The Oaks" as the twilight was beginning to set over the Medellin horizon. I have already reminded you about the half a mile distance between the bus stop and the entrance to the camp. Now, let me add a few details. As you make a right onto the gravel road that leads to the camp, you drive or walk through a densely wooded area, then through a clearing that was once used for cattle farming, but the Center acquired years ago, in case they need to expand in the future.

The clearing is approximately a quarter of a mile. After it, you begin to ascend to the camp, once again passing heavily wooded areas at both sides of the road. Near the top of the incline, you come to a metal fence, which is never closed. When the place was first built, Fr. Garcia thought about building a guard house for security reasons, but the place was so quiet and isolated that in the many years the Center had been opened, there had never been a break in. Soon the idea was abandoned, and the gate left permanently open.

A few hundred feet after the gate, you begin to pass the camp's buildings on the left. The back door to the kitchen is the first entrance you see as you begin to drive the steeply curbed incline to the visitor's parking lot and main entrance, a few hundred feet away. As you pass the kitchen, you begin to see the roofs of the chapel, the Alpha, Beta, Gamma buildings on the left, and more wooded area on the right.

Just around the bend, you come into a modern multi-car parking lot, an entrance archway, and the chapel. A cement staircase to the left of the chapel leads visitors to the administration building and kitchen, and a straight walk from the chapel leads visitors to the ABC residential buildings. About three quarters of the way to the ABC, on the left hand-side of the walkway, there is a steep cement staircase leading down to the quads and the soccer field.

All visitors to the Center were required to enter through the main archway, right off the parking lot. The kitchen employees, staff, and Leadership School students could come in through the back kitchen entrance since most of us walked or were dropped off by parents, and the cars could easily turn around in the loading dock outside of the kitchen.

Many years before, a walking trail had been developed from the loading dock to the quad buildings. Although nobody used it anymore because it had become heavily wooded. The trail was still walkable, and it offered a shortcut to the quads and the soccer field and, if you kept walking, you could even come around to the back of the ABC buildings.

I had William drop me off at the kitchen entrance. He turned around and waved at me before heading back to the highway. I waved back, grateful for his incredible help. I was tired and hungry, and I had been promised a dinner plate, which I could find in the staff's refrigerator in the kitchen. When I reached for the door handle of the kitchen, I realized that it was locked. This was unusual because there was always someone around until 8:00 pm and it was only 7:15.

Since none of the students had a key for this door, I knocked loudly, but no one opened the door. I waited for five minutes and decided to start walking the steep incline to the parking lot. About halfway to the main entrance, however, I could see the tail end of a car I recognized, parked towards the archway entrance to the building. I froze and hid in the woods. As I inched closer a few more feet, I recognized Machado's grey sedan, parked next to three other cars I recognized because they belonged to the staff.

I quickly retraced my steps, returning to the kitchen, where I tried the door handle one more time. Then I decided to walk the dark, dense trail to the residential buildings, trying hard to remain as hidden and as quiet as I could. You and I had walked this trail before, and I knew it well. Of course, we had never walked it in pitch-black darkness, and I did not carry a flashlight.

I reached inside my backpack, pulled out a cigarette, and lit it. My box of matches had seven short matches, and I was grateful for them. I decided to save them in case I needed them later. In the meantime, I used the faint glow of my cigarette to provide a little light. After a few minutes of a painfully slow and careful walk, I arrived at the bottom of the staircase that led to the north section of the campus -the same staircase, Ivan had climbed months before when you threatened to jump off the roof of the bell tower.

Instead of taking the staircase, I quickly got out of the bright light by the stairs and continued straight, finding coverage in darkness once again a few seconds later. I walked the circular path I knew would eventually bring me to the bottom of the hill behind the ABC buildings. Once I reached the back of my building, I hid behind a tree and stared up at the buildings.

I could see that all the lights of the empty buildings were on. In the Alpha, the building closest to the chapel, there were two men dressed all in black, going from room to room, turning over all mattresses, emptying all dressers on the floor, and violently inspecting all drawers and closets. Outside Alpha, facing me and not seeing me, there were two other men, Machado, and a young, tall, handsome boy I recognized well.

Machado was holding a sub-machine gun, ready for an unexpected southern invasion I knew would never come. Cesar was unarmed but was just as attentive. The two men doing the damage inside the rooms were the same I had seen entering the library that afternoon, my friends from the Castle Ridge Security Consultants.

I remained very quiet as Black Suit #1 and Black Suit #2, the two inside men, joined the two outside men and all four of them moved to Beta. They took their designated positions, and started tearing the building apart, room by room. Finding nothing, they followed the same procedure and went inside Gamma, the building our room was in. I was at the bottom of the hill, looking straight at them, but I was well hidden and there was no way for them to see me, unless they found reasons to inspect the hill below. I remained very quiet, frozen in place by fear.

Suddenly, inside our room, Black Suit #1, found an envelope inside one of the drawers in the dresser where you used to store your clothes and contraband. He ordered Black Suit #2 to do something, but I couldn't hear what they were saying. Black Suit #2, knocked on the window loudly, getting Machado and Cesar's attention. The two of them walked towards the building and joined the men inside. I could see all four of them engaged in conversation through the large window that faced the hill below.

Machado snatched the envelope from Black Suit #1

and opened it. All men gathered closely together to grab a view. There seemed to be several documents in the envelope because each of them grabbed a piece of paper and dispersed throughout the room. After each had read their respective document, the men huddled again and started an animated conversation. Satisfied by the success of their mission, the men placed the documents in a suitcase that miraculously appeared from somewhere and left Gamma, not bothering to inspect the last room.

My soul dropped to my knees. I realized that I had been too late in coming to "The Oaks," and I had lost all the evidence you had left for me. I may never find the truth about what happened to you, and this made me as sad as the realization that you were gone forever. Whatever you had found in that building in La America was dangerous enough for this assault on a peaceful religious institution that had served the city with distinction for almost a quarter of a century.

I felt intense anger begin to rise within me, but I knew this was not the time for reaction. Putting a twist on my sainted mother's most common expression, "God would provide the opportunity somehow to take all these sons-of-bitches down!"

Quickly and quietly I began to climb the hill, but I remained out of view until I saw the lights of a car reversing in the parking lot, making a U-turn, and heading back towards the highway. I cautiously walked towards the chapel, looked inside it for a brief second and found it empty. I carefully walked down the steps to the administration building and walked in. I tried to turn the knob of Fr. Garcia's bedroom, but it was locked. The office next to the priest's room was locked as well. I crossed the living room, down the corridor, and tried to open two more doors. All were locked and dark. I opened the door that connected the admin building to the dining room, but the place was dark and empty.

I continued straight until I entered the kitchen. At the opposite end of the room, in the chef's small office, I detected light coming out from the gap at the bottom of the door. I opened the door and gasped as I saw a group of six terrified staff, huddled together by a desk, comforting each other. Several of them screamed when I opened the door, and one of the youngest counselors, holding a broom, came towards the door ready to attack, until he saw that it was me. Two of the younger female staff were crying, and the old cook, who had been sitting on the desk chair at the center of the huddle, exclaimed a joyous, "Alleluia! Praise Jesus!"

Chapter 28

The first phone call the staff made after the break in was to Fr. Garcia, who had accepted the invitation from Fr. Bedoya to stay overnight at the rectory and to join him for supper that night. In fact, knowing that I was heading to the Center that afternoon, the good priest had sent me a note with the staff which read, "Rest tonight, we will talk tomorrow."

I was grateful that Fr. Garcia was not at the Center because I know he would have resisted the attack somehow, and these were not the kind of men you resist. Fr. Garcia and Fr. Bedoya decided to come to "The Oaks" after receiving notice of the break in. They spent several hours, inspecting the damage throughout the place and comforting the shaken staff.

The second call the staff had made was to the police. Within ten minutes of that call, two patrol cars arrived, with a total of eight agents. They asked us to remain in the admin building while they did a thorough search of all the buildings and grounds. A senior officer stayed behind at the administrative building to take our statements.

The staff's account could be summarized in several statements of fact: (1) Around 6:15 pm a dark grey sedan had arrived at the Center, (2) Two masked men had entered the administrative building. One of them was holding a sub-machine gun. Two more remained outside and could be seen through the windows. They too wore masks. (3) The armed men inside the building had rounded up the staff and put them in the chef's office. (4) They had threatened to shoot them dead if they left the room. (5) The men had unplugged all phone receivers from the rooms and had locked them up in Fr. Garcia's office. (6) They had locked all offices that could be locked. (7) The men had been gone for almost two hours, wandering around the Center, looking for something or someone, by the time I opened the door and let the staff out. (9) None of the staff could recognize any of the intruders, and (10) I added a most believable lie that I had arrived at the Center around 7:50, had dismissed the taxi from the main parking lot, was surprised that the place looked abandoned, and ultimately had found the staff in the chef's office. I added that I had not seen any cars leaving the premises as I was driving in.

Fr. Wilbert Garcia was a man of great resources, which means that he was a man of great influence. Within a few minutes of receiving a call from the staff, the good priest had called the Diocesan Bishop and had hired a private security force to protect the Center until appropriate repairs could be done to the almost non-existent security systems and protocols.

These Rent-A-Cop men looked more like a "Rent-A-Mercenary" commando, dressed in military uniforms and displaying their weapons visibly on shoulder straps over their uniforms. The new security force took over the entire campus, carefully supervising every entrance point, making rounds of all the buildings twenty-four hours a day, and writing the names and drivers licenses of visitors and vendors on clipboards.

While this level of supervision was happening, within two weeks of the incident an entire construction crew built a tall adobe wall on both sides of the gate. They replaced the old, rusted gate with a new gate that could only be opened from the brand-new guard tower, right inside the wall. Finally, they placed a permanent guard on rotation from six in the morning to eight at night, seven days a week.

If the gate had to be opened before or after these hours, a call button would alert a designated duty officer at the Center and the gate was opened remotely. Once the new gate system was finished and the regular guards hired, the Rent-A-Mercenaries left "The Oaks" to the relief of all the staff and visitors.

The break-in at the Center shook me deeply. I began to realize for the first time that I could be in serious trouble with whoever was looking for the evidence you had taken from La America. If they thought I had anything to do with the theft or I was holding the evidence for you, there was nothing Juan Machado or the Castle Ridge Security Consultants wouldn't do to get the evidence back or to silence me.

I suddenly realized it was getting late, and I hadn't called my mother as I had promised. I also thought of a very sly and conniving cousin, who had married rich and moved to the coast, but who had been a police officer in Medellin for many years before he found a way out. It occurred to me that cousin Fernando may know about Lt. Jaime Castro, the name on the calling card the librarian had given me, or Machado himself. At nearly 10:00 pm that Saturday evening, I called my mother from the camp.

"Where in the name of God have you been?" Were the first words my angry and concerned mother uttered. "You left here fifteen hours ago, and you waited until now to call your mother? You better have a great excuse, mister."

"I spent most of the day with Alex's parents. I am sorry I lost track of time. I just got here a couple of hours ago but found the place in shambles. Someone broke in and stole a bunch of stuff while the staff were at the funeral." I half lied, being terrified of my mother. Okay, I three-quarters lied.

"Are you okay? Are the staff okay?" she asked quite concerned.

"We are all okay; we were not here when the break-in happened. The police showed up to take our statements, but there was nothing we could tell them. Anyway, we have been busy cleaning up the place." It was amazing how I could lie to the woman without feeling guilty.

"Well, I'm glad you called. Your dad is back from the farm and I didn't know what to tell him about your whereabouts. How are Alex's parents doing?" she asked.

"They are obviously upset, Mom. We all are. Just keep them in your prayers." I answered as honestly as I could.

The truth was that Missy and Arturo Cuevas were going to need my mother's prayers if I found out they had something to do with what happened to you almost five years ago. I may have been outmanned and outgunned, but I had a weapon they didn't know I had. They underestimated my tenacity. Even if it would take me a lifetime, I would eventually take them all down. I had time and I was patient.

I decided to ask my mother the question I had in mind, "Mom, one of my friends is going to Cartagena on vacation, and he is looking for someone to talk to about safety concerns in the city, good hotels, transportation, and that kind of stuff. Would you happen to have cousin Fernando's number?"

I knew she had the information because Fernando

had always been her favorite nephew. She responded, "What a coincidence. I just spoke to him about an hour ago. He is doing so well. Did you know Marta is pregnant again?"

"That's awesome," I said, not really caring. "Let me call him to congratulate him and ask him if I can have my friend's parents call him."

"Sure, honey. His number is 312-611-3074. If you call him now, you'll catch him for sure." She added, helpfully.

"Thanks, Mom. I'll call you tomorrow. I promise."

After I hung up, I wrote a few questions I wanted to ask Fernando. This was necessary because the only way to speak to my cousin was to interrupt his never-ending monologues at crucial points. I wanted to be ready to catch him with the right question when he paused to take a breath, when I noticed a dip in his tone and could cut him off, or when, however long it took, he was done making a point.

I am not going to re-tell the entire conversation because, even though you have been dead for over a year now, there is only so much pain I can cause you. The man is the world's most long-winded individual. After listening to him tell me everything he could tell me about life in Cartagena; his beautiful and rich wife, who was almost ten years his senior; and his two children and "one on the way," I found the right time to ask him. "Hey, I met a friend of yours the other day. Does the name Juan Machado ring a bell?"

As a miracle too rare to describe in words, Fernando had nothing to say for nearly fifteen seconds. Thinking he hadn't heard the question, I repeated it.

"That piece of shit is not my friend." He responded angrily, as though I had touched a very raw nerve.

The forcefulness of the statement was not lost on me because Fernando was a newly converted Evangelical of the Assemblies of God persuasion, and he didn't drink, smoke, lie, or curse. At least not in public.

He continued, "Is he back on the force? I thought he was

doing private security now? He's lucky he is not in prison. When I was in the force, Sargent Julio Rodriguez, from Internal Affairs, was on the verge of filing charges against him for corruption. Even though he left the force soon after that, the investigation was still unfolding when I left. You know some us believed Machado was involved with the death squads. He is a dangerous man, Joe. You stay away from him."

I started thinking about the name. Where had I heard that name before? While Fernando was still talking about whatever he was talking about, I looked inside my wallet and found a business card someone had just given me a few days before. The former Sargent of Internal Affairs, Julio Rodriguez, was now Colonel Julio Rodriguez, the head of the entire Medellin police force. I had met him briefly after your death. He had given me the card to call him personally if I remembered anything else about the case. I filed this name in my brain for future use.

I interrupted Fernando with another question, "Do you know a Lieutenant Jaime Castro?"

"He wasn't a lieutenant when I knew him, but, yes, I know the guy. He was a street cop like I was. I didn't know him well, but I remember his face. Why are you asking me about these guys, Joe? Are you in trouble?" Fernando was concerned for someone other than himself for the first time in my life. I thought this showed some progress, and I was happy for my narcissistic cousin Fernando. Perhaps a costal life was good for him after all?

I responded, "Me? In trouble? Come on, I'm just a kid. No, I met these two guys at a party at Alex's house, and I thought I would ask you about them. They said they work for Castle Ridge Security Consultants. Do you know them?"

"They are a foreign company that does security for American diplomats and high value customers. They have been pillaging good officers from police stations and military installations all over the country. They offered me a job once, but I had already met Marta and was on my way out." He said and I understood what he meant. Why do dangerous work when you can marry an ugly girl with millions to her name?

Politely, I excused myself, listened to another five minutes of goodbyes, and hung up. I had a headache and I was starving. With all the excitement of the day I had forgotten to have dinner.

With the staff's permission, I settled in the only room in Gamma that wasn't destroyed by the Castle Ridge guys. I reached inside my backpack and took out the three guava pastries William had given me earlier and ate them in three giant bites. I smoked one last cigarette and lay down on one of the two beds in the room.

Within minutes, I fell asleep until around 9:00am the next morning, when one of the counselors woke me up with a hot cup of coffee and the promise of bacon, eggs, and re-fried beans.

Chapter 29

I received two calls that Monday that proved to be very helpful to my search for answers about whatever nightmare you had gone through. Before I describe these phone calls, let me summarize where I was at in my investigation the morning after the break-in at "The Oaks." This is what I knew:

1. The planning for your suicide had most likely begun at "The Oaks" during the last weekend of our fall program. This explains your mood on Saturday and Sunday, your giving presents to folks, your loving and grateful behaviors towards the staff and peers at the party on Saturday night, your request to sing "When a friend Goes Away" during the closing Mass, your visit to Ivan on Monday and Tuesday, and your phone call to me. I believe drinking and doping were ways for you to find the resolve and courage to do what you knew you were going to do but were not the cause of the event.

2. Beginning with your revelations to me on Friday during our poetry game and followed by your finding out about the existence of pictures, you had spent a lot of time coming to terms with what happened to you around the

age of ten. As you forced yourself to think about the event, you started planning a way to make the truth known, and perhaps punish those responsible.

3. The memories most likely began to come to you several months before when an episode happened that made you feel replaced, "retired," and betrayed. To cope with that episode and the flood of memories about the trauma, you had turned to drugs, starting with cocaine and finishing with the deadly bazuko. As a result, you had become withdrawn, paranoid, and angry during the last months of your life.

4. You broke into an office in La America to retrieve the evidence you knew existed and were seen leaving the building. Within several minutes, the guards discovered the theft and realized you had taken the evidence. They started looking for you at first, and, after your death, they began to look for the evidence.

5. You had anticipated that these people would do all in their power to find the evidence, which is the reason why you chose to divide it into several sets. You left me two articles to translate, mailed a package to someone else, and left some documents at "The Oaks." You may have left more clues that I had yet to find.

6. Cesar was involved and, judging by the fact that Machado was your family's driver, so was your mother and maybe even your father. I also assumed that one or both of Cesar's parents knew what was going on or was involved. I was beginning to formulate theories about what was happening at your home, but, by Monday of that week, I still had a few questions to answer before I got the whole picture. I suspected your father would prove useful in getting the information I needed.

7. Your mother was either having an affair or had become romantically involved with someone at some point during the last few years. There was someone with the initials YM who might have the key to unlock Pandora's box.

8. Whoever was hunting for the evidence had hired their own "Rent-A-Mercenary" firm, called Castle Ridge Security Consultants. I had learned through my cousin that those guys were mostly former police and military and, therefore, highly trained and dangerous. I also knew that Machado was much more than just a driver and appeared to have a substantial role

in the evidence "search and destroy" mission. He may have been involved with the famous death squads, which means he may have a connection to either "The Boys from Medellin" or some other outfit.

9. Whatever was going on had started outside of Colombia or had international connections.

10. Finally, your ace detective was an emaciated fifteen-year old, who had exactly the equivalent of three dollars in his wallet, did not speak English, and was so out of his depth that anyone with a brain would wonder if you were insane when you got him involved in your plan. To make matters worse, all he had to go on were two newspaper clippings in a language he couldn't understand.

This brings us to the first call I received that Monday morning at 10:23 at the camp. The whole place was frantic with activity. There was a dozen or so volunteers from around the Diocese, cleaning the destroyed rooms, putting new furniture together, unloading new mattresses from a delivery truck, and painting designated areas. In the kitchen, the staff were busy cooking for all workers and volunteers. In the office, several leadership school students, who had been called to return to the school, were manning three telephones, which kept ringing every few minutes as more people found out about the break in.

"The Oaks" community was large and, regardless of profession or age, we had something in common: We all loved Fr. Wilbert Garcia and the incredible piece of paradise he had created. The last group of people at the Center were the security forces and the workers assessing the upcoming improvements to the Center's security systems.

I was assigned to the office staff, which means that I spent most of the day answering phones, directing donations to the Diocese, and creating a calendar for volunteers who would be arriving over the next few days.

At around 10:23, Hernando, one of the other office workers tapped me on the shoulder and said, "This one is for you, Joe. It's a girl."

He said it a little too loudly, as though he had just discovered my secret lover. Others around us looked at me and laughed, not because it would be impossible for me to have a girlfriend at the time, but because in all the time at the Center, I had never received any calls from anyone other than my family. I had a simple rule I lived by. I gave no one my number at "The Oaks." My time at the Center was mine alone and I did all I could to protect it.

Hernando and I traded places and took each other's receivers. I answered the phone with a tentative, "Hello?"

"This is Elvia Gomez, from the Inter-American. I was told by my cousin Lucia to call you. You have a translation job?" she said in a beautiful soprano voice.

"Yes, of course. Thanks for calling me back. I have two newspaper articles written in English, and I need to have as faithful a translation as I can have." I said, rather hurriedly.

"Do you have a fax machine where you are?" Elvia asked.

"Unfortunately, we don't have one yet," I responded. The technology was ascending in popularity in the city, especially in banks, hotels, and hospitals, but the Center still didn't have a machine. I added, "Can I bring you the articles in person tomorrow morning?"

"Tomorrow will be a very busy day for me because we have a large group from America coming for a textiles conference and I need to translate. Can you bring them this afternoon with the payment? I will work on them this evening and leave them for you at the hotel's front desk. You can pick them up in the morning." She volunteered.

"Let me see if I can arrange transportation for this evening. How late will you be at work today?" I asked, trying to figure out how I might get into the city without William and without much money for taxis.

"I'll be here until six. The fee is 1,000 pesos per typed page. Depending on how big the newspaper clips are, it will cost you between 6,000 and 8,000 pesos." She stated quite casually.

Eight thousand Pesos would have been roughly twelve dollars at the time, which doesn't sound like much until you realize that the average well-paid worker earned the equivalent to thirty dollars a month. The translation would cost almost half a month's wages, and there was no way I could come up with this money. Not wanting to lose the opportunity to have Elvia's help, I made a quick decision.

"I'll meet you before six at the hotel. What's a good number to call you in case I need to talk to you before I see you?" I asked and the young woman proceeded to give me her office number at the hotel. With that, I said my goodbyes and hung up.

Hernando chimed in, getting one more laugh at my expense, "So, Joe. Did I hear you correctly? You are meeting a beautiful woman at 6:00 pm at a fancy hotel? Can I come, please?"

Everyone was laughing in the room while my face became as red as a tomato. Not amused by the insinuations, I stood from the chair and said to Hernando, "Can you, please, grow up? This is how rumors start. I'm doing a project for school, and I need something translated. So, just shut it."

I walked out of the room, stating, "I need a smoke." With that, I left a group of laughing, hormonal teenagers behind as I walked out of the admin building.

As soon as I opened the door, I came face to face with Fr. Garcia who was just coming in. He gave me the type of smile a parent gives a child they haven't seen in a long time. He gave me a quick hug and said, "Do you have some time to talk?

"Sure, Father. Can I see you in five?" I desperately needed a cigarette.

"Sure, I'll be in my study, come see me when you're done smoking your cigarette." He said, smiling.

He knew me well and assumed I was leaving the building for a smoke. From the very first day of operations, Fr. Garcia had instituted a non-smoking policy in the admin building, all classroom areas, the cafeteria, and the chapel.

Nicotine and caffeine are lovers. They have as close a relationship as peanut butter and jelly, rice and beans, and chips and salsa. Smoking my cigarette and drinking a black cup of coffee, I contemplated what my next steps should be. I needed transportation, I needed money, and I needed support. After all, every superhero needs a team, and I knew it would take supernatural abilities to do whatever you had had in mind. I was as far away from a superhero as you could possibly imagine, but you had left me no choice.

This would be a step-down fight. In other words,

while the powerful worried about exposure, people without power and status, and a backer no one expected, would launch a fight from the shadows. I had already learned enough to create a chain reaction that would topple whatever version of hell the Castle Ridge Consultants were trying to protect.

I had several people in mind to enlist in my own band of shadow fighters: A thirty-five year old driver I suspected was an evening drinker, a soccer phenom who was most definitely going places, a college student from Rio Negro who had loved you before I knew you, and an intrepid priest who had spent most of his life protecting the underclass and training the next generations of Medellin's leaders. And, of course, a 110-pound, wee little mouse from the wrong side of the city.

I knew that for the plan to work, I had to have a heart to heart conversation with Fr. Garcia, whom I hoped would provide the financial backing we were going to need.

Chapter 30

I knocked on Fr. Garcia's door around 11:15 that morning. The priest was lost in one of his books and didn't hear the knock. This was not uncommon. There were two things Fr. Garcia loved about as much as he loved his God: His job and his books. I had never seen the old priest as contented as when he was nose-deep in a classic book. He loved Latin American authors, but, being a fluent Latin and Italian reader, many of his books were classics in the original Latin language and modern theology and literature works in Italian.

After the second, louder knock, the priest called out, "Come in."

The otherwise humble priest was as sophisticated as a lord in Victorian England when it came to his study. Two of the walls had floor-to-ceiling, custom-made, oak bookshelves, lightly tinted in a burgundy color. Against a third wall there was a beautiful leather sofa that could seat at least three overweight giants. To the left of the over-stuffed couch, there were two leather arm chairs, which matched the couch in style and color. On the fourth wall, the priest had a beautiful cedar desk that had belonged to his grandfather. It was believed that the first document ever signed on behalf of "The Antioquia Beverage Company," had been signed on that giant desk.

The chair that went with the desk had no arms because the priest's grandfather had been quite rotund and required more rump and body space than the average human. The chair had been specially made for the occupant in New Orleans at the turn of the 20th century. It was built of solid cedar with burgundy leather upholstery, which Fr. Garcia had restored to its original condition when he built "The Oaks."

At the center of the room there was a famous icon of the Holy Trinity, which had been sewn at the center of a beautiful carpet, somewhere in Jerusalem in the early 1930's. The priest had placed a beautiful glass table over the image of the Trinity because he didn't think it was appropriate or respectful for anyone to walk over God's own image.

The result of the clear glass table was that anyone seated at the desk, couch, or chairs could have a direct view of God's image. The priest would often turn to the icon when counseling students and say something like, "I wonder where he is in this?" Or, "I wonder what he would want us to do?"

Fr. Garcia was seated on his desk chair, facing the door. As soon as I walked in, he pointed to the couch, but I walked past it and sat on an armchair directly in front of the priest. I was a little unsure about involving him in these matters because he had been in ill health for a while, and everyone at the Center protected his time and energy-levels like Fort Knox protects its gold.

No one was allowed in his side of the admin building between 12:30 and 2:00 pm when he was taking his nap, and calls were often withheld from him under the excuse that, "Father is indisposed at this moment, may I, please, take a message?" Mundane messages would be passed down to staff to handle, and the important ones were given to him only after Sister Celeste, the nun who managed the office, made sure he was having "a good day."

Yet, here I was, about to talk to him about conspiracies, dangerous people, our poetry game, and your telephone call to me a few days before.

Sighing deeply, I started, "I'm so sorry to bother you, Father, especially after you are so busy dealing with the break-in. Are you strong enough to talk to me or should I come a bit later?" I said respectfully to a man who had become a second father over the last two years.

"No bother at all, Joe. No bother at all!" He said buoyant. He seemed to be having one of his good days. He continued, "It may sound strange, but his break-in may have been a blessing. The truth is that I have been praying to God for a new project, and he has given me one. I feel as invigorated now as I felt when I built this place. I am a builder at heart and this crisis will give us a chance to paint some of the buildings, make the place more secure, change the old furniture, and spruce-up the place a bit. I am even thinking about building a basketball court. What do you think about that?"

I sucked at basketball, but I knew some of my friends would be thrilled with the idea. I smiled appreciatively for two reasons: first, I loved how Fr. Garcia always found the silver lining in everything and, second, I was glad he was feeling healthy. I silently prayed that his good health would continue after I was done with my story.

I said, "A basketball court would be awesome. You spoil us, Father."

"Nonsense." He exclaimed. "You are all my family

and, if you don't take care of your family, who are you going to take care of? Now, tell me, Joe, how are you doing?"

"I don't really know, Father. I cry sometimes, I laugh when I remember his silliness, I pray for his salvation sometimes, I worry about his family, I cry again, then I laugh again. It is like one of those roller coasters I've read about. Ups and downs," I answered honestly.

The priest smiled and said, "Welcome to grief, my boy. I have lost many people I loved and that is exactly how I have felt each time. It is a crazy ride, but it gets better over time. He loved you dearly and he knew you loved him too."

I started crying once again and the priest pushed a box of tissues gently my way, not to cause me to stop, but to prevent me from using my need for a tissue as an excuse to get up, go to the bathroom, and compose myself. In a way, the box of tissues was his permission for me to cry it out without embarrassment. He waited patiently until I was able to speak again.

I asked him, "Father, I have a story to tell you, but it sounds paranoid and crazy. You will think I have lost my mind and you may feel like you need to call my mother to take me to a psychiatric hospital."

The priest interrupted me in his typical fashion. He gently raised his hand in a "stop" motion at the opportune time.

Then he said, "You are one of my most sober, serious, and responsible students. 'Paranoid' or 'crazy' would be the last words I would use to describe you. So, please, go on. Tell me your story and don't stop until you have reached the end. I will take some notes, as I always do, and will review my comments with you when you are done. Does that sound okay with you?"

"It does, Father. Thank you." For the next hour and fifteen minutes, I told Father Garcia everything about your behavior changes for the last three months, our poetry game, your phone call the day you died, your visit to Ivan, the poem you left me, my visit to the library, the men who looked for me there, and the envelope with the two newspaper articles. I also told him about William's involvement in the events of the day before, my spying on the men who broke into the Center, the Castle Ridge Security Consultants, my discovery of your friend Cesar at "The Oaks" and my belief he may be involved somehow, my theories about what was happening at your home, the translator I had to see that evening, my lack of money to pay the lady, and what I believed needed to be done next. In other words, I opened my heart to the priest in order to enlist his help.

At 12:30 sharp, Sister Celeste knocked, opened the door without waiting to be invited in, and announced that it was late for Father's lunch and nap and this wasn't healthy for him. If her eyes had been guns, I would have been shot about one-hundred times in the two seconds she was in the office. I kept my head down and Fr. Garcia smiled at her, as a child who has been caught with his hand in the cookie jar.

He spoke to both of us at the same time, "This is what we will do: I will go and have lunch with the sisters while Joe gets some food in the kitchen. After this, I will take my rest until around 2:30 pm. At 3:00 pm, Joe and I need to go to a meeting off campus and will not return until later in the evening. So, please, don't prepare any dinner for me, Sister." Then, looking at me, he asked, "Is this okay with you, Joe?"

Surprised and grateful, I said, "Yes, Father. That's perfect. Thank you."

I left the priest's office, heading down to avoid Sr. Celeste's annoyed look of disapproval. I went straight to the kitchen and the elderly chef welcomed me as a distinguished dignitary and served me a heaping plate of roasted potatoes, steak, and salad. For desert, she shared her special carrot cake, which she sneaked in for Fr. Garcia from her house occasionally. The old cook avoided Sr. Celeste as one avoids the plague, so she never served the priest his cake when Sister was around. Fr. Garcia knew, however, that on special occasions he could visit the kitchen to "check on things" and be treated to a large slice of the magnificent cake. To be treated to "Father's Cake," was a treat reserved for special people. In the eyes of the staff, I had become a very special boy, indeed.

Chapter 31

For an old man, Fr. Garcia was as good a driver as William, maybe even better. He eased in and out of traffic with the dexterity of a Formula One driver. And he loved to speed. This was well-known in the Center and those with a weak constitution often chose to drive with a staff member rather than the beloved priest. He was also a quiet driver. He believed that driving allows the right side of the brain to be in charge, lessening its grip on the left side of the brain. Since dealing with complicated manners often required left-brain work, the priest refused to listen to music or engage anyone in conversation.

Driving was precious time for his left brain to do the thinking and processing that was required to solve a problem. Of course, driving in complete silence was very uncomfortable because I didn't have a book to read and I had left my backpack at the Center, along with my cigarettes, and chewing gum.

The drive was long but familiar, as we were driving in the direction of Bello. For a while, I thought the priest was taking me home, where two men dressed in white lab coats would be waiting for me with a straitjacket. When we passed Bello and continued driving on the North Highway towards Copacabana, I began to think that he was taking me to Ivan's house to corroborate my story with his good friend Luisa Santos. When we passed Copacabana, I realized I had no idea where we were going. Outside, the scenery was becoming more rural, sparse, and beautiful: Luscious farms, rolling hills, and oceans of perfectly green savannas that could rival the Irish or Scottish countryside.

When we arrived at the beautiful mountain town of Girardota, about ten miles north of Bello, the priest drove straight to St. Therese of the Child Jesus church. He parked in the church's parking lot and we both entered the massive church. Although the priest had called in advance to announce his visit, we were told by a cleaning lady that the rector was on vacation until Friday. This was okay because we were not here to see the priest. In fact, after about five minutes of quiet praying in the back of the church, Fr. Garcia touched my shoulder and whispered, "Please follow me quietly and quickly and don't ask any questions until I tell you."

With that, he left the pew and I followed. We walked deeper into the church towards the altar. At the foot of the altar we made a right turn, walked about one-hundred paces, and exited through a side door, directly into a dark green Jeep parked right outside. The priest gently pushed me inside the back seat of the car and followed me, closing the door quickly and quietly.

As soon as we were inside the car, the silent driver drove to the bottom of the street, made a left, and jumped back on the same highway we had used on our way to the church, but in the opposite direction. He drove approximately 1.5 miles and took an exit onto a gravel road. He drove on the gravel road approximately three miles, arriving at the bottling plant for the "Antiochia Beverage Company." Next to the large plant there was a three-story high building, with its own parking lot. He pulled in, drove to the end of the lot, parked in front of the last entrance to the building, and turned the engine off.

The driver turned around and said, "Sorry for the cloak and dagger stunt, but one cannot be too careful these days. Go right in Father. He is waiting in his study."

Fr. Garcia, looked at me, smiled, and told the driver, "Good afternoon to you too, Julio. This is Joe, one of my students. It's nice to see you. How are Olivia and the kids?"

"You know how they are because you just saw them last week. Stop fooling around and get inside." The driver ordered and I was shocked that he would speak to Fr. Garcia that way.

Fr. Garcia started laughing, looked at me, and said, "Julio is my nephew. He likes to pretend he is in charge around here. But I let him believe it because he is my only nephew, and I feel bad about his lack of manners."

Julio gave us a faint smirk and said, "Will you please get inside?" Smiling again, Fr. Garcia left the car and I followed him.

I believe there are names that command respect. For example, I would never offend someone whose name is Spartacus. The person we were coming to see on that Monday afternoon had one of those names that inspired respect. His full name was even more impressive. He was Dr. Julius Arthur Garza, III and he had been the corporate attorney for ABC Cola for almost a quarter of a century. The English middle name notwithstanding, Dr. Garza was the prototypical Colombian intellectual, down to the tweed jacket with patches on the elbows, the bowtie, and glasses hanging on the tip of his nose. More university professor than corporate counsel, Dr. Garza had an affable, grandfatherly look, that obscured a sharp mind and a calculating and rigid personality.

Dr. Garza had had two jobs in his lifetime: To protect the country from enemies domestic and foreign, and to protect with ruthless precision the interests of the Garcia family and the ABC cola companies. He performed his first job for almost twenty years, rising through the ranks of the Colombian Secret Service, reaching the rank of Colonel at the rightful age of thirty-eight. While advancing in his career, he had married, raised two children, and completed a degree in corporate law.

He had performed the second job with distinction since Fr. Garcia's father had recruited him in 1957 to lead the Legal Affairs department of the growing company. At the age of 64, Dr. Garza had two loves, his growing family and everything and everyone associated with Julio Garcia, his much younger boss. Fr. Garcia often made fun of his nephew by saying, "I don't know what Julio would do without Julius." The play on words always sounded hysterically funny to the good priest.

Dr. Garza's love for Julio was fully reciprocated by everyone in the company and their boss. The old man had achieved legendary status at the company and everyone, including Julio, did as he commanded. Everyone that is, other than the rebel priest who technically owned everything until the moment he took his last breath on this earth and left 90% to his beloved nephew and 10% to a trust fund for the future maintenance and care of "The Oaks."

Julius, welcomed us into his rather utilitarian office and boomed across the room, "Where is your escort, Padre?"

One of the calls Fr. Garcia had made the moment he learned of the break in at "The Oaks" was to his good friend Julius. It had been the lawyer who called in the cavalry, using the same "Rent-A-Mercenary" firm the company had used several times before. One of the immediate instructions of the lawyer was that Fr. Garcia was not to travel outside of the

Center without an armed guard or, preferably, two. Yet, by leaving through the kitchen door, where he had parked his car, Fr. Garcia had ditched his escort. The lawyer was visibly frustrated because he still didn't know if the break-in had been a failed kidnapping attempt on Fr. Garcia.

The priest, on the other hand, had done an incredible job hiding his interests in the company by naming his nephew as the president and CEO, and by removing himself from any marketing materials related to the business. In the eyes of the world, the Diocese, and the staff at "The Oaks," the company was owned by Julio Garcia, who was generous enough to indulge his uncle by supporting his pet projects and the beautiful conference center he had founded and where he spent most of his time.

The first call the Father made after our conversation earlier that day was to his good friend Julius. The priest had told the lawyer everything he had learned about the break in at the Center and his suspicions that a highly dangerous security firm had been involved. He wanted the lawyer to find out who the firm's client was, whether they posed any additional threats to "The Oaks" or him personally, and whether something could be done to prevent any danger to the students, staff, or clergy.

Chapter 32

Dr. Garza offered us a chair around a small conference table and introduced himself to me with great respect, as though I were a Supreme Court judge who had chosen to honor him with a sudden visit. He cleared his throat and began to speak.

"First, a bit of good news." He said in his booming voice. "The break in had nothing to do with the Garcia family or with ABC Cola. I was led to believe that it was a one-time thing, never to be repeated. Our security firm has a contact at Castle Ridge and their boys are very sorry for the break-in. Supposedly, it was a last-minute idea of a third party who doesn't work for their company. Their boys had no time to check in with headquarters. The employment of both people involved has been terminated. The fourth person involved is a minor. They believe he is the son of the third party. Castle Ridge didn't know there was a connection between 'The Oaks' and ABC cola. They have volunteered to pay for all the damage and make a substantial contribution to the Center."

All due respect to Dr. Garza, calling those thugs "boys" and apologizing for their behaviors sent chills down my spine. So far, I had not learned anything I didn't already know, and, perhaps, I knew more than he did. For example, I knew that Cesar was not Machado's son, but, perhaps, Machado's boss. In either case, I remained quiet and allowed the lawyer to continue his monologue.

He picked up his story where he left it off, "Now, for a bit of concerning news. The third party, the one who ordered and participated in the break in, is bad news. And when I say bad news, I mean he is the type of threat this company has never faced." Garza took a brief pause for effect and continued, "His name is Juan Manuel Machado. He is as ruthless and as corrupt as they come. Prior to working in private security, he used to be a big wig at the Medellin Police Department, which he used as his private hit squad. Our sources believe he is behind some of the most publicized kidnappings in the early 1970's, when he was still in the force."

The lawyer took a sip of his cold coffee and continued, "Machado retired a few years back, when he was on the verge of being indicted for corruption. It is believed he bribed a few prosecutors, kidnapped the son of a judge, eliminated a few witnesses, and intimidated fellow officers until all charges were dropped. He was never charged, and he has never served a day in jail. He is in private security now, but he works solo. When he needs back up, he calls Castle Ridge or the boys we use, but most of the time he is a lone ranger. Castle Ridge has disavowed him, but there are plenty of other people he can call on."

The lawyer took a break, pressed his intercom and ordered fresh coffee for everyone, and continued, "I have no doubt this man would not hesitate to return to 'The Oaks' if he feels it is necessary. As such, he presents a danger for us and for you personally." He looked at Fr.

Garcia when he made that last statement. He added, "It is my recommendation that we keep our boys in place until we have dealt with Machado. And I strongly recommend you always have armed guards with you, Padre."

Father Garcia nodded in agreement, looked at me, smiled, and asked his friend a follow-up question, "Do we know who Machado's employer is?"

"We do and we don't. Let me explain. According to Castle Ridge, the invoices were paid by a company called 'South American Real Estate Investments.' The checks have always cleared, and they had no cause for suspicion. The problem is this. The company does not exist officially. It has never paid any taxes; it has never registered as a business entity with the State or the National government; and its banking history only shows payments to consultants, maintenance firms, or cleaning services. No mortgages, no real estate investments, no payroll payments, nothing. Not even utility bill payments. Basically, the company is nothing but a checking account they probably set up with fraudulent documents. We don't even have an address or a telephone number. Whoever these people are, they are ghosts at this moment."

Once again, all due respect to the wise lawyer, these folks were not ghosts. You had known them by name. You had interacted with them. They had hurt you. And, one day soon, they would be made to pay. The question in my mind was whether your parents were behind this mysterious bank account. After all, I knew who Machado worked for. At least I knew who he pretended to be a driver for. In this respect, I still knew more than the lawyer, even though he had revealed some valuable information I could use later.

Julio Garcia had been listening to the lawyer's presentation from the back of the room, but he had been so quiet that I didn't even know he was behind me. When he spoke, he startled me. Thankfully, he ignored my jerk reaction.

With a grave look on his face he asked his friend and

lawyer, "Can we have our guys look into this Machado character? I don't ever want him near my uncle or his kids."

I loved the expression "My uncle and his kids" because that was exactly how the old priest saw us. We were his kids. I also loved that the safety of the people at "The Oaks" was so dear to Julio. I felt that if anything ever happened to our beloved benefactor, the Center would be in safe hands under the watchful eye of Julio Garcia.

Dr. Garza thought about his boss's question for a few seconds and answered, "I believe this is wise, but I advise caution. This man is sly, and he may have contacts we don't know about. The moment he realizes we have people looking into him or following him, he may turn his attention directly in our direction. At that point he will become even more dangerous. Rather than having our people involved, I suggest we farm this out to one very special player we have used before. He is not associated with any of us and his payment can be handled discreetly."

At this point, Father Garcia stood from his chair, turned to his nephew, and said in a measured but chilling tone, "No violence this time. I mean it."

Julio Garcia defensively responded to the implicit accusation in the cleric's statement. "That was self-defense and you know it. Don't we have the right to defend you or ourselves if our lives are at risk? Even the authorities sided with us. We will do nothing that reckless this time, but if your life is in danger, we will act. You can give me absolution later. Honestly, I can handle your recriminations if I know I can keep you on this earth a little longer." He looked at his trusted lawyer and asked, "I thought he was out of the business?"

The lawyer responded, smiling. "He lives here; for us he will end his retirement as soon as we make the call. He has a lot to be thankful to this family for."

With one simple sentence, Julio Garcia, unleashed a

holy terror Juan Manuel Machado never expected on this side of hell. He said, "Make the call today."

The issue of Machado having been decided, Fr. Garcia addressed the lawyer. "We have another little favor to ask you. We need to arrange a private meeting with Armando Cuevas, and we need you to accompany Joe to that meeting. This must be handled with absolute discretion until the actual meeting. You will be there as Joe's lawyer and you can't disclose who hired you. As far as the parents of the students are concerned, I am just a humble priest who spent every penny building "The Oaks." I don't want the Center's name or ABC Cola associated with this. But Mr. Cuevas must allow Joe to tell his story, and, if Joe's theory is correct, I suspect Mr. Cuevas will become a powerful ally. Bring couple of guys with you. There is strength in numbers. It is important that Mr. Cuevas know we are serious. Tell him Joe's patron is willing to go the distance to find out what happened to Alex, but don't threaten him. And, please keep me informed, but be discreet when calling the Center."

I had no idea Fr. Garcia and Julio had hatched this plan before we left "The Oaks." I was impressed, however. This was a great idea. If anything, your father was a businessman and to have the most respected corporate attorney in the city with me would make him more willing to listen and take me seriously. If, as I suspected, he had nothing to do with what happened to you, he might choose to help us after listening to me. If, on the other hand, he was guilty of some misdeed, his survival instincts would prevent him from acting against me, especially if he didn't know who Garza's boss was and how much he knew. Great empires can be toppled overnight if the right amount of pressure is applied. This was a clever idea and I was grateful I had the Garcias on my corner, but for their plan to work, I had to keep this meeting secret even from William.

"I will handle all the details. Joe, please stay put at the

Center until I call you or leave a number with Sr. Celeste where I can find you. Give me through Thursday to set this up. I will call you then. And, please, don't take any unnecessary risks until we sort this out." The lawyer stated in a serious tone.

"What about the driver?" Fr. Garcia asked suddenly.

The lawyer answered, "He's clean. We looked into him. He has no criminal history, lives alone, and has no money problems. He owns his own home, is an only child, and visits his mother regularly at a nursing home nearby. He has no connection to the Castle Ridge boys or any other security firms we do business with. He is a good worker who is fanatically loyal to Arturo Cuevas. He drinks a little too much but is well-liked by neighbors. He is kind of a loner in the love department, and there are no known girlfriends. Lastly, he is a very good driver."

The lawyer looked at me and said, "My suggestion is that you continue to use him, feed him some information, but not everything, and continue to assess. You're a smart kid. If you notice anything that makes you uncomfortable, just call me." At that point Dr. Garza placed his business card in my shirt pocket.

I was beyond impressed. I had finished my conversation with Fr. Garcia at 12:30 pm, we had left the Center at 3:00 pm, it was now approximately 5:00 pm, and Dr. Garza had already managed to learn a considerable amount of information on Machado, Castle Ridge, and even William. I remember your father's comment about money and my own thoughts concerning the power money allows and the doors it opens.

As if to confirm my thoughts, Fr. Garcia asked his lawyer, "Did you call the young woman I mentioned?"

"Yes, everything is set. But you must leave soon. Julio had our people drive your car back to 'The Oaks.' For the foreseeable future you ride with us, Padre," the lawyer said.

Before Fr. Garcia had an opportunity to object, a security detail composed of three very tall, well-built, and serious looking men approached the table. They had been as silent as statutes, but they had been in the room the whole time. I thought it was outright terrifying how well-prepared Julio Garcia and his lawyer had been. These men knew how to be in control and were experienced at anticipating even the craftiness of the rebel priest who paid their salaries. Fr. Garcia looked at his nephew with a look of disappointment.

Julio returned the priest's glare, approached him, gave him a hug, kissed his cheek tenderly and said, "No objections. You are too important to us. We will take no risks tonight. And please don't request a change of itinerary, the men have their orders."

The priest kissed his nephew back and held him in his arms for a few extra seconds. After this, he did likewise with his old friend, confidant, and corporate lawyer, and, lastly, he spoke to his security detail. "You can guard me, but I will be driving tonight."

The lead officer looked at Julio, who bowed his head slowly. Both Julio and Julius shook my hand with affection, offered their support for anything I might need, and vowed to stay in touch. After this, we followed the security detail to the cars.

Chapter 33

From the outside the two Jeeps looked like normal four door, hardtop, late-model Jeeps. What was obscured from anyone who was not an expert in security was the fact that both cars were custom made to include an extra layer of re-enforced steel that could stop almost any type of bullet. The tinted windows were likewise reinforced with bullet-proof glass. The tires were specially made to prevent perforation by knives, spikes, or bullets, but in case they were deflated for some reason, the driver could ride the vehicle for fifty to seventy-five miles before the rims would break. And each vehicle had a small arsenal concealed in places no normal passenger would ever find.

Fr. Garcia and I drove in the second vehicle with one of the three men seated in the passenger seat, which means that I sat in the back seat, a practice I had successfully prevented up until this moment. The team leader and a third agent rode in the vehicle in front of us. The two vehicles drove close to each other, which means Fr. Garcia was forced to mind the speed limit, to his utmost disappointment.

By the time we reached the Inter-American Hotel, it was almost 6:30 pm. To my surprise the vehicles parked in reserved locations, and the hotel manager herself met us at the lobby. She was an elegant woman in her mid-forties, tall, dark hair perfectly styled in the puffy style of the 80's and dressed in an impeccable, pricey pant suit.

The manager recognized Fr. Garcia immediately and gave him a hug. She said, "Everything is set up, Father. Please follow me."

One of the security men followed the manager ahead of us. In the middle, Fr. Garcia and I were busy trying hard to avoid people's stares. The two other security people followed us close behind, eyes in every direction, closely watching everything, and assessing possible risk at every step of the way.

The manager opened a small, but elegant conference room where a young lady, had been patiently awaiting our arrival. The leader of the security detail walked into the room first, let the rest of us in, and promptly closed the door. The two other men stayed outside the door.

The young woman stood, walked to us, and said, "You must be Joe? We spoke this morning. I am Elvia." She walked to Fr. Garcia and said, "You must be the Padre. Thank you for your generosity." Then, pointing to a table at the end of the room, she said, "As instructed, we have set some dinner for you and your men. This will take some time, so, please, make yourselves as comfortable as you can."

At this point, Elvia took the newspaper articles I had carried in my back pocket all day, sat at the small desk located opposite to the food table, and started working.

The food consisted of a generous assortment of sandwiches, salads, pastries, and beverages. We ate in silence for a few minutes, after which I filled in Fr. Garcia on my visit to Ivan's home. Fr. Garcia wanted to know how Mrs. Santos was coping with the added responsibilities of being a landlady, especially since Alfredo's promotion demanded longer hours and weekend work.

I was impressed that the cleric knew as much about Ivan's family as he did, but this was normal for him. He cared deeply about people, and Ivan's family had contributed generously to the Center and had volunteered for functions over the last few years.

After dinner, I excused myself and went to a smoking lounge for a smoke. One of the security men outside the door followed me closely and stayed within view, while I smoked my cigarette. This was a new experience for me, and I wished I could have the company of these men for the rest of my life. The truth was that I seldom felt safe in Medellin, and I hated going outside unless I absolutely had to. Life would be better with this kind of muscle following me everywhere.

When I returned to the room, Fr. Garcia invited me to sit next to him and said, "I feel I must explain something to you, Joe, but you must swear you will never share this story with anyone for as long as I am alive." I nodded and he continued, "A few years back, someone who used to work for us planned a sophisticated kidnapping plot to extort money from my nephew. A co-worker who had agreed to help in the plot changed his mind a week before I was to be taken. Julio and Julius hired a Chilean man known for very specialized security work.

I was ordered to continue my daily routine as usual, but of course there were at least six pairs of eyes on me at all times. When the day of the kidnapping came, our Chilean friend impersonated me, dressing in the same way, altering his weight through specially made clothing, cutting and dyeing his hair to match mine, and even imitating my walking cadence.

As we all expected, the kidnappers thought he was I

and snatched him outside my office at the Diocesan Center. This was a reckless move, but our Chilean friend believed this would be the best way to know where the kidnapers were working from, who else was involved, and whether we had any additional dangers to worry about. The unsuspecting kidnappers took their hostage to a home in a small house in Liberty Town, without realizing that a small army was following them. When the kidnapers arrived at the home, our Chilean friend took both down, disarming but not killing them."

The good Father stood up from his chair, stretched his muscles briefly, sat back down and picked up his story where he had left it, "Unfortunately, a third man had been smoking a cigarette in an outside patio and, when he heard the struggle inside, he came in, gun drawn and ready to shoot. Before he was able to fire his first shot, our Chilean friend placed two bullets in the man's forehead. I was devastated and secretly investigated the man's background. Julius found a way to help his wife and two children with the funeral and some money for expenses. I felt guilty for months, but I have learned to see this episode as proof that a man reaps what he sows."

I was both horrified at how close Fr. Garcia had come to danger, and grateful for the Chilean's special abilities, which had kept the priest safe. Fortunately, the horrible episode had worked well for Fr. Garcia. I had known of other cases where the victim is killed in botched rescue attempts, or when the kidnapers suspect they are at risk of being caught. Ransom money is only helpful if you are alive and out of jail. Kidnappers don't take unnecessary risks and are very quick at eliminating danger by killing their victims.

Filled with emotion, I said, "Thank God, you were safe, Father."

"Thank you, Joe. We live in a dangerous world, and, unfortunately our country is becoming more difficult to live in with every day that passes." Responded Fr. Garcia.

Just as the priest had finished this sentence, Elvia, the

translator, interrupted us saying, "I just finished the first newspaper article from *The London Bugle*. It's rough." She stood up from her desk, walked towards us, and handed the article to the priest, saying, "I would read it first before sharing it with the boy."

Fr. Garcia smiled knowing how the translator's condescending tone would sting me. He placed the neatly translated pages on the flat surface of the table, and we both reached down to read it together.

The article read as follows:

London "Pedophile Cult" exposed as Police Warn More Victims Remain Unidentified
By Leslie Warden: Home Affairs Correspondent
Friday 12 June 1975

"Thirty-one boys and girls between the age of nine and thirteen have reported being drugged and raped by a group believed to be operating out of upscale flats around the city.

Detectives believe the numbers will grow and appeal for others to come forward, after arresting three men and three boys at a flat near Stratford. The men were caught in the process of abusing the children. They were taken into custody, but their names will not be released until the investigation is completed.

Police are already arresting over two-hundred men every month over child sexual exploitation in England and Wales, but the local ring managed to elude the authorities for over four years, according to the testimony of some of the victims who have been involved with the group since 1971.

Detective Inspector George Sumpter, of the Metropolitan Police's Sexual Exploitation Team, said an operation codename Stratford Ring was launched after the first four victims came forward separately in South London. One of the victims led the authorities to the flat in Stratford where the first arrests were made.

Sumpter stated, 'All the victims report meeting well-dressed men at local parks and ice-skating rinks from several weeks to several months before the abuse. At first the men offered the youth meals, clothes, and money, without acting suspicious or requesting anything from the would-be victims. The kids were even treated to hotel nights and innocent stays at the men's flats, where at least two of the boys met the men's families. When the men had established trust with their victims, they took them to the homes of other men the youth had never met. These men drugged the kids and transported them blindfolded to parties at flats throughout the city. Once at the party, the children were additionally drugged and given alcohol. We think the scale of the crimes is wider than initially thought, and the number of victims will increase.'

Investigators say these bands of grooming men prey on young street children, youth who reside in foster care, and children in dysfunctional homes.

Authorities believe some of the victims were taken to London from places as far as Northern Ireland and Scotland on promises of vacations and shopping sprees. Once in the city they were transferred to men who housed them and took them to these parties at flats across the city.

The children are believed to be 'Party Models' -targeted by groups of men who lure them to gatherings with offers of money, drugs, and drink.

Chief Constable Simon Chesney, the National Police Chief's council lead for child protection, said, 'There is an element of cult practices at these parties. Some of the victims describe the men as dressed in white and black robes with carnival-like masks on their faces. One of the children described how they were taken into the parties in single file and the host, wearing a red robe and red mask, introduced each child to a guest, who then took the child for the night. In the morning, the children were dropped off at Metro stations around the city, still drugged and confused.'

Deputy Constable John Steam, from Suffolk Station, believes the three suspects arrested in Stratford will lead the authorities to a detailed list of the guests at these parties. He said, 'Although the robes and masks make it difficult to identify the guests, the men at the Stratford flat and the dozen arrested men believed to be part of the 'grooming gangs' will share information soon enough, especially when they are charged with multiple counts of child sexual abuse and exploitation, kidnapping, and providing illegal substances to minors.'

Inspector Sumpter believes the three men arrested on Wednesday are all associated with the fashion industry in the city, but their names are at present withheld until the investigation is completed. He said, 'We have a problem here and we intend to get to the bottom of it. In the meantime, we warn all parents and charities working with children to educate them about the risk of predators and groomers. Parents need to be more 'hands-on' about their children's friends. And we invite all members of the public to contact us if you have any information regarding this case!'"

Fr. Garcia made the sign of the cross and said, *"Mio Dio!"* I was speechless, but a thousand questions were swirling around my mind. Was such a ring operating in Medellin? How could you have become involved with such a group? You did not fit the type at all. You were not a street kid, did not come from a dysfunctional family in the classic sense, and you were not in foster care. How could such a group be able to recruit you, especially because at the age of nine, according to your father, your mother had an obsessive grip and control over your life, even cutting your steak into perfect little squares, if I remember correctly. That kind of care and concern does not scream, "Neglect."

Deep in thought, I also realized there was a piece of the puzzle Fr. Garcia didn't know about, and I chose to wait until I knew more before I shared this with him. That piece of the puzzle was Cesar. He had grown in London, his parents were in the fashion industry, and they had moved to Medellin in 1976. Could they have been involved in this ring? These were all terrifying questions for which I had no answers yet.

With deep sadness in his voice, Father Garcia stated, "This type of evil is infecting the very soul of our society. May God have mercy on us all." He stood up and went back to the food table to get a refill of his coffee.

I excused myself and, guard in tow, went to the smoker's lounge for a smoke. I felt defeated and dirty, as if I had encountered such pure filth that I needed a long shower with some strong detergent. The idea that such a gang would set shop in Medellin was not surprising. Our fair city is known for the large number of young children living on the streets, under bridges, covered with carton boxes in abandoned buildings, and sleeping on park benches across the city. Take those kids out of the gutter, bathe them, feed them, and buy them some new clothes, and suddenly you have a ready work-force for domestic and foreign pedophiles. Add a dose of drugs, intimidation and violence to the grooming process, and you could do whatever you wanted with them: trade them, sell them, prostitute them, and serve them on a silver platter to deviant men in expensive residential buildings across the city.

Unfortunately, the authorities have demonstrated over the years a terrible lack of care and concern for the needs of these street kids. In fact, back in 1980 there was a killer who preyed on street kids, torturing, killing, and displaying them in public parks. It took the police almost nine months to find the man, even though they had received hundreds of clues, several well-drawn renderings, and credible evidence of where the man lived.

Crimes against children were seldom fully investigated, as though these street kids, who survived by sniffing glue and begging, didn't deserve police attention. If Michael Walters was behind this ring, then his business model had evolved to include a trade more profitable than the garment industry, in a city filled with discarded children, and under the neglectful cover of a corrupt government who simply didn't care.

Tired of waiting for the translator, Fr. Garcia was on the phone conducting remote business with the staff at "The Oaks." I sat next to the translator. I asked her if I would distract her if I used the telephone on the wall behind her.

She said quite calmly, "It will not bother me at all, but keep it short. I'm almost done here."

I called home and spoke to my mother. After our customary greetings, she said, "You sound awful. Have you eaten yet?" Satisfied with my answer, she continued, "Did you receive my message at 'The Oaks'? I left it about two hours ago."

Surprised, I said, "No, I've been with Fr. Garcia all day at the Diocesan Center. What was the message about?"

My mother sighed and said, "I swear, I know nothing about your life. You drive me crazy, Joe. I thought you were doing a retreat with the staff? Traveling around the city, working, and doing stuff at the Diocesan office doesn't sound like a relaxing retreat. Maybe you should return and help Fr. Gaviria in church. God knows the man needs you."

Terrified I might have to return home, I lied to my sainted mother again, as I had done so many times during that last week, "We are on retreat, mom. Most of the staff is with us here, and this evening we will return to continue our retreat at 'The Oaks.' Remember how I told you there was a break in? Well, they are fixing the place today and we were in the worker's way."

"Okay, relax. No need to get upset. I'm just worried about you. You sound exhausted and sad. That's all. Now, where did I put that message?" My mother put the receiver down on the table, and I could hear her moving lamps and chachkies around.

Eventually, she came back on the line and said, "Here it is. A young woman called you this afternoon. She said Alex had mailed something to her house, and when she opened it, there was a letter for her and another sealed envelope inside addressed to you. She wants to know if you want her to mail it to you here or at the Center. What do you think this is about?"

"I have no idea, Mom. You know how strange he was sometimes. Did the young woman leave a name and a number for me to call her?" I asked, knowing at least half of the answer in advance.

"Are you ready to write it down?" She asked, anticipating my need to get a pad and pen.

"Hold a sec." I said, smiling at her clairvoyant ways. After I got a piece of paper and a pen from the translator, I said, "Go on."

My mom said, "Her name is Julia Salcedo. She was calling from Rio Negro. Her number is 301-531-4582. Don't call her too late. She said she was a college student."

I thanked my mother and called Julia Salcedo, as the translator said, "Two minutes." I gave her a thumbs up and made the call anyway.

Julia answered at the second ring, "Hello?" She said in the tired voice of one who had just returned home from a long day of school and work.

"Julia, this is Joe Cardenas. I understand you have a letter from Alex?" I said causally, without letting the young woman know how apprehensive I felt about the contents of the envelope.

Julia said, "Hey, Joe. Nice talking to you. Alex used to talk about you often. He really liked you."

Surprised by the young woman's revelation, I asked, "You were still friends?"

Julia broke out in laughter, "He said you would be surprised. He knew you well. He called you his Jiminy Cricket." She laughed again and added, "No, Joe. I wasn't his friend. I was his much older lover. Didn't he talk about me?"

Unsure about whether she was poking fun at my expense, I asked, "When did you see him last?"

Another laugh, Julia answered, "Right before he went to 'The Oaks' in early November. Anyway, listen. I don't have a lot of time tonight because I have company, but I want to talk to you soon. I don't have school until the afternoon tomorrow. Can we meet somewhere?"

"How about I drive to Rio Negro tomorrow morning and I'll meet you at your home?" I said, anticipating a use for William, who thought he was taking me to meet the translator the next day.

"That would work, but you must be here early. It takes me almost an hour to get to school, and I want to be there no later than noon. But, Joe? We will just be talking about Alex tomorrow, I already mailed your letter to 'The Oaks' after I spoke to your mom, and she said you would be there all week. You should get it Thursday or Friday. I didn't want to keep it with me until I saw you. But, please, come. I want to meet you, and there is something I need to show you." Julia said.

Disappointed at the fact that Julia had already mailed

the letter, I said, "I'll be there around 9:00 am and we will give you a ride to school. I have a driver."

"Awesome," She said. "I'm looking forward to meeting you."

I said my goodbyes and hung up because the translator was signaling for me to join her and Father Garcia at our table.

Chapter 34

Not bothering to caution Fr. Garcia about protecting the young boy, the translator laid down the translated pages on top of the table for us to read. The article from *The London Daily News* was shorter than the one from the *Bugle.* It read

High Fashion House to Leave London
Becky Smith Jones: Fashion Editor
14 January 1976

"Tiffany Walker, a spokeswoman for the prestigious Walters Fashion Corporation, announced yesterday at their headquarters in Chelsey that the company intends to transfer its manufacturing operations to South America by the end of the first quarter of this year.

Renowned for high profile fans like Hollywood elite, European royal families, and a distinguished clientele throughout the world, the Walters company came to national attention last year when three of their executives were caught up in the net of a Government operation, famously called, 'The Stratford Ring.'

In total fifty-one men from around the country were found guilty of having sex with under-aged children, as young as nine years of age. The investigation that led to the arrest of the men discovered the men had relied on well known 'grooming gangs' to provide them with a steady supply of young boys and girls for their entertainment. The famous 'Model Party Kids' as the media have called them, were often kept against their will in flats around the city, and were given drugs and alcohol as means of control. In total 152 children came forward and testified against the men.

Early during the investigation, Michael Walters, the Chief Executive Officer of the giant fashion house, disavowed the behavior of his executives and pledged his full cooperation with the authorities.

Deputy Constable John Steam, from Suffolk Station, who was a crucial part of the original task force, stated that Mr. Walters had cooperated fully, giving the authorities access to employee files, and answering all questions candidly. He said, 'At this point in the investigation, there is no reason to believe any other employee of the Walters Fashion House was involved in the ring and the company is no longer under investigation.'

The spokeswoman for Walters told our reporter the move was necessary to distance the company from this scandal, which has seriously affected the company's relationships with designers and costumers in Europe. She said, 'It is a regrettable move because we love London and feel very committed to our three hundred and fifty employees. We know they will face hard times and we have set up a special fund to provide training and career counseling to help them secure other sources of employment. The company and Mr. Walters remain deeply grateful for the support we have received in England, and we assure our customers in England, Wales, Scotland, and Northern Ireland that we will continue to provide them the quality garments they deserve and have come to expect from us.'

The employees of the Walters Fashion House have expressed their sadness to see the company leave England. 'They were a great company to work for,' Stated Jane Houssel, who worked as a seamstress for Walters for the last three years. This sentiment was shared by Jacob Whetersby, who was a machine repairman for Walters for the last two years, 'This is a damned shame, if you ask me. The company was crucified in the media because of three bad apples. I don't blame Walters for leaving, and I wish I could go with them.'

Requests for a comment from our mayor and city council were not returned as of the time of this edition, but some in the city blame London officials for not doing enough to protect The Walters Fashion House or their affiliates. This may prove to be unwise in an election year where many are looking for a more business friendly atmosphere in our city.

As for us, we are sad to see the fashion house go and we remain grateful for the many iconic looks they gave our fashion stores."

Fr. Garcia, lost in thought, looked at me and said, "Okay, Joe. What don't I know? These two articles make no sense to me and I wonder why Alex left them for you to translate."

Uncomfortable, I said, "Michael Walters is the father of a good friend of Alex. In fact, he is the same boy I saw at 'The Oaks.' I believe the note Alex attached to the articles says it all. He said that it all began in London. I think Walters may have been responsible for what happened to Alex almost five years ago."

"But these men preyed on street kids. This doesn't fit our Alex." Fr. Garcia said, beginning to show signs of exhaustion.

"I know, Father. It makes no sense to me either. Maybe the package Alex mailed out from central station will give us the answers." I said, not telling the priest about our morning appointment with Julia Salcedo.

"Do you have a fax machine in this hotel?" Fr. Garcia asked the translator.

"Yes, Father, we do." She responded.

"Can you please take me to it? I must send these faxes to an old friend to look into them." With that, Fr. Garcia left the room accompanied by the translator and two of the security escorts. To the last escort he said, "Please take Joe to the car and stay with him. We will be with you soon."

A few minutes later, Fr. Garcia came back and asked, "Do you mind if I keep these originals, Joe? I want to put them in my safe. I have a suspicion these documents are dangerous, and I don't want them in your possession."

I nodded and the priest told the security man, "Do you mind driving? I am exhausted." Silently, the security man exchanged places with the Father and started following the lead Jeep to "The Oaks."

After a few minutes of silence, the priest asked me, "Will you join me for Evening Prayer when we get back?" I nodded again, and we rode in silence the rest of the way.

Chapter 35

William arrived at the Center by 7:00 am on Tuesday, as I had asked him to do when I called him after Evening Prayer the previous night. He was waiting on the same spot he dropped me off at on Sunday evening. He was holding two cups of coffee on both hands, and he had ditched the corporate uniform, settling for jeans and the soccer jersey of a local team.

He smiled when he saw me and asked, "Are you ready to get some translations done? I can't wait to see what those newspapers say. I haven't stopped thinking about them since Saturday."

I smiled back and said, "Do you mind a change in plans? We are heading to Rio Negro. I will bring you up to speed in the car."

William seemed surprised at the change of plans, pointed to his car, and smiled again. He said, "Remember I told you today was my day off? Well "day off" means private car. Meet Roxanne, my 1974 Simca model 3. This is an upgrade from the car I was driving when I got fired from the club and started working for Steerco. It is not a limousine, but it rides like shit." He seemed very pleased with his joke and laughed loudly as he unlocked the passenger door from inside the small cabin of the car.

The Simca was everything the limousine was not. It had one of the smallest cabins I had seen in a car; it was compact and uncomfortable; and it had the distinction of smelling like old French fries and burgers, which at the time, was a smell I wasn't accustomed to. Fully accepting the premise that beggars can't be choosers, I showed my appreciation for the car by saying, "If it can take us to Rio Negro and back, I will be happy."

"What's in Rio Negro?" William asked more curious than concerned.

"Have you ever heard the name Julia Salcedo?" I asked, hoping that William may have met the young woman and could give me some information about her and her mother.

"Sure, I have." He said smiling. "She is the ballbuster who used to screw Alex since he was old enough to have erections. I drove them to the movies and out to eat a bunch of times at the request of his dad, when she was 'babysitting' Alex. I knew the relationship was more than babysitting, but I said nothing.

"Of course, when Mr. Cuevas found out the two were having sex, he let Maria, the girl's mother, go. I was always very discreet about the whole thing. Julia was proud of her much younger lover, and Alex felt experienced and important with a much older girl. That was the main reason I never said anything to Mr. Cuevas. I think, in a way, she was good for him. At least he seemed happy when he was with her, and she could match his sense of humor, his irreverent comments, and his disdain for his mother. She acted like she liked Mrs. Cuevas, but she couldn't stand her."

I was curious about this bit of information, so I asked William, "Did she have any reason to dislike her boss?"

William thought about it for a second and responded, "Mrs. Cuevas used to have guests at the house all the time. Julia always felt like the men looked at her in a weird way. In fact, one of them grabbed her ass one time when she was helping her mother serve the table. The girl claimed that Mrs. Cuevas did nothing to correct the behavior and just laughed it off. The girl ran to the kitchen and let her mother serve the rest of the dinner. But she never forgot, and she was cautious around the men when they came around again, which was often."

I remembered William had said a few days before that your mother preferred the company of politicians and real estate moguls over the company of her husband and son. Certainly, she also allowed some of these men liberties that placed those in her household at considerable risk. I was beginning to get a picture of your mother that I didn't quite like.

William asked the obvious question before I had to tell him the reason why we were driving to Rio Negro. He asked, "Did Alex mail Julia the packet he took from La America?"

"I believe he did. I spoke to Julia yesterday, and she says she needs to show me something. I promised her we would be there by 9:00 am, but I want to scope the place out and make sure no one is watching it before we see her. I am still a bit rattled by the men in the gray sedan."

I did not tell William about the assault to "The Oaks" because I didn't want him to say anything to your dad before Dr. Garza and I had a chance to meet with him officially. I also chose not to tell him about the Garcias' full involvement because I didn't want to place Fr. Garcia in any additional danger. Until I knew more about your dad's involvement, I chose to limit the information I gave William.

It was not that I didn't trust him or like him. I felt completely safe with him, and I knew he had nothing to do with your death. But, as hard as he tried to keep things confidential, William liked to talk, and I knew he was fiercely loyal to Mr. Cuevas. Now that the Garcias' safety had been compromised, I needed to be extra careful.

We drove in silence for a few minutes, after which William, asked, "So what about the translations?"

I filled William on the highlights of the articles, lying to him that one of the counselors of "The Oaks" had given me the money, and the translator had a cancelation that evening, which allowed her time to do our work. We had waited for her to finish.

William listened intently and then said, "Holly Shit. Are you thinking what I am thinking?"

"It's too early to speculate, but it looks like Alex discovered some stuff about Cesar and his parents and there may be a connection between his dad and this ring. I'm hoping Julia will shed some light on the whole mess," I said evasively.

We drove in silence for a couple of miles and William said, "The space you occupy determines your behavior in the space. If you're in church, you keep silence. If you're in a soccer match, you scream your heart out and drink beer until they roll you out in a wheelbarrow. If you are in Arturo Cuevas' car, you listen to his stories about new deals, expansion plans, interesting people he has met along the way, and the like. If you are in my crappy old car, you listen to *musica vieja*, or old timey music." With that, William turned the cassette player on in his car and started playing his favorite songs.

The first song, *Las Acasias*, is a sad melody about a grand old home on the side of the road that after much life now remains abandoned. The grain silos have been destroyed, and the crumbling walls are now a testimony to the home's state of disrepair. The only sounds heard are generated by the acacia bushes forced by the wind to beat against the opened doors. Towards the end of the song, a former inhabitant, visiting the abandoned home after a life filled with heartache, listens to the stories the acacia bushes tell: "All the joy and the lively sounds are dead. Those who were the very happiness and warmth of the home have left, either because they died or because their souls were already dead when they finally abandoned the place. They left the home, never to return."

The song made me think about that feeling of rootlessness that sometimes we experience when we wander too far afield and become disconnected from others, from the places that nurtured us as children, and even from ourselves. The yearning for home is a common experience that never goes away. Some of us feel alone in the universe, precisely because we have lost that sense of home. You were one of those souls, my dear friend. Surrounded by glamour and privilege, you often felt lost, disconnected, and unloved.

Listening to that song, I prayed you had finally found your home.

As if to cheer me up, William played, "Black Soul," a depressing ballad about a woman who cheated on her husband and later returns, begging to be taken back. "Today your pride has reached a new low and you drag your haughtiness and arrogance back to me. But all of this is fruitless, you will never convince me to take you back... I tell you truly, I am surprised by your visit, you have a black soul, and I no longer want your love."

Very cheerful indeed.

What was that about Latin Americans having a tragic sense of life? Well, any interested student who wants to prove this theory just needs to dig through the noise of the festive arrangements and read the lyrics of our folk songs. There he will find the wounded soul of our culture.

As if to prove my dark musings correct, the next song, simply called, "Fatality," narrated the story of a man who, in the dawn of a cloudy morning, remembers a lost lover.

Theirs was the type of love you only experience once in a lifetime. Destiny, the cruelest of all enemies, separated the two lovers, and now he lives in perpetual anguish, alone with his memories. Fate gave him the greatest of ecstasies, only to take it all back again, leaving him in a persistent state of anxiety and loneliness.

The seductive guitars of our music obscure the pain and anguish of a culture that has for centuries felt oppressed by those in power, controlled by forces beyond their control, and abandoned by those charged to protect them. We translate these overall emotions through songs that speak of loss, abandonment, betrayal, unfulfilled dreams, and the prototypical need for revenge and retribution. The longing for something permanent and affirming is as deep as the longing for home.

Unfortunately, many of us have lost the roadmaps that lead us back to a place of meaning and belonging.

After many of these songs, we began to see the outer edges of Rio Negro. The town is a farming community, filled with lush greenery, exquisite farms, and prosperous dairy plantations.

The town still shows the charm of many old-Spanish towns you find on the countryside of Madrid and other European cities: A central plaza with its church, government building, police station, and several shopping stores welcomes visitors to the town. In typical fashion, the town grew from its central plaza in all directions via narrow streets that take you to residential communities. Homes share a common wall with neighbors, use adobe roofing tiles, and are built of clay or cement materials, painted in deep reds and oranges. Some have balconies, but not all. Some have second floors, but not all. And some have backyards, but not all.

Chapter 36

William and I took the directions we had written down from a Rio Negro map and within a few minutes we parked the car approximately two blocks from where we knew the humble home would be located. We started walking in that direction. At some point during our walk an older, tall, well-dressed man passed us, looked at us curiously, and said, "Good morning." We responded in kind and continued walking behind the man, until we lost him because he was walking much faster.

Around half a block from the address we stopped at a small coffee shop across from where the home was located. We sat by the shop's window and ordered breakfast which for William was sausage, eggs over easy, freshly made corn arepas, two buñuelos, and hot cocoa. For me it was toast, guava jelly, and black coffee.

The breakfast arrived within ten minutes, primarily because we were the cafe's only customers. As we were about to finish our food, we noticed two patrol cars and a small ambulance drive past our restaurant and stop at Julia Salcedo's home. William and I looked at each other and stood up at the same time. William threw some money on the table and we walked out, made a left, and started running towards the home. As we arrived, a group of onlookers were beginning to assemble.

We approached one of the police officers and William lied to him quite dramatically, "What's happened? Please tell me, I am Maria's younger brother?" Not registering any recognition from the policeman, he said, "The woman who lives here is my sister. What's going on?"

The policeman said, "We just got a call from a neighbor. I am sorry to tell you that both women were assaulted and beaten. The medical people are with them now. It looks bad."

William and I looked at each other and paled in fear. William continued to put pressure on the policeman to let us in or give us additional information. I took the time to survey the scene. I looked at the crowd; then I looked past them to the end of the street in both directions. I didn't see anything suspicious at either end. I noticed that I was trembling in fear. Whatever we came here to see could have caused Julia and Maria their deaths. I felt somewhat guilty and wondered if anyone knew we were there. I felt we needed to leave as soon as possible, but first I needed to know what had happened to the two women.

The young policeman was saying, "I'm sorry, but I can't let you in until the detectives give me permission."

I managed to sound as pathetic as I could, "Please tell us what happened to my auntie and my cousin. Please? Please? What happened?" I started tearing up, which wasn't a total act. I was feeling deeply sorry for the vivacious young lady with whom I had spoken the day before.

Unsure of what to do, the policeman whispered, "They were roughed up and the house was ransacked. There is broken furniture all over the place. Do they have any enemies?"

William responded, "Not at all. Did anybody see anything?"

I thought this was an excellent question and I quickly I added more validity to our story by saying, "Everybody loves them."

The policeman said, "A neighbor saw a car leave the premises about thirty minutes ago, but she didn't see who was driving and she doesn't remember the make or model. All she can say is that it was grey. That's all we know. Please wait behind the line until I can let you in."

Just as we were talking, two gurneys were being rolled out of the small house. The women had been cleaned up some, but we could see blood all over their clothes, just underneath the soaked white sheet they had placed over them. Their faces were disfigured, their eyes almost closed shut, and there were cuts on their lips.

Maria was unconscious and taken into the ambulance first. Right behind her, Julia made the same journey to the ambulance. As she passed right by me, I exclaimed to William, "Julia!"

To my great astonishment, the woman opened her left eye slightly and asked, "Joe?"

Quickly, I said, "Yes. it's me. I'm so sorry about this."

Julia said, "They took everything, Joe. I'm sorry. They know we spoke last night. They wanted to know where you were. Sorry, Joe."

With that the young woman was lifted into the ambulance, which drove away in a hurry, leaving police investigators behind to do whatever it is that they do in these cases.

William and I looked at each other and, perceiving danger, left the area, walking fast to our car, looking in all directions, and preparing ourselves to run the rest of the way to the car if necessary. As we passed the coffee shop, we saw the same well-dressed man who had passed us before, sitting at the same table we had occupied, looking at the scene unfolding a short distance away.

I was feeling defeated once again. We lost the evidence at "The Oaks." Now we had lost the evidence at Julia's house and the lives of two innocent people had been in grave danger. Whatever was going on was dangerous beyond expectation. I was beginning to wonder how deeply this went and how many people were involved.

As we made it to the car, William whispered apprehensively. "I think we are being watched. Get in the car quickly and put your seatbelt on."

Terrified, I did what he asked me. Without much warning, William sped out of the lot, made a quick right, came to the bottom of the hill, turned right again, and within two blocks took the entrance to the highway that had brought us to Rio Negro.

As he was about to enter the highway, I looked through the rearview window and saw the grey sedan. We were being followed, and I recognized the car immediately. It was Machado's sedan, or a very similar car. I could also see a dark-colored Jeep, following close behind the grey sedan. I closed my eyes and prayed that William could drive the old Simca well enough to get us out of danger.

Expertly, William exchanged lanes, passed vehicles with great precision, and braked and accelerated as needed, putting some distance between us and the grey sedan. The mountainous terrain was dangerous on any given day and passing on curves was an extremely risky maneuver, but William continued to speed on inclines and declines, and continued to pass on curves, barely missing oncoming traffic. Through it all, he remained calm and focused. He was a true professional and I was glad he was driving the car.

The problem with high-speed chases is that success

depends as much on your car as it depends on your driver. There is no way the grey sedan could ever catch up with us if we were to rely exclusively on the expertise of the driver. But there was no way the Simca could outrun and outperform the late Mercedes Benz sedan chasing us, or the solid and well-built Jeep behind it. I knew we were in trouble, and I started praying in my mind for safe delivery. Thinking about you brought me some comfort, but not enough to calm my nerves and reduce my anxiety.

Chapter 37

The distance between Medellin and Rio Negro is only thirty-two miles approximately, yet it takes an hour to an hour and a half to drive to the city. The reason is that Interstate 60 travels through the central mountain range of the Andes, passing Marinilla, Dos Erres, La Ramada, Guarne, and Bello. The high altitude of the mountain range demands that vehicles traveling in both directions share narrow passages with steep drops on both sides. Any car that loses control on this highway and falls off the cliff, most certainly would kill all passengers immediately.

William's goal was to drive down from the mountain as fast as he could because it would be easier to withstand a rear-end impact in the plains near Guarne and Bello than on the mountain range near Marinilla and Rio Negro.

Approximately ten miles from our entrance to Highway 60 in Rio Negro, however, I spotted the grey sedan three cars behind us. They were gaining on us and we were still high on the mountain. "They are three cars behind," I said, but William had already spotted them on his rearview mirror. We could not see the Jeep, which was good news for us.

William replied while in absolute control of the vehicle and his emotions, "I see them. Hold on, little man. Let's see how fast we can go."

He floored the gas pedal, but within three additional miles the grey sedan was two cars behind us. Four miles after that there was just one car between us and the grey sedan. William continued to swerve in and out of lanes at speeds that would have made a race car driver envious. The grey sedan attempted to pass the car in front of them, but, quickly, they had to return to their place because of oncoming traffic. We could now see the Jeep about a car behind the sedan. I kept praying mentally and remained very quiet not to disturb or distract William.

Our luck ran out about three miles later when the car behind us exited the highway, leaving the grey sedan directly behind us. William noticed this and floored the gas pedal, but soon the car was just a few meters behind us. The green Jeep had advanced positions as well and was now right behind the grey sedan.

About a mile later, as we were entering the plains near Guarne, the grey sedan rear-ended us, causing the Simca to abruptly drive out of the paved highway onto a gravel road. William was able to remain in control, but, a few seconds later, the sedan T-boned us on the back-left side of the car, causing the Simca to fly in the air, roll twice, and land on its roof, still moving in circles on the gravel road.

Everything went by so quickly that by the time I realized what had happened, the car had already stopped. There was shattered glass everywhere, and I noticed that William had lost consciousness. He was bleeding from his forehead, held in place by his seat belt, head touching the ceiling of his overturned car.

I felt disoriented and confused. Nothing was hurting, but I couldn't move. I felt held in place by an immovable force. Outside of the car I saw two men get out of the grey sedan and begin to approach the Simca. I called for William, but he didn't respond. I focused on the men and recognized them immediately. They were the same two men who had looked for me in the library and had nearly destroyed "The Oaks."

I thought I was hallucinating because Dr. Garza believed these two men were no longer involved with Machado. They had been fired from their jobs. Why were they here now? Panic began to seize me when I noticed both men were carrying guns. I tried hard to untie my seat belt, but it was somehow jammed. I called for William again, but there was no response.

I closed my eyes and prayed for God to deliver us. I thought of you and prepared myself to join you this very moment. I thought of my poor mother and felt deeply saddened. "She will have to plan my funeral," I thought. How would that feel like? Losing a fifteen-year old son in such violent way. I thought of Julia and her mother, Maria, agonizing in pain in a hospital in Rio Negro. I thought of my brother Juan having to grow up without me. Tears were now flowing down my cheeks. I didn't want to die, but I saw no way out of the situation.

I opened my eyes and prepared to die. If these men were going to kill me, the least they could do was to face me. I would force them to look at me in the eye, to carry my last accusatory and terrified look with them to their graves. I wouldn't make it easier for them.

As I watched the men approach, I saw in the distance the green Jeep stop. Black Suit #1 turned around to inspect and came face to face with a bullet on his torso. Black Suit #2, turned around, shot once wildly, and underwent the same fate as his partner, falling just inches away from Black Suit #1. I closed my eyes as two men ran out towards our car. I felt lightheaded and I knew I was about to faint.

The last thing I heard before I fainted was the clear Chilean accent of the tall, older man we had met on the streets of Rio Negro. He told his partner, "Hurry, help me get them into the Jeep."

As I drifted off, I gave thanks to God for the special talents of a Chilean man who had chosen to return from retirement to help a weakling like me.

Chapter 38

I woke up in a small, rural hospital in Guarne several hours later. There were two people I loved sitting on chairs by my bedside. The first was my mother and the second was my friend Ivan. I was confused, disoriented and my head hurt.

My mother jumped to her feet when she saw me open my eyes and exclaimed an excited, "Thank you, Jesus!" She then asked me, "How are you feeling, honey?"

"Thirsty," I replied.

She immediately went to the small table by the door of the room and served me half a glass of water. I drank it gratefully and asked her, "How is William?"

Ivan broke in and answered, "He's good. He broke two ribs and his left arm, but the doctors patched him really well. He is resting in the next room. You really gave as a scare, buddy."

I said, sadly, "He's dead, Ivan. He left us."

Ivan responded, "I know, Joe. I just found out yesterday

morning. But we must worry about you now. How are you feeling?”

“I’m good. Some pain, but I’m fine.” I answered,

At this point, my mother said, “You’re lucky, Joe. All you have is a few scratches where the broken glass hit you. There’s nothing broken, honey. The doctor said you are just in shock, but there is no reason to keep you. You might get to come home tonight. I haven’t told your siblings about your accident. I didn’t want to worry them.”

I didn’t know how much my mother knew about what had happened to us. So, I said nothing.

Noticing the need for a backstory, Ivan said, “That was a crazy accident. I arrived as the cops were leaving. They told me a truck driver fell asleep at the wheel and hit William’s car, causing it to drive off the highway and roll over a couple of times. Some nice drivers who saw the accident stopped and brought you here.”

“Does Fr. Garcia know?” I managed to ask still parched and pointing to my mother for more water.

Giving me a smile and a knowing glance, Ivan answered, “He knows. In fact, it was he who called your family. He will be here in a few minutes to visit you. The family wants to take you home, but he wants the sisters to nurse you to health. After all, you were on Center’s business, coming back from delivering all those posters to the churches in Marinilla and Rio Negro.”

Grateful for the backstory, I suddenly realized that if my mother took me home, the safety of the entire family would be at risk. I thought of Julia and her mother. We would be sitting ducks in Bello. Somehow, I had to convince my mother to let me return to the Center.

I said, “Mom, you know best. If you want me to come home, I will. But I was beginning to get back into the swing of things at ‘The Oaks.’ Fr. Garcia and I have been meeting regularly, and the counseling is helping a lot. I still miss Alex, but I am less sad."

My mother gave me an "I wasn't born yesterday" look but said nothing as she brought me my water.

I greedily drank the water as a doctor dressed in a white lab coat, entered the room. However, I knew that face well and I knew he was not a doctor.

He quickly surveyed the room and said slowly in a beautiful Chilean accent, "Hey, Joe. I just want you to know we are outside if you need us. I am glad you are awake. You took quite a hit."

"Thank you for everything." I said in a code only he could fully understand.

"It really is our pleasure. You will receive the best care as long as we are around. There is nothing to be afraid of. By the way, your friend is doing great. We might be able to send him home tonight as well."

At that point, I realized that William lived alone, and his life would be in danger as long as Machado was still hovering around. I said, "Do you think he is well enough to go on a ride? If Mom lets me, I would love to take him to 'The Oaks.' The sisters will take care of him. I don't want him alone in his house."

The doctor-who-was-not-a-doctor responded, "I think that's a great idea. He will need some rest and someone to care of him for a few days."

I looked at the suspicious lady holding the cup of water and tentatively asked, "Mom?"

She said, "Let me talk to Fr. Garcia first. I don't want to presume on his generosity until I talk to him."

"If your mother agrees, I will let our ambulance drive you both to the Center and I will personally set you up in their nurse's office. Better to be safe than sorry." The doctor-who-wasn't-a-doctor interjected.

As if on cue, Ivan stated, "And I'm coming with you, buddy. I have no games for a week, and I want to be with you."

I had never seen a more coordinated attack against my poor mother, but I was grateful for this plan, which obviously had been hatched while I was still unconscious.

"There you are, Joe. Said my mentor, Fr. Garcia. He came to the bed and gave me a quick hug.

He turned to my mother and introduced her to his lawyer, saying. "Mrs. Cardenas, it is so good to see you. I am so glad our Joe is doing well. This is my good friend Julius."

Julius shook my mother's hand, and she became instantaneously uncomfortable because the old lawyer looked like an old money oligarch. "My pleasure meeting you, Mrs. Cardenas," The lawyer said.

"Likewise," said my mother uncomfortably.

Fr. Garcia noted my mother's discomfort and said, "I wonder if I could have a word with you, Mrs. Cardenas?" Gently walking with her to the hallway, he left the room. Right outside the door, he said, "I feel so sorry about this unfortunate incident. We wonder if you will let us take Joe to the Center. We have a great nurse and both sisters are trained in emergency medical care. You are welcome to visit any time, of course, and I will personally keep you informed of his progress. We love your boy and we want him to recover properly. He has had a very difficult week."

My mother said nothing, she just reached out and gave the cleric a hug, crying, "You are the best thing that has ever happened to that boy. He loves you as a second father. You are a Godsend, Father. Please take good care of my boy."

Fr. Garcia was choked up by the sincerity in my mother's words. He said, "He is my son. and I will take excellent care of him. Now, we better go, it's getting late."

Within a few minutes, William and I were moved to gurneys, loaded on an ambulance rented by the Garcias, and taken to "The Oaks." I kissed my mother before I left and I begged, "Please don't tell the family anything. I'm fine, really. I don't want to worry them."

My mother smiled and said, "You are a good boy. I won't tell them anything, but you better call me every day, mister."

"I will, I promise." I said, as the doctor-who-wasn't-a-doctor jumped in the back of the ambulance with us, followed by two other doctors who were not doctors, and Ivan, who obviously had been introduced to all of them and acted very comfortable in their presence.

Fr. Garcia and the old lawyer first offered my mother a ride, which she declined; then they left with their security personnel and followed behind the ambulance. A block away, a dark green Jeep turned into the street ahead of the ambulance, and we followed it all the way to the camp. Next to me William slept comfortably, aided by enough sedatives to take down a small elephant.

Chapter 39

The take down of Juan Manuel Machado was a systematic work of art, which deserves to be studied by all police academies and organized crime groups alike. The first action by the Chilean, just barely two days before, was to assign a very discreet duo to follow Machado around the city, whether he was driving for the Cuevas family, visiting friends, or paying a short visit to one of his two young mistresses.

The duo had talents few people have. For example, they were excellent photographers who had their own black room and could develop their film within minutes of taking the pictures. This is how by 10:00 on Monday night, barely twenty-four hours after Machado had launched an assault on "The Oaks," his irascible and mob-connected wife received several color pictures of her husband having amorous relations with a woman twenty years his junior. Furious, the rather overweight woman had kicked her husband out of the house and forced him to stay at a hotel in the city.

Her threats of retribution by her brother, the mention of whose name brought fear to any living soul in Medellin in 1981, were enough to cause Machado to look over his shoulder for the next few days. It was well-known in the city that the cartels protected members of their families as well as they protected their money. There was no extent to which they wouldn't go to avenge an offence, real or imagined, to one of their siblings or children. On occasion, this courtesy even extended to cousins and other members of the extended family.

Next, came a frontal attack on Machado's finances, the afternoon after his goons had assaulted two innocent women in Rio Negro and had tried to kill William and me.

Several hours after dropping William and me off at the hospital in Guarne and calling enough reinforcements to keep us safe, a very smart Chilean man, who was a master of disguise and an expert at blending-in, moved to the next phase of his plan. At 1:15 in the afternoon, on Wednesday, December 16th, 1981, a man looking exactly like Juan Manuel Machado entered a branch of Banco Popular and transferred all the money in his checking account to an offshore account in Belize, from which the money was transferred twice that afternoon, ending up in an untraceable account in Chile.

The man was able to produce all legal paperwork, account numbers, and codes necessary for the transaction and, by 5:00 pm that evening, as the Machado-who-wasn't-really-Machado was driving to the hospital to check on his patients, who were not really his patients, the real Machado had the equivalent of one-hundred American dollars in his bank account.

The next step in the coordinated, yet silent attack, came as a courtesy of the Castle Ridge Security Consultants. Feeling responsible for the behaviors of their former employees, the C.E.O had personally contacted all the reputable security agencies in the city and obtained from them a solemn promise that they wouldn't work for the man. If Machado needed muscle, assuming he could pay for it, he would have to go local, which meant less trained and committed, and, therefore, more difficult to manage.

Part two of the Castle Ridge Security Consultants revenge was to raid an apartment in Envigado, where one of Machado's mistresses lived, and where he had stored over twenty million pesos, the equivalent to $25,000 American dollars, under a false bottom in the unsuspecting girl's closet. This substantial amount of money in 1981, was Machado's "Petty Cash" and crucial to his day to day operations. The security firm had known about the place for over a year and knew the young mistress's schedule in detail. By the time the Machado-who-wasn't-really-Machado was driving to the hospital to check on his patients, who were not really his patients, the real Machado's petty cash fund had exactly the equivalent of one American dollar.

The very next attack on the man was taking place this very Thursday morning as Dr. Garza and I, accompanied by two younger lawyers and several bodyguards, were making our way in the two dark green Jeeps to the headquarters of Steerco.

Your father's calendar showed that at 10:00 am, he was meeting with a Bolivian food conglomerate who wanted to secure the distribution rights for Steerco products in their country. This was a pre-planned meeting which, unbeknown to him and his executive team, had been replaced with a meeting with Dr. Julius Garza, a well-known corporate lawyer and friend of his father.

I was brought up to speed on all these moves by Dr. Garza himself in the car. The lawyer explained that this coordinated attack on Machado was important because he would need influence and money to launch any kind of coordinated attack against us. Take away a man's financial resources, make him a pariah to his business partners, remove the support of powerful benefactors, and watch the man crumble.

To make matters worse for Machado, Michael and Cesar Walters had taken a sudden trip to New York City that same morning and would not return for almost a week. When the time came to take Machado down, he would be completely unable to offer any resistance. And, the best part of it, was that he would never know the real source of the attacks on his wealth and power.

The lawyer also fed me a story that by now he and Julio Garcia had insinuated to their boss, "I've been informed the men who tried to kill you survived their wounds and are in a private hospital under guard, until the authorities finish their investigation. They have been identified as the men who assaulted the two women in Rio Negro. The authorities have enough to send them away for a long time. You no longer have to worry about them."

All due respect to the good lawyer, I knew how the game was played and, although this story allowed his sainted boss to sleep well at night, I knew there was a very strong possibility that the naked, decomposing bodies of the two men, lay on a garbage hill somewhere near Guarne. I never asked or cared to find out what really happened to the men. They are just blurry faces, part of the new scenery in a country greedy for blood - a country that has become a nightmare-making factory.

We arrived at Steerco at 9:45 and were asked by the receptionist to wait until your dad arrived. At 9:55 all four of us were taken into a small, but elegant, conference room and offered coffee, which we all accepted. The bright room had floor to ceiling windows, facing a perfectly landscaped courtyard adorned by a beautiful pond with a water fountain at its center. The fountain was timed to shoot spurts of water high in the air at variable intervals. The chairs butted against the round table were dark blue

Corinthian leather, with elegant stitching on all sides. On the opposite side of the table, there was a breakfast bar filled with coffee, tea, and pastries. Next to it, there was a small, but elegant, desk with a telephone, paper pads, and pencils with the Steerco logo prominently printed on their surfaces.

I sat giving my back to the front door because I didn't want to be the first person your father saw as he entered the room. Let him see the expensive suits across from him before he is introduced to their client, the same young person he refused to assist on a dark street in Envigado when a deranged man attacked him.

At exactly 10:00 am, your father entered the room and closed the door. He introduced himself to the group, looked at Julius and said, "I know you. You used to be friends with my father. Are you representing Bolivian Foods in this deal?"

Julius responded, smiling. "I used to have drinks with your old man in his study when you were in diapers." Then walking towards the door, he extended his hand and said, "Julius Garza, nice seeing you." After shaking hands, the lawyer continued, "No, we are afraid we have deceived you, Arturo. We are not representing the Bolivians. We are representing a young man you know well. His name is Joe Cardenas."

Since I knew that was my cue, I stood up, turned around, and said, "Good morning, Mr. Cuevas."

Still standing by the door, your dad, responded quite confused. "First, Joe and I have no business deals, and second, this time slot has been reserved for the Bolivians for weeks."

He was visibly annoyed. Someone had come into his private domain and rearranged his schedule without his express consent. This was an insult to his authority and an act of disloyalty from the well-compensated secretary who made the change in secret, calling the Bolivians to postpone to the next day. They, in turn, were grateful for an extra day of sight seeing at their client's expense, but the switch was an inconvenience for your father.

Noticing your father's displeasure, the lawyer stated, "Please give us a few minutes, Arturo, and everything will be crystal clear to you. We had to keep this meeting under wraps because we believe your family may be in danger. Please give us a few minutes."

Your dad looked at me and asked, "Joe?"

"He's right, Mr. Cuevas. I believe you are in danger and all I want is a few minutes of your time." I answered.

Your dad took one of the chairs and said. "Okay Julius, talk away. I can give you ten minutes."

"You will give us as much time as Joe needs, Arturo. Now, let my client talk," Julius responded forcefully.

Your father looked at the two other attorneys and addressed one of them, "I know you, don't I? We interviewed you for our legal department a year or two ago, but you turned us down. I was really disappointed."

The young lawyer smiled and said, "I was given a better offer. Nothing personal."

Not impressed with his answer, your dad looked at me and said, "Go ahead, Joe, unburden yourself, but do it nicely. Contrary to what your lawyer may think, I don't like to be bullied."

Chapter 40

Julius and I had practiced a script and the old lawyer had given me a few questions he wanted me to ask your dad. I began to give your dad a brief recap of our conversation at "The Oaks" and your last call to me in the early morning of Wednesday, December 9, 1981. Slowly and systematically, I told him about the real clue in the poem, Machado's visit to the library, our meeting with Luisa Santos at Ivan's house, the assault on "The Oaks," and Machado's role in it. I also related the translated articles, the assault of his former maid and her daughter, and the attempted murder of William and me.

Your dad was shocked and confused. He looked like a man who was just given all the secrets of the universe and now didn't know what to do with them. He had a million questions, which I answered patiently to the best of my ability. The water fountain was strangely soothing, and I was bone-tired of carrying all these secrets with me around the city. This unburdening, as he had called it, was as much for me as it was for him.

At some point, he jumped in and asked, "Are you trying to tell me, Joe, that my boy was abused?"

"Yes. He told me he had been raped when he was ten. That was his word, 'raped.'" I answered him, and it felt good to finally put a word to the tragedy that had changed your life so radically.

At the sound of that word, your dad slammed the desk with great force and said, "Who? You better tell me, Joe. Who's the son-of-a-bitch who raped my boy?"

"I'm sorry, but we don't know. That's what we are trying to figure out," I answered honestly.

"And Julia and Maria were assaulted? Almost killed? By my family's driver?" He shot in rapid succession, not wanting to believe any of it.

"We know the men worked for Machado because they were the same two men at the library and at the Center," I answered.

"And this sex ring, did they rape my boy too?" His voice breaking, your dad took his napkin out of his suit jacket and dabbed his eyes.

I couldn't help but put myself in his shoes. How would I feel if someone in my family had gone through the nightmare you went through? How would I feel about the information if the person was already dead and I had no chance to comfort them? What would I do with the guilt these revelations left behind? He was your father; you had been abused; and he wasn't able to protect you.

"We don't know, but he may have been. We are still looking into it. Now, Mr. Cuevas, I need to ask you an important question." I paused, took a sip of my coffee, stared at the fountain for two seconds and asked, "Whose idea was it to hire Machado to drive the family?"

"He used to drive for Michael and Linda. About a year after we met them, Missy announced that the man was going to start driving for us. I didn't pay much attention to it. I always leave home matters up to my wife, as I told you before, Joe.”

“Did you know he was a high-level security consultant and not just a driver?” I asked.

“I knew the man could handle himself. He had that air of confidence about him. There were times he seemed outright dangerous. But I just assumed he was a bad-tempered son-of-a-bitch.” Your father answered, feeling taken, lied to, duped, and somehow manipulated by his own wife and driver.

“Do you know how much he gets paid?” I asked as the lawyer had suggested.

“I’ve no idea, Joe. But I can check. We handle all payroll from this office, although we keep the houses on a separate budget.” He said, picking up the phone on the desk and contacting someone from finance. Within a few minutes a young woman, dressed in a business suit, entered the office with a set of spreadsheets.

Your dad reviewed the spreadsheets and said, “This must be a mistake. The man gets paid more than ten times the amount of money the other drivers make.”

“Do you know if Machado and the Walters are close?” I asked, knowing the answer.

“Thick as thieves.” He said angrily. “Michael used to brag that the best favor he ever did for us was letting us steal his favorite driver. Steal, my ass! I will fire that son-of-a-bitch today. He’s gone.”

At this point Julius intervened, “Arturo, we believe this man is involved in what happened to Alex. But we have a theory and a plan. Just listen to the boy.”

Your dad looked at me and said, “Sorry, go ahead, Joe.”

“I believe Machado was a plant in your house. I think Michael Walters placed him there to spy on you. I think your phones are bugged and there may be recording devices throughout your house. Machado has been communicating with Walters about your daily comings and goings. This is my theory and we can use this to our advantage. If you and your family suddenly take a four to five-hour trip and have Machado drive you, we can have people look at your lines, trace them until we find the recording devices, and listen to see if he and Walters implicate themselves. If they do, they both can be arrested. If they don't implicate themselves, you can fire the bastard when we are done."

Your dad broke out in a loud laugh. "Joe, you sound like a junior detective. How did you hatch this plan?" He asked.

"I had a lot of time in hospital beds to think about it." I said angrily, still feeling some pain from my bruises.

"We'll get the sons-of-bitches, Joe." He said with great emotion. The he added, "I just have a question, Joe. Why not come to me directly? Why hire lawyers? I know where you live; there is no way you can pay Julius and his associates. Why go through the trouble?"

His comment about my home and social class was made so casually that he didn't realize how profoundly it hurt me. Now more than ever before, I realized that your father had seen me as no better than one of his servants from day one. His trip to Bello and the breakfast at the club had been information-fishing expeditions. He had always known his place and mine. I was grateful for his kindness, but at this very moment, it felt like cheap charity.

Smarting from his question, I answered, "I didn't know if I could trust you. Having Dr. Garza with me made sense. I may not be wealthy, but I have a very wealthy patron. We are prepared to go the long way to find out what happened to Alex. Having his law firm witness this conversation and carry out my plans if anything happens to me or my family makes perfect sense. It's not personal, Mr. Cuevas."

Your dad smiled and said, "I feel you have just handled me like you handled that bum in Envigado. You have the killer instinct, Joe. Next time just call me. I promise you, I am on your side. When do you want us to take this trip?"

I looked at Dr. Garza to confirm and said, "How about tomorrow afternoon, say from 12:00 - 5:00 pm? And, Mr. Cuevas, please keep this meeting confidential. We still don't know if we can trust your wife. I hope you understand our concerns. These are dangerous people."

"You got it. But I want something in return." He said looking at Julius defiantly, "No more surprises. From today on, I am a part of the team. Here is my private number Julius. You call me any time day or night. And please thank your benefactor for his concern for my boy."

Julius shook your dad's hand and said, "I think you are a far better businessman than your dad ever was. Nice to have seen you again. I will keep in touch."

Your dad looked at me and said, "I wish I had such a loyal and determined friend as you are to Alex. Thanks, Joe."

After this, we left your dad to plan his family's trip for the next day.

Chapter 41

We arrived at "The Oaks" around 12:30 and the chef prepared us a delicious lunch of chicken salad, homemade potato chips, spinach and tomato salad, fresh dinner rolls, and coffee. The sweet, buttery smell of the rolls filled the entire kitchen with a homey, comfortable feeling. The good lawyer chose to pay a brief visit to his friend and boss and the two of them ate in Fr. Garcia's study. I suspected this was a debriefing session. The rest of us ate with the chef in the dining hall.

William joined Ivan and me at lunch, even though he had already eaten. I was glad to see him doing so well physically. Emotionally he was still a mess. He seemed ill at ease as the guest of a religious institution surrounded by nuns, priests, and weirdly religious kids. I suspected William was not the churchgoing type and the place was getting on his nerves.

Another reason for joining was the fact that both Ivan and William were curious about our meeting with your father. I gave them a brief synopsis of your father's reaction and his promise of cooperation, but I kept from them our plan for a detailed inspection of your home, the family's out-of-town trip, or how any of this fit into our plan to take Machado and Walters down.

As soon as we sat at the dining room table, William said sheepishly, "I'm sorry I almost got us killed. My crappy little car just couldn't keep up."

I smiled and said, "You're kidding me, right? You were great. Without your excellent driving, we would have been killed up in the mountains. You got us to level ground. You are the best driver I've ever known."

"Thanks, little man. I mean it. I've been feeling all sorts of guilt. But, listen, now that I see you, maybe you can help me. I'm having a little problem. I've got to go to work, and I no longer have a car. Can one of the people here help?" he asked hopefully.

At this point, Ivan jumped in and said. "I've been given one of the Center's cars to drive while I am here. I'll be glad to take you, if it's okay with Joe and Fr. Garcia."

"I'm sure Fr. Garcia will not object, but you have a broken arm and two cracked ribs. You need to take some time off to rest. If you want, we can call Mr. Cuevas and explain," I volunteered.

"I love Mr. Cuevas, but here is the thing. I've already used my sick time to care for my mom. What this means is that if I don't work, I don't get paid. If I go back, I know they'll put me on light duty, and I'd rather be working any way. I'm going nuts sitting around here, doing nothing." He added.

I suspected he was missing his mother, his evening drink, and his soaps. The dirty little secret of Colombian television in the 1980's is that the men were as hooked on telenovelas as the women were. "The Oaks" had no televisions in the rooms and only one area in the whole campus with an antenna, which led to a theater in the quads. The infirmary, which was in the Admin building, had no televisions, radio, and no Aguardiente.

"We think Mr. Cuevas is okay. But you need to be careful with Machado for a while. Don't take stupid risks. Are you sure you can't stay with us a little longer?" I asked, thinking about his safety.

"I'm staying with my mom for a while. She'll take good care of me and I want to keep an eye on her."

I thought this was a good idea. Finally, I asked, "What are you doing for transportation in the next few weeks?"

William answered, "Mr. Cuevas is letting me take the car to Mom's until I buy something else. You know how it is. I'll be okay."

By this he meant that he didn't have insurance for his personal car. In fact, most Colombians do not have auto insurance. The car-owning process is actually very simple: You save your money, buy your car, fix it yourself when it breaks down, and you replace it when the old one dies. In the meantime, you try hard to avoid accidents, and if you have one, you either leave the scene and keep on driving, or you stop and negotiate with the other driver about damages. These negotiations often end in heated arguments, threats, and violence, which explains why so many people flee the scene and dodn't wait around for the police to show up.

I said goodbye to William at the main parking lot as he entered Ivan's car. Hugging him, I said emotionally, "Thanks for saving my life. You were amazing. You have balls. I've never seen someone that cool under pressure."

"Thanks, little man. It means a lot coming from you, because you, my midget friend, have cojones of steel," William replied.

It was like hearing you all over again. I laughed until the car made a right turn out of the parking lot and took William away. That was the last time I saw one of the kindest men I have ever met.

Chapter 42

When I walked through the arches back into the campus, I was feeling responsible for William's injuries and his emotional state. I wondered if I had exposed him to danger unnecessarily. Certainly, there was a less dangerous way to open the lid on this nightmare. I prayed silently that William might recover soon, and I prayed for his safety.

Lost in thought, I did not hear a voice calling me from the admin building, until the voice repeated her question. It was Sister Celeste. "Joe, can you please join me for several minutes?"

Sister Celeste was a small-town woman who had never left the small town. Educated in a monastery barely three blocks away from where she grew up, she had never traveled outside of the city, even when her order had attempted to send her to Rome for additional training. She fought change with fierce intent, and she saw traveling as a futile exercise in wastefulness. She believed that "God provides what we need where we are, and we don't have to go anywhere to get it."

This philosophy made Sister Celeste rigid, uncompromising, suspicious of anything new, and resistant to innovation in all forms. Still a young and attractive woman under her veil, she managed to find creative ways daily to disfigure her appearance, as to look haggard and old at the age of thirty-four. One of these ways of disfiguring herself was a perpetual frown, which made her look like she was always sucking a lemon.

Overwhelmingly feared by staff and students, the Sister was a huge asset to Fr. Garcia because of her fastidious and obsessive organizational skills. Without Sister Celeste, the Father would be so lost and disorganized that little would get accomplished at the Center. This was the message Fr. Garcia gave the Sister almost daily, but, of course, some of us knew the truth. The reason Fr. Garcia endured the insufferable nun was not her organizational skills, but the fact that Sister Celeste was the niece of one of his best friends in seminary who was now dead. He tolerated her out of love and respect for her uncle.

Terrified that I had done something wrong and was about to be scolded, I quickly asked, "Is everything okay, Sister?"

"Everything is fine, Joe. But there is something I need to show you." The sister answered without giving me any details.

Sister Celeste's office was small, simply decorated, and a mish mash of furniture passed down from former occupants. It was as though the nun's space had taken the same vows of obedience, celibacy, and poverty the Sister had taken. For years the sister had fought against Fr. Garcia's attempts to bring a little color into the space, to the point that the good father had given up after the desk-chair incident.

Several years before, Sister Celeste had complained

of lower back pain, which she attributed to her desk chair. As a Christmas present, Fr. Garcia had ordered her a beautiful leather, high back chair, with whatever lumbar support was known at the time.

Several days after returning from vacation, Father Garcia found the chair in the middle of his study with a note attached to the back with a clothes-pin. The note read, "If the good Lord would have wanted me to spend my life sitting on this chair, he would have made me a man and a priest."

Point well taken. The chair made its rounds from desk to desk in the admin building, until it ended on the desk of the old chef, who had appreciatively used it ever since. The nun, for her part, stopped complaining because, "Every time I complain, he buys another contraption I don't want." For his part, Fr. Garcia left Sister Celeste to enjoy her misery in peace.

"Come this way," the Sister said as I entered her office. Then pointing to a folding chair next to her desk, she said, "Sit, Joe." Then she said, "Do you remember the day before we closed for the session? The day of the party?"

"Yes, Sister, I remember." I said.

"Well, as you know, that is also the day when students return any books they have borrowed from the library or from Father's study. That morning, after rehearsal, Alex returned Father's copy of *The Divine Comedy*. Since Father was not here in the morning, I took the book from Alex, but I totally forgot to give it to him. I found it this morning in one of my bookshelves, over there." She said, pointing to an old bookshelf across the room.

She continued, "As soon as I took it, this letter dropped out. It is from Alex, and it is addressed to you. Do you know what this is about?" She asked, filled with curiosity.

Since Sister Celeste didn't know much about the events that had transpired over the last week, I lied, "I had asked him to review a project for school. He was such a good writer. That's probably what it is." I took the envelope from her and quickly put it in my back pocket.

Not happy with my behavior, she said, "All in all, we better open it. Just in case it explains why he did what he did."

Not wanting to be rude, but also not wanting to bring the Sister into your story, I simply said, "It's okay, Sister. I'll read it later and if it is not my project for school, I will return the envelope to you."

"Do you promise, Joe?" She insisted.

"Absolutely," I lied.

"Should we let Father know about this unusual place to leave your school project? I mean, why wouldn't he have just given it to you that Saturday? This makes no sense, Joe." She pressed on,

I thought that in addition to celibacy, poverty, and obedience, the Sister had taken a vow of nosiness. I said, calling her bluff, "I think that's a great idea, Sister. In fact, let me talk to him right now." I said standing up. "Thank you, Sister." I added out of respect for the nun and walked out of her office, out of the admin building, up the cement steps, left to the Gamma Building, and into my room. I locked the door and drew the brand-new curtains down. I sat at my desk, lit a cigarette and, filled with anxiety, opened your letter.

"Dear Joe,

Your poetry game was a big help last night. I promised you that soon I would tell you the whole story. I'm sitting alone in the chapel, waiting for choir rehearsal, and I believe this is as good a time as any. I don't know when or if you will get this letter, but I hope you do and quickly. I have made a decision about how my story will end, and I know this letter will answer many of your questions.

First, I'm really sorry for what I'm about to do, but, please know that I'm at peace, and I'm not afraid. I know

I can't go on like this and I always knew someday I would end my life. At a time when all choices have been taken away from us, this is the only choice that will be truly mine to make. Sounds crazy, right? Well, I've been feeling kind of crazy lately. Please don't blame yourself, midget! There's nothing you could have done. This is my choice and not your failure."

Unable to continue reading, I stood, went to the bathroom, closed the door, let the water run from the faucet, and wept loudly, without reservations, without guilt, and without shame. After a few minutes, I dried my tears, closed the faucet, and returned to my desk. I took another cigarette out, lit it, and continued reading,

"Last night I told you something happened to me when I was little. This is true. But I knew it was coming for a while. To explain, I must tell you a story that will sound like paranoid rantings. I hope by now you have received the letter I left for you at Ivan's house. If you haven't, please call Mrs. Santos. In either case, that note, and this letter are part of the same story. I hope you won't hate me for what I'm about to tell you.

Michael Walters, Cesar's dad, is into kids. By that I mean that for years he has used children for sex and has provided kids to powerful people for the same purpose. He was almost caught in London a few years back, but when he set up shop here in Medellin, he changed a few rules.

First, he kept his club of weirdos small. Second, he demanded of all members two things, a tribute and an insurance policy. This was his way of avoiding betrayal from anyone in the club, as he had almost faced in London. Back then, it had cost him almost a million pounds to bribe, intimidate, and physically force three executives in his company into silence.

The tribute was someone between the ages of nine to thirteen who was either related or known to the member. This

was important because this demonstrated the member's commitment to the exclusive club. Michael used to call it, 'Having skin in the game.' The tributes were almost always used once, photographed with the member, and let go. I was a member's tribute when I was about nine and a half, but, in my case, Michael Walters did not let me go. For six months he groomed me, showing me all sorts of attention, complimenting my looks, buying me stuff, giving me alcohol, and letting me smoke at his house. He introduced me to pot when I was twelve, and I snorted cocaine for the first time at a party with him and his friends at thirteen.

I was a stupid kid, so I loved the attention. Since I was Cesar's friend, I had an excuse to be at his house all the time. And, since Michael came to our house often, he had unlimited access. The behaviors became more sexual overtime, until the day before my tenth birthday, when I went to his home for a sleepover with Cesar.

Around 3:30 am Michael came to Cesar's room, woke me up and took me by the hand to his study, where he abused me. From that time on, he used any excuses to be with me and his 'special game' went on for several years. I know it sounds stupid and I know you'll hate me for this, but I convinced myself that I loved the guy and I went to the home voluntarily a bunch of times.

When I turned thirteen and started growing up, he began to lose interest in me. Michael started spending more time with other boys his club recruited in poor towns and the streets. I protested several times and he would agree to see me each time. About three and a half months ago, he sent me away because I was "too old." When I protested, he threatened my family. He said he had insurance that could send my folks to jail for many years, and I would lose everything. I believe our driver is secretly working for him, but I have no proof of this.

I believe his insurance has something to do with pictures. On one of the times I threatened to expose him, he gave me the picture in this envelope. I have been carrying this with me for a while. I don't remember when this happened, but Michael has threatened to send it to the media if I make noise. He says he has hundreds more. I know he kept stuff related to his 'club' in one of his buildings in La America and I'm planning to investigate. Please be careful, Joe. These sons-of-bitches are dangerous.

I'll call you soon with instructions. Thank you for your friendship. Take care, buddy. Remember that life is precious, and we need to hold on to those we love. Your friend, Alex."

Trembling, I reached inside the envelope and took out a 5x7 photograph of a fully undressed child of about 10 holding the hand of an older man. The man was smiling, the child looked frightened. You were the boy, and the man was Manuel Escobar Estrada, the State's Secretary of Education, and your uncle.

Chapter 43

The destruction of Juan Manuel Machado and the club of pedophiles he protected continued on schedule. Your family left exactly at noon to their emergency visit to your father's aunt, Lucrecia, in Santa Rosa de Osos. Your mother had received a frantic call from the town's hospital announcing the 87-year-old had been admitted for dehydration. The doctors needed to speak with the next of kin and Arturo Cuevas appeared in their records as the only survivor and inheritor. Your mother, unaware of such a relation, had called your dad at work, which meant that Machado had heard a complete recording of the call.

Your father confirmed the existence and vast wealth of the fictitious relative as instructed, and your mother eagerly planned a family trip for the next day. The promise of additional wealth was too high a temptation for your mother to resist. Unbeknown to them, the fictitious patient would feel much better by the middle of the afternoon and would check out of the hospital against medical advice, failing to leave an address where she could be reached. Your father would direct Machado to drive to the last known address in the center of town, where he would learn that the elderly aunt had moved out five years before and had not left a forwarding address.

About three minutes after the couple and their faithful driver, who was much more than a driver, left their garage for their trip, a highly specialized group of lawn maintenance professionals, who were not really lawn maintenance professionals, began to inspect every room of the vast home systematically. Within an hour, they found the extensive wiretaps Machado had set-up throughout the house.

Within thirty minutes after that, they found the expensive recording studio he had set in the bedroom the family had given him years ago. He had convinced the family that this room was necessary to store all equipment, cleaning supplies, and maintenance items necessary to keep the cars in proper working order. He also used the room for those occasions when he had to work late, and it was just easier to stay on the premises. This was a standard practice in large households, where the staff's quarters often included rooms for the maid, the cook, and security guard.

Stored in a large plastic bin, hidden in a closet, there were hundreds of compact cassette tapes that documented the family's calls from 1978-1981. Each cassette case was labeled with the date by week, month and year, four to five tapes per month, for four consecutive years. Machado and his bosses knew every fight, complaint, argument, and decision that was ever discussed over any of the multiple telephones in your home.

Acting as ordered, the team replaced the tape in each case with a blank tape, making sure not to disturb the case. They then placed all the recordings in new cases, marking them with the corresponding date. Using a two-way recording system, they brought with them, they made copies of the two tapes that corresponded to December 1981 and left the originals intact. They knew that if Machado suspected an intrusion, he most likely would check the newest recordings first to make sure everything was in order. This would buy the team some additional time.

Making sure they left everything as they had found it, the team of lawn maintenance professionals left your house, without raising any suspicions in any of the neighbors, who by now were accustomed to the vans, with the green thumb logo stenciled on the side, working on most of the homes on this block.

Within an hour of leaving the house, a team of twelve highly specialized professionals, were sitting on comfortable chairs in the administration building of the Antiochia Beverage Company's headquarters in Girardota, going over the hundreds of tapes.

They had devised an interesting system: All tapes that contained any embarrassing information about your family were set aside in Pile One and marked with a small red sticker on the cover. Tapes that contained incriminating evidence about illegal behavior, were set on Pile Two with a blue sticker. Tapes that showed any communications between Machado, either with members of the family or outside parties, were set on Pile Three with a green sticker, and tapes that contained conversations between any other third persons, were set on Pile Four and marked with a yellow sticker.

By Saturday at 4:00 pm, when Machado began to suspect that his life was in danger, the exhausted technicians, who had worked around the clock for nearly twenty-four hours, had finished their work and were ready to present a report to their bosses.

Chapter 44

After analyzing the hundreds of hours of tape recording, the team arrived at the following conclusions,

(a) Machado had been a plant in the Cuevas' home since several days after your "initiation" into the club. The reason was not specific to your family. The club had plants in each of the homes of their twenty-four members, from cooks, to drivers, to security guards. All the plants were former police men and women, highly trained, fiercely loyal to Michael Walters, and very dangerous. Many tapes later, a complete list of these plants was developed because, ironically, all twenty-four were friends, had recommended each other for the jobs, and freely spoke about their "assignments" on the phone.

(b) Over eighty percent of the tapes were mundane conversations between your mother and father, business calls to your father from Steerco, calls from you and to you at "The Oaks," calls from maids to their homes to check on sick children, telephone orders from cooks to local markets, friends looking for you, Cesar frantically checking on your whereabouts, etc.

(c) About ten percent of the tapes had serious incriminating information from the twenty-four plants about "operations," payments to low level informants, payments to hundreds of boys and girls throughout the city for "services rendered," conversations about the various residential buildings and the security that would be needed for each building and "gathering," and, most concerning, specific information about the extra-curricular activities of the plants in relation to the boys and girls recruited for the club. One of Machado's mistresses, for example was only sixteen and had been "used" by the club for well over four years. He had been "seeing" her on the side, without the club's knowledge, and had gotten her an apartment when she "graduated" from the club. The other twenty-one men and two women had also used the "merchandize" at some point over the last four years.

(d) About three percent of the tapes had conversations between Michael Walters and your mother. These were the more surprising to me because I hadn't expected what the tapes had to offer. Walters had terrorized your mother for years. Your mother never knew your uncle had touched you inappropriately since you were about six years old and had personally delivered you to Walters as a membership tribute when you were nine and a half. But, early in March of 1979, when you had turned twelve, your mother began to suspect that there was something sexual going on between you and Cesar. She called Michael to voice her concerns.

A brief recap of the call, just showing your mother's side for brevity, goes like this: "Michael? This is Missy. How are you? Yes, well. Thank you. Listen, I am calling to ask you something kind of embarrassing. Have you noticed anything strange going on between Alex and Cesar? No, not that. I mean, something, sexual? Don't laugh. You can be such a brute. No, listen. Alex has been using words that are kind of inappropriate for a kid his age. The other day he asked the babysitter for a 'blow job.' Oh, stop it. No, really, I'm worried. I asked him, but he just laughed it off. Can you please look into it?"

After this call, Walters called Machado and the two discussed how Missy Cuevas needed a conversation with the "club president" about her precious older brother.

Walters stated angrily, "I need Alex's involvement with the club for a bit longer. She can't mess this up. I tell you, if the bitch stops letting us see the kid, I will go postal. You hear me?"

A conversation in a tape about ten days later, recorded Walters, calling Missy at the home. "I know you're upset by the pictures I showed you of Manuel. Obviously, I can't tell you how I got these photos, but what I can tell you is that I'm willing to use them if you interfere with Alex's relationship with Cesar. My boy is a fragile, lonely kid. I think your suspicions about sex are bullshit, but I will keep an eye on things. Be smart, Missy. Let things be. The boys are great friends, and this is good for them. And, obviously, if you let Arturo or Linda know about the photos or this conversation, your brother will have a very public dismissal from his job. On the other hand, the boys at the Central Jail in Niquia will throw him a great welcome party. They will love some fresh meat. If you know what I mean?"

A tape about six months later, had a frantic Missy call Walters to complain about his threats, "You're going too far. You are an evil man. What would happen if Arturo saw this stupid letter? Stop your damn pranks. I have never been your mistress and I will never be. And what that hell does Y.M. mean, anyway. What? You're not my master. Stop these nonsense letters or I'll swear I will speak to the authorities, Manuel be damned."

From this tape forward, a frequent line between Machado and Walters was, "How's the bitch behaving?" This was always followed by laugher and a simple, "Behaving," from Machado.

About the time you started attending "The Oaks" and you started seeing less of Cesar, Walters' threats began again. Your mother was under a lot of stress, which increased her pleas for you to return Cesar's calls. Ironically, the threats during these tapes were not about "the club" as Walters was beginning to lose interest in you. He really was worried about his son's misery over your unexplained interest in the ministry. It was obvious too that Cesar's mother, Linda, felt offended that your "Working class trash of a mother thought you were too good for her son, all of a sudden."

(e) The last seven percent of the tapes were the most dangerous to "the club," its members, its founder and president, and the twenty-four security people whose contacts secured a steady supply of minors for the club's gatherings. In these tapes, there were hundreds of calls between Machado and Walters about each man by name. It was obvious that Machado was Michael Walters' right-hand man, oversaw all the other plants, and kept a close eye on all the club's members.

After a brief meeting between Dr. Garza, the Garcias, the head of the audio technician detail, and me, it was decided that the more than eighty percent of tapes that contained private, common, uninspired banter would be destroyed. The three percent of compromising tapes involving your mother would be kept at a specific safe until all parties were arrested, after which they would be destroyed. We didn't know yet if your mother would cooperate with our plan or somehow run to her brother's aid and deny prior knowledge of his deviancy. These tapes could put pressure on her to finally do the right thing and expose her brother. The additional seven percent of the tapes would be given to the authorities.

I interjected at this point, "I have an idea about how we could do this." I looked at Dr. Garza and asked, "Would you mind representing your client Joe Cardenas just one more time?"

The lawyer smiled and said, "What do you have in mind?"

Chapter 45

Juan Manuel Machado knew his life was about to end as soon as he arrived at his apartment from driving his bosses to Santa Rosa de Osos, a five-hour waste of time. Stressed and tired, he decided to spend the night at one of his mistresses' apartments, rather than going to his hotel for the night. His wife was still mad at him, and he knew to keep his distance when she was this angry. He also needed to replenish his petty cash because he hadn't had time to go by the bank that afternoon.

The first thing he noticed as he parked on the side of the road, were the blinds of the house across the street from his mistress's apartment, quickly open, and close, as though someone had been caught spying on the place. Then, he noticed a dark cargo van parked down the street about half a block from the apartment. Being a cautious man, he decided to go inside the apartment, get his money, and leave to his other mistress's place.

He walked into the empty apartment and was immediately angry that Olga wasn't waiting for him. He then remembered that she visited her mother in Sabaneta every Friday afternoon and usually didn't return until Saturday. He went straight to his closet and found seven hundred pesos at the bottom of the drawer, the equivalent of one American dollar.

Enraged, Machado kicked the drawer to shreds and began to suspect that his brother in law, Jaime, was coming for him. The ungrateful pissant turned capo had forgotten who had introduced him to "The Boys from Medellin." He now thought he was big shit. He would show him soon enough who was the real threat. Jaime didn't know whom he was dealing with. He was a man with powerful friends, and he still had millions in his bank account. For now, he needed to get to safety.

Filled with rage, he called one of the security agencies he dealt with and asked for a back-up team to meet him outside Olga's apartment in an hour. Unfortunately, the secretary informed him that all executives of the firm had left already and that all security personal had been assigned to weekend jobs. He called four more agencies and was given the same excuse. By now, he knew for sure that Jaime was seriously coming after him.

Next, he called two teenage boys who had done small jobs for him in the past and they agreed to come immediately. Unfortunately, their motorcycle was stopped a block away from their destination and the elegant man's modern weapon and distinctive Chilean accent convinced the boys to return home and never to take Machado's calls in the future. After waiting for his back-up for almost an hour, Machado left the apartment, entered his car in almost complete darkness, and drove as fast as he could.

He felt safe after not detecting any tails for several blocks, but, out of the corner of his eye, he saw the cargo van trailing him several cars behind. He needed to leave the streets as soon as possible. He needed a phone desperately. And he needed a drink.

As the expert driver he was, he changed lanes several times losing his tail in the process. Of course, his tail, who was not mob connected at all, was there just to inflict maximum psychological torture on a man who had dared violate their boss's sanctum at his camp. They never intended to catch up with him, to inflict any damage, to arrest him, or to stop him in any way from reaching his destination. In fact, for the man's paranoia to continue to increase, they needed the man to reach his destination.

Machado arrived at his second mistress's apartment in El Cedral, quickly parked the car in an abandoned lot half a block away, and, under the cover of darkness, entered the place through the back door. Sofia, the twenty-six-year-old brunette, jumped and screamed all at once.

She said, "Juan, you sacred the crap out of me. I wasn't expecting you."

Machado demanded under great duress, "Get me a drink. Now."

The young woman, who by now was familiar with his violence, detected grave danger in his tone. She quickly got up from her chair, where she had been watching television, and got her lover a half a glass of whiskey on the rocks.

Machado downed the drink in one gulp and asked for a second one. The young woman repeated her earlier routine and Machado drank the second drink in one swift motion, beginning to calm down.

He went to the phone and made a call to The Walters Fashion House in Envigado. A security guard answered that all the office staff had left for the day and that Mr. Walters was not working late that evening. He called the Walters' residence and was surprised that Linda Walters answered the phone.

She said, "I am so sorry, Mr. Machado, but Michael and Cesar left for New York this morning. I am not expecting them back until Tuesday or Wednesday next week. Unfortunately, I don't have the number for their hotel. I will let him know you called when he checks in."

Machado gave the woman his number at his mistress's apartment and hang up.

Machado looked at his mistress and asked her, "Has anyone called me today or come to visit?"

The young woman responded, "No to the first and yes to the second. About an hour ago someone dropped this off for you." The woman pointed to a small box on the kitchen counter.

Machado quickly opened the box and saw two severed chicken heads wrapped in newspapers. Next to them there was a note, "I know what you've done. You may hide, you may run, you may call an army, but I'm still coming for you. And please tell Rosalba I love the new curtains."

Confused, he looked at the windows of the apartment and saw brand new dark blue curtains. In anger he asked, "When did you get those?"

"The curtains?" Rosalba asked.

"Yes, the fucking curtains. When did you get them?" he repeated frustrated.

Terrified, the young woman answered. "They arrived yesterday, but I just hung them up this morning."

Without saying a word, Machado ran out of the back door, ran a half a block to his car, drove as fast as he could, and made the one-and-a-half-hour drive to Fredonia, a town approximately thirty miles south of Envigado, where he had a hideaway house.

Chapter 46

The Inter-American Hotel was busy that morning, but the meeting had been arranged, and the manager waited at the ap-pointed place in the lobby. When Colonel Julio Rodriguez walked in, alone and wearing civilian clothes, as he had been instructed by the old lawyer the day before, he was greeted by the manager and taken to the same small conference room we had used for the translations. The only difference today was that, lying on the small table were dozens of tapes and a set of listening headphones.

Sitting around the table, Dr. Garza, the same two young lawyers who accompanied us to Steerco, your dad, and I were waiting for the highest-ranking police official in the city of Medellin.

As soon as Julio Rodriguez was seated, Dr. Garza made the introductions, ordered coffee for everyone, and began a careful, slow, and systematic narrative of all the facts as we knew them, providing available evidence to substantiate each fact. He produced your letter to me and the original articles in English; the picture of you with your uncle; the translated documents from the papers in London; the additional pictures from Julia, which had arrived at the Oaks with the Friday mail and showed at least six different men, including Walters, in the company of undressed children; and, the coup de grace, the selected tapes that proved the conspiracy and all the criminal behaviors of the organization. In addition to these, a list of the twenty-four security plants, and a list of the twenty-four members of the club were also produced by the lawyer.

When Dr. Garza had finished his presentation, Julio Rodriguez asked, "May I use a telephone?" Directed to the same phone I had used to call my mother from this room, Julio Rodriguez repeated most of the information given to a silent listener on the other side of the line, and within thirty minutes he received via a private courier a set of subpoenas for all buildings and homes associated with Michael Walters, The Walters fashion house, the building in La America, and Walters' home. Rodriguez was about to call the cavalry to execute the subpoenas, when Dr. Garza intervened,

"All due respect, Colonel. But, if Michael Walters and his son are in the United States as we are told by our sources, shouldn't we wait until they are on Colombian soil before we scare them off?"

"You are wrong, Dr. Garza. You forget how difficult extradition is in Colombia, if not virtually impossible. Additionally, with the kind of power Walters has, it will be a matter of days before he buys, intimidates, or eliminates any witnesses to get away with this. The best thing to happen to us is for him to get arrested on American soil. We will send one of our men to the United States to share this evidence, once he is in custody. We will have forty-eight hours to make that happen, which is plenty of time. I have a suspicion this man has other victims in America. And don't forget, the English will have plenty of reasons to extradite him, which, again, would be hard to do from Colombia."

The Colonel added, "Our State's attorney will make the call to the FBI via our people at the embassy in Bogota. He will be picked up at his hotel in New York within the next two hours. I have an American visa which I might just need to use for this important state business. Heck, I might even take the wife." He added with a smile.

After receiving notice that Michael and Cesar Walters had been detained by the FBI in New York City, the Colonel Julio Rodriguez, followed by over one hundred police officers, executed warrants and subpoenas throughout the city, arresting over sixty people associated with Walters' club. Warrants for several fugitives were issued and within several weeks they had been arrested.

The news media were in a frenzy, but they were never told who the whistleblower had been and how the investigation had commenced. As expected, the British media descended in Medellin like vultures, making a connection between the two sex rinks and demanding the immediate extradition of Michael Walters to England.

The Colombian authorities responded that they would not object if the Americans extradited Walters to England on condition that the British courts considered the great damage this man had done in Colombia when they sentenced him.

Michael Walters seemed to be heading to England, when the FBI discovered at least ten cases in Atlanta that were connected to Walters and his father, dating back to when Michael was a freshman in college. Most of the identified victims picked Walters in several lineups and he was officially charged and denied bail because of his immense wealth and extensive international connections.

Within ten months of his arrest, Walters was tried, and the majority of his American victims testified against him. By then the case had become a sensation in England and the United States. Sadly, we had worse issues to deal with in Colombia and the entire affair was reduced to one newspaper article in Medellin: *Walters found guilty of all charges.* In a gesture of international goodwill, the judge allowed impact statements from the victims in England, and a summary report from Colombian prosecutors, in the sentencing portion of the trial. Walters was given 40 years in State prison.

Within two weeks of the arrest, Cesar was brought home by his distraught mother, and the family was not present for the trial or the sentencing of Michael Walters.

Chapter 47

Juan Manuel Machado had to avail himself of a public defendant for his trial because he was penniless, and his friends refused to come to his aid. He was found guilty and given twenty-five years in a maximum-security prison in Medellin.

He was in fact assassinated by his brother-in-law, but not until almost a year later, when Machado decided to turn state witness against Jaime in exchange for a pardon. Before the deal with the state was signed, his associates were informed of the negotiations by a prison warden on the Cartel's payroll, and the apparent suicide by hanging of Juan Manuel Machado was announced to the media several days later.

In a rare act of gratitude, Colonel Julio Rodriguez shared with me his last encounter with Machado. Apparently, after the raids in the city and all its major suburbs, Colonel Julio Rodriguez decided to take a trip to the country side of Fredonia, Antioquia. He felt he needed a break from all the activity before he and his wife flew to Atlanta to meet with the Americans. When asked by those close to him about the trip, he simply said, "I'm searching for a big fish and they tell me there is good fishing in that part of the state."

After watching Machado for several hours on that Sunday, December 20th, 1981, Julio Rodriguez casually approached him as Machado was entering a local diner.

"We have to talk. Don't make a fuss, you are surrounded, Juan. It's good to see you, old friend," said, Rodriguez.

Machado tried to move away from the man, not recognizing him in civilian clothes at first. Jamming his service pistol into the man's ribs, however, Rodriguez said, "That would not be advisable, my friend. Let's talk, we have a deal to offer you."

Machado tried to speak that he had done nothing wrong, that he was just a driver for Walters, that he had no idea what the American was doing, and that he was an innocent bystander.

Rodriguez listened patiently and said, "Be that as it may, we need you to listen to us."

At this point, a non-descriptive Jeep pulled up, and the two men entered through the back door. The car drove to Machado's house, where two men had done a thorough search and found a cache of weapons in a closet and dozens of neatly stacked packs of money in the wooden subfloor of the kitchen.

As soon as Machado saw they had found his weapons and money he became crestfallen and threatened to have the police men's badges pulled. "I still have friends in this town!" he grandstanded.

"You mean Jaime Carmona? Funny you should think of him at this difficult time, Juan. You know he has been looking for you, right? In fact, maybe I should just call him right now and tell him we found you. I'm sure he would be very grateful for the information. After all, your wife misses you greatly, Juan."

At the mention of his brother-in-law, Machado paled, lost his balance, and fell heavily on his couch.

The Colonel continued, "We can offer you a deal, Juan. First, we need you to take us to Manuel Escobar Estrada's hideaway. If you do, we promise you we will keep you in protective custody at the Estate's Jail, in a place where your brother in law will not be able to find you. If you don't, you are going into general population, where you will last about five minutes. I'll give you a chance to think about this.

Without much thought, Machado agreed, and the group left in the same Jeep on their way back to the city and to a second-floor apartment where the State Secretary of Education was hiding until he could leave the country.

Estrada had not left the apartment since the raids began. Neither his sister nor his brother-in-law were returning his calls and he knew he was running out of time. All his political contacts were refusing to return calls and even the Governor was unavailable. They had all abandoned him, leaving him alone, pissing in the wind. "After all that I have done for this State. Ingrates! This country is going to hell." He thought to himself, right before a thunderous noise sent shreds of door flying in all directions.

Terrified, Estrada dropped to the floor and rolled under his bed, from which he was dragged out by several police officers. He was taken to the kitchen where Colonel Rodriguez was having a whiskey on the rocks. "Please take a seat, Secretary." Rodriguez ordered the terrified man.

The police men sat Estrada on a chair and held him in place. Rodriguez offered him a drink and, surprisingly, the man accepted it.

Rodriguez said, "Juan, you may be wondering why we

have kept your name from all newspapers, radio and television interviews, and public statements. In fact, in the eyes of all good people in this state and in the country, you still are an upstanding public servant. Do you know why we have done this, Juan?"

Estrada said nothing. As a good politician he knew he needed to keep his mouth shut if he was ever going to survive this.

Rodriguez continued, "We have done this, Juan, because this Governor is the only decent politician, we have had in this state in twenty years and we need him now more than ever before. The cartel boys are afraid of him and he's got the balls to take them on. We can't afford to have any of this blow back on him. You do understand, right?"

Again, absolute silence from Estrada.

Undeterred, Rodriguez continued, "No. We think the best course of action is for you to die a hero, Juan. We all know how depressed you have been since the suicide of your nephew. As one of the only males in his family, you feel responsible for not providing proper guidance and support. Your life has always been about the care and protection of children and, to have failed your nephew, has been weighing you down. You have missed a few days of work and you are terribly depressed. Your family and friends have been deeply concerned about you."

"Today, as your beloved sister came to visit you at your home in El Poblado, where we will take you a little later, she discovered you dead on your bed. You had taken an overdose of pills and alcohol. On your nightstand they found a very sad note in your handwriting. The letter will be released to the media, and the state will declare and official day of mourning on Monday. Schools will march with their bands during your funeral procession, and the Governor himself will eulogize you at your last Mass. It will be very sad, but you will die a hero for children's education."

As Rodriguez was speaking, Estrada began to feel very tired. He looked at his empty whiskey glass and mumbled, "You, bastard." After this, he collapsed on the table, dead before the glass reached the floor and shattered in a dozen pieces.

Chapter 48

I never learned the name of the Chilean, but about three months after the lid was opened on the entire Walters Affair, as it was called, I received a note in the mail, which read,

"Joe, as I wrap up the last details of this peculiar assignment, I wanted to inform you of a few decisions I have made. This very day, I have informed Julia Salcedo and her mother, Maria, that an account has been opened in their names at Banco Popular and the balance is fifty percent of the money I removed from the account of a certain former security officer. They will never have to worry about money for the rest of their lives.

I have sent your friend William the other half of said money. He has been promoted to head of the motor pool at Steerco and spends a great deal of time traveling. The money will pay for full-time caregivers for his mother. He also informed me that he will buy himself a new car to go with his new home.

Disregarding the instructions of the good priest who signs

my checks, I have left the twenty million pesos we took from the apartment in Envigado in Ivan's care for you. Our priest friend believes you will reject the money as 'blood money,' but I had to give it a shot.

I'm so impressed with you and how you handled yourself throughout this whole affair. I guess the saying, 'never underestimate the young or overestimate the old' applies in this case. You are a cool operator. Best of luck to you. I hope you do become a priest someday. We need a few good men to help us overcome the pain caused by so many of the evil people I must deal with. Keep safe. Your friend from Rio Negro, T.C."

The Chilean was right. I never took the money for myself, but even blood money can be used for good and that's what I did. Three and a half blocks away from the State's Psychiatric Hospital, I found a humble, but comfortable three-bedroom home. I had Julius purchase the place in Uncle Pedro and Aunt Irene's name. I lied one more time to my mother, making her believe that the place was a gift from your father, after he heard Irene's story and felt moved by her lack of proper medical care.

Your parents are working through the trauma of your suicide and the "Walters Affair." They had a second child they named Matilda. She is barely 2 months old and beautiful. You would love her at first sight. Steerco is on its way of becoming a multinational company, as they recently broke ground for additional manufacturing plants in Mexico and Chile. Your parents are just as busy as ever, with a growing company and a new baby. I visit them at least once a month and we have long conversations about the Alex I knew. They still miss you greatly, but I know time will heal their wounds, as it will heal Colombia's own wounds. I am a person of faith and hope is the last resort of the faithful.

As for me, I was hired by "The Oaks" as a counselor, which means that I am officially on the payroll. I still have plans to enter seminary next year, when I graduate high school. I miss you terribly and have become somewhat of a loner, but I am still doing what I love, and Fr. Garcia and the Center have become my family since my parents left for the United States a few months back.

Eventually, I will have to make my way to the United States, since my family has worked very hard to make this possible. I know I will miss my life here and I hate leaving you behind, but life in Medellin has become untenable.

My future is uncertain at this point, but I am excited to see what God does with me next. After the tragic events of December 1981, I am certain of only two things: First, life is precious, and we need to hold on to those we love. Second, I can't wait to see you when we wake.

Acknowledgements

There are so many people involved in the process of writing a book that listing them all by name would be almost impossible. Having said this, I would like to thank my children, Emily, Rebeca, Austin, and Sarah who have heard snippets of this story through the years and who encouraged me to write this book. Special thanks to my beautiful wife, Chris, who read and corrected numerous versions of this story over the last year. Thanks to Kelly Ward and Dr. Olivia Pass for reading my manuscript and providing valuable feedback. Your friendship and support is deeply appreciated.

Finally, thanks to those who were there when the real "Alex" lived among us. Your love has made all the difference in my life.

Contact Information:

R.D.Roldan
PO Box 3093
Saint Francisville, LA 70775

Email: author.rdroldan@gmail.com
Website: www.rdroldan.com
Facebook: https://www.facebook.com/AuthorRDRoldan
Twitter: https://twitter.com/Author_RDRoldan
Instagram: https://www.instagram.com/r.d.roldan/

What inspired you to write your book?

I think I have been a story teller all my life, and I have told my children many bedtime stories from my childhood, including some of the stories in this book. As my children grow up, some of these stories have stopped, which is both natural and sad at the same time. About a year ago, I realized that some of these foundational stories of my childhood needed to be preserved for future generations of my family. As I began to retell these stories to yet-to-be born descendants, something magic began to happen to me: I began to rediscover my own roots and I began to reconnect with a past I had tried to forget. My mother used to say that before you knew where you were going, you needed to know where you came from. This book is my attempt to rediscover where I came from and how the places and events of my childhood have influenced my life.

How did your friend's suicide impact you in such a way that you had to write his story?

Teenage suicide has been a taboo in our culture both in Colombia and the United States, yet suicide affects everyone in the person's family, friend group, and community. I have carried the pain of Alex's suicide in my heart for over 37 years, waiting for the right opportunity to tell his story. The recent epidemic of teenage suicides in America have inspired me to tell my story, hoping that it might resonate with others who have lost loved ones to suicide. We must not allow the voices of those who have taken their own lives to go silent forever. Their stories deserve to be told and their voices need to be heard once again. This is my attempt to allow Alex to make us laugh and cry, as he allows us a birds-eye view into his tragic life.

Why is Alex's story important to the average person?

It has been 25 years since Pablo Escobar was assassinated on a rooftop in Medellin, Colombia, yet he remains one of the most talked about, studied, and hated Colombians in the history of our nation. In fact, Escobar is so recognized that the millions of stories that took place in Medellin during his reign of terror are ignored, unless they have something to do directly with the Cartel and the eccentric psychopath who made our lives miserable for so long. This book allows the reader the opportunity to read a story that took place during the same period, on the same streets, and in the same town where Pablo lived, yet is not about him and his men. This story is important because it is a story of loyalty, love, and grief and these are themes common to our human experience regardless of setting, age, or political backstory.

How will this book change the hearts of readers?

Guilt is the daily bread those who have lost loved ones to suicide eat. We blame ourselves for not having said the right words, not having seen the signs, and failing to comprehend the pain our friends are feeling. Yet, no one can truly prevent the suicide of those whose minds are set and who see no other way to end their pain. I want to shine a light on that survivor's guilt many of us feel and I want to whisper in the reader's ears, "It's not your fault. There is nothing you could have done. It's not your failure!" Beyond this humble aspiration, I want readers to pledge to live by the book's ultimate premise: Life is short, and we need to hold on to those we love.

Why is suicide so important to you, personally?

I have been a Clinical Social Worker for twenty-five years and an Episcopal clergyman for twelve. I have heard countless stories of the guilt families feel when confronted with suicide and, through this book, I want to say, "I understand, I empathize, I've been there." The effects of suicide never go away, but time and the empathic support of friends, help us all cope with our grief. I hope my experience will help the reader feel less alone and more supported.

About the Author

Starting off his life in a small town outside of Medellin, Colombia, R.D. Roldan, a first generation immigrant, became a social worker, clergyman and Doctor in Theology. A personal project, meant to share stories of his youth with his children, has turned into a rediscovery of his roots. Growing up in the 1970's and 1980's Medellin of Pablo Escobar, R.D. Roldan recounts his own experiences in light of a painful period of Colombian history. The author now resides in St. Francisville, LA with his wife and 4 children.